"Are you from Intelligence?"

"Yes. You talked to that couple that was just here, didn't you? You told them everything you know about the Citadel?"

"What are you going to do? Court-martial me?"

"I don't have a problem with you talking to them. In fact, I sent them to you."

"Then what do you want?"

"I want to make sure you don't talk to anyone else." Royce stepped up to the confused old man and lightly slapped him on the back of the neck.

"What the hell was that?"

Royce slid off the metal ring he had on his middle finger, carefully avoiding the small barb that protruded from it. He slipped it into a metal box and put it in his pocket. "Good-bye, Colonel."

"What did you do?"

"Killed you," Royce said as he turned for the door.

He pushed it open and left the dead man behind.

THE CITADEL

Also by Robert Doherty

ROBERT DOHERTY

THE
CITADEL

HARPER

An Imprint of HarperCollinsPublishers

This is a work of fiction. Names, characters, places, and incidents are products of the author's imagination or are used fictitiously and are not to be construed as real. Any resemblance to actual events, locales, organizations, or persons, living or dead, is entirely coincidental.

HARPER

An Imprint of HarperCollins*Publishers*
10 East 53rd Street
New York, New York 10022-5299

Copyright © 2007 by Robert Mayer
ISBN: 978-0-06-073585-2
ISBN-10: 0-06-073585-6

First Harper paperback printing: April 2007

HarperCollins® and Harper® are registered trademarks of HarperCollins Publishers.

Printed in the U.S.A.

Visit Harper paperbacks on the World Wide Web at www.harpercollins. com

10 9 8 7 6 5 4 3 2 1

THE
CITADEL

PROLOGUE

"You've got to be joking?" President Harry S Truman stared at the document on his desk with undisguised surprise. He looked up from it at the men gathered in the Oval Office and knew the situation at hand was no hoax, given the power that was concentrated in the room.

"Even the information about the atomic weapon—" Truman began. He stopped to gather his thoughts. After Roosevelt's sudden death on April 12, 1945, Truman had received numerous briefings on matters he had been kept ignorant of, the most shocking of which was the development of those terrible weapons he had subsequently made the decision to use against Japan. He'd told reporters that he "felt like the moon, the stars, and all the planets had fallen on me."

Now it appeared they literally had.

Truman looked at the document once more. "July eighth? That was two months ago. Why wasn't I told earlier?"

"We've been evaluating," Sidney Souers said. He was the man Truman had appointed as the director of the newly formed Central Intelligence Agency. There were three other men scattered about the room: Dr. Vannevar Bush, Chairman of the Joint Research and Development Board; James Forrestal, the first man to fill the newly developed slot of Secretary of Defense; and General Vandenberg, now Chief of Staff of the Air Force, but Truman knew him better as Chief of Military Intelligence during the world war. The man who knew all the secrets. The man who had been part of the small group who shocked him with the news about the development of the atomic bomb shortly after Roosevelt's passing.

"And your conclusion?" Truman demanded. He shook the folder. "You're telling me we have a damn craft of some sort that crashed in New Mexico, and it wasn't made by us, wasn't made by the Russians, indeed you say it was made by—" He peered through his reading glasses for the line. "—nonhuman, non-Earth entities. What the hell does that mean?"

Vandenberg's deep voice echoed through the Oval Office. "Aliens, Mr. President. Creatures from space. We believe this craft might have been on a reconnaissance mission. Small ship and a small crew numbering only three."

"Reconnaissance for what?" Truman asked.

"Invasion," Vandenberg simply said.

Forrestal cleared his throat. "Now, General, we don't have any evidence of that."

Vandenberg's large head swiveled toward his civilian superior. "What the hell else do you send a recon for?"

"To find out information," Forrestal said. "To explore."

Vandenberg's snort of derision indicated what he thought of that. "While this is the first craft with crew we've managed to recover, this alien activity is not an isolated incident, Mr. President. Throughout the war and several times since, Allied pilots—and from what our spies tell us, Russian pilots—were often trailed by alien craft."

Truman removed his reading glasses. "What kind of craft?"

"Small glowing balls, about three feet in diameter," Vandenberg said. "No visible propulsion system." He pulled a folder out of his briefcase and slid a photo out. "This was taken by a gun camera in a P-47 Thunderbolt in 1945 over the Rhine River in Germany. This is the only picture we have, but there are almost fifty other reports of pilots who saw something like it.

"The pilots nicknamed them 'foo fighters.' At first we thought they were German or Japanese. Secret weapons. And because they were suspected to be Japanese and German, all information concerning them was classified. The reports on these things started in late 1944. They were described as metallic spheres or balls of light. Since the aircrews that reported them were usually veterans, and a gun camera recorded one, giving factual support to those accounts, the reports were taken seriously."

Vandenberg took the photo back out of Truman's hands, which irritated the President. The Air Force general was like many others in Washington who saw him as an interloper, a poor replacement for the President who had led them through the war.

"It was serious," Vandenberg continued. "We lost eight aircraft to these things when they challenged them and fired at them. After the war we found out from going through their records that the Japanese and Germans had the same encounters and didn't know what the damn things were either. So we knew then that they didn't make them, which made us wonder who the hell did."

He slapped down another photo. Truman put his glasses on, and his eyes widened at what he saw.

"*They* did," Vandenberg said, tapping a finger on the alien body laid out on an autopsy table. The general leaned over the President's desk, putting both fists on it. The photo wasn't the clearest, but the gray figure on the table was obviously not human. "I don't think their intentions are good. When the *Enola Gay* flew the first atomic mission toward Hiroshima on August sixth, 1945, it was accompanied the entire way by a foo fighter. The mission was almost scrapped when the sphere appeared, but the commander on the ground at the departure airfield at Tinian decided to continue it. There was no hostile action by the foo fighters, and the situation was repeated several days later during the mission to Nagasaki."

"Why wasn't I informed?" Truman demanded.

The lack of any answer was insult enough.

"But you say they did nothing to stop the mission, so why do you believe their intentions are not good?" Truman asked.

"I'd ask the dead men who flew those eight planes the foo fighters took out that question, Mr. President," Vandenberg said.

Truman sighed and leaned back in his chair, rubbing

his eyes and putting more distance between himself and Vandenberg. "What now?"

Vandenberg backed off slightly, removing his fists from the desk. "We want to form a special committee to oversee everything to do with these aliens. And to prepare countermeasures and emergency plans in case of invasion. We want you to authorize the formation and the funding of this committee—which will have to be extensive, Mr. President. This might be the gravest threat mankind has ever faced."

Truman glanced over at Forrestal, the only man among the three facing him that he trusted. It was hard to judge the Secretary of Defense's face. "James?"

Forrestal looked left and right, at the other two men, and then nodded. "I think it makes sense, Mr. President. Always better to be prepared."

Truman turned back to Vandenberg. "What exactly are you talking about doing?"

The Air Force general pulled out a piece of paper. "This is an overview. We plan on calling the oversight group Majestic-12, composed of nine other men besides the three of us. Our headquarters will be set up in a very isolated site in the Nevada desert on the Nellis base range at a place called Area 51."

Truman was staring at the paper. "You're asking for six *billion* dollars?"

"Most of it will come from the Black Eagle Trust," Vandenberg said, "not the taxpayers.

What we need is authorization to use Defense Department assets to support this."

Truman scanned down the page. "What's this about a second base? And in Antarctica?"

Vandenberg glanced over his shoulder at Dr. Bush, who fielded the question. "Sir, we also think there is a need to establish an emergency base, sort of a bastion of last resort for the human race."

Truman looked up from the document. "My God, you really believe the threat is that serious?"

"It has the potential to be," Bush said. "If these aliens can travel across the stars, we have to assume they have incredible weapons, the likes of which we most likely can't even comprehend, never mind defeat. That is why we want to set up this Citadel in Antarctica."

Shaking his head, Truman pulled out his pen. He scrawled his signature on the bottom of the document. "Where is the copy for my records?" he asked.

Vandenberg took the signed paper out of the President's hands. "Sir, it's better if there is no paper trail. We need this"—he held the paper—"to get things going, but the only eyes that will set sight on it are the members of Majestic-12."

"I want a copy," the President said simply.

"Sir—" Vandenberg began, but Truman cut him off.

"Are you saying you don't trust me?" Truman said in a level voice.

Vandenberg's face flushed red.

"Give him a copy, General," Forrestal said.

The room was still for several moments. Reluctantly, Vandenberg pulled a copy of the order out of his briefcase and handed it to Truman.

"And if that is all," Truman said, "I have other business to attend to."

Vandenberg stiffly saluted and led the other men out of the office.

Finally alone, Truman stared at the paper in his hand. He began to put it in his classified out box, then paused. He folded the paper in half, then in half again, and slid it into his suit pocket.

* * *

As their car exited the East Gate, Vandenberg turned to Dr. Bush. "Is he going to be a problem?"

Bush frowned at the question. They had left Forrestal at the drive, the Secretary taking his own car back to the newly built Pentagon. "Are you referring to Truman or Forrestal?"

"Good question," Vandenberg said. He flipped up the left lapel of his suit jacket, revealing a finely worked small brooch. It consisted of an iron cross overlaid on a circle of silver. He ran his fingers over it lightly. "Neither are of the Organization, but we need them."

"And if either become problems?"

"They'll be taken care of."

"And the Organization?" Bush asked.

Vandenberg nodded. "As we discussed. We tell Geneva about Area 51. But not about the Citadel. It's our ace in the hole. Just in case."

Bush looked uneasy. "This is a dangerous ploy."

"It's a dangerous world."

Washington, D.C.
22 May 1949

"I'm not crazy, you know." The twitch under James Forrestal's left eye seemed to contradict that statement.

"Of course not," the young doctor said. The small nameplate on his white coat indicated his name was Lansale.

This late at night, just before midnight, the normal sounds of Bethesda Naval Hospital were muted. A corpsman came by every fifteen minutes and peered in the small window set in the steel door of Forrestal's room. "Cell" would have been a better term, but no one used it out loud, at least not around the former Secretary of Defense. The occasional sound of a car on the road outside was muted this high up on the sixteenth floor.

"It's been a bad year, two years," Forrestal said, taking Lansale's agreement as an indicator to keep talking. He'd been denied visitors for months and he was desperate to share with anyone, even this new night shift psychiatrist.

"The goddamn Air Force," Forrestal began. "Money. Money. Money. That's all they want. And Truman wants a damn balanced budget, yet he keeps signing allocations pouring the money out. And they hate me. The Joint Chiefs. They hate me. They have me followed. Followed me right to the doors of this place.

"Men. Dressed in dark suits. They were everywhere. Watching me. And then when Truman removed me, fired me, replaced me. They were in the car after the ceremony. Waiting. Drove with me back to the Pentagon. They told me."

Forrestal fell silent, and Lansale waited with the patience of a man who was working the graveyard shift and had nothing better to do. But after the silence stretched into several minutes, he finally bit. "Told you what?"

"The truth," Forrestal said simply.

Lansale fired up a cigarette and offered Forrestal one. He shook his head. Lansale inhaled. "About?"

"Majestic-12."

Lansale's eyes narrowed. "What?"

"They wanted to scare me, and they did. I was a loyal fellow. Loyal."

"I'm sure you were," Lansale said.

Forrestal snorted. "Aliens. That's what they used as a smoke screen. Even Truman bought into it. Fool."

Lansale glanced down at the medical folder. "It says you tried to kill yourself not long ago."

Forrestal's head snapped up and he stared at Lansale. "That's what they said. But I didn't. Never. I was a loyal fellow. Always will be. No matter what they're planning on doing out there."

"Out where?"

"In the desert," Forrestal said. "And in the icy wasteland."

"This also says you tried to jump out of the car several times on the ride over here last month."

"I was a prisoner," Forrestal said. "I am a prisoner. They won't let my family see me. My friends."

"You're a patient, not a prisoner," Lansale said. "You have involuntional melancholia."

"I have a mind that knows too much," Forrestal countered. "My brother told me that Truman's men took my diaries. They've been reading them."

Lansale became very still. "When was this?"

"On the phone yesterday." Forrestal smiled. "My brother is coming tomorrow. He told me that also. He's getting me out of here. I've been better. They know I've gotten better. Tomorrow I leave this prison."

"We know about your brother coming," Lansale said. He closed the file and stood. "Would you like to go with me and get some food in the diet kitchen across the hall?"

"A last meal?" Forrestal joked as he stood up. He tightened his bathrobe around his waist with its cord.

"Yeah," Lansale said as he pulled out his key ring and unlocked the door.

They crossed the hallway to the small kitchen that

served the floor. Lansale let Forrestal go in first, and then locked the door behind them. As Forrestal went to the small cabinet near the window, Lansale reached out and pulled the cord from the small loops of the bathrobe. Forrestal turned, confusion on his face, one hand holding the robe closed, the other holding a can of soup.

"What are you—" Forrestal never finished, as Lansale looped the cord around his neck and stepped behind him, back-to-back, and bent, lifting Forrestal off his feet with the cord. The former Secretary of Defense flailed about, gasping for air. Lansale had already prepared the room: the window was wide open, and he hauled Forrestal like a sack of potatoes on his back toward it.

Forrestal grasped at the edge of the window and managed to get a momentary grip as Lansale spun around trying to toss him out. The former Secretary of Defense teetered in the window, half unconscious from the cord around his next, one hand holding on.

Lansale let go of the cord, stepped back, and then snap-kicked Forrestal in the stomach. With a strangled shriek, Forrestal flew out the window and into the darkness, arms flailing. Seconds later there was the dull thud of his body hitting the ground sixteen stories below.

Lansale exited the room and briskly walked down the corridor, removing the white coat as he did so. He pocketed the small nameplate and tossed the coat in a trash bin. He went down the fire stairs, all sixteen floors. He ignored the growing commotion and walked over to a dark sedan that was waiting, engine running, across the street from the hospital. He slid in the backseat and the car pulled away.

"Any problems?" the man in the front passenger seat asked without turning around.

"None in the mission," Lansale said. "But he said that Truman has his diaries. And I think he's talked about both Area 51 and the Citadel in there."

There was just the sound of the car's engine and tires on asphalt for several minutes as the man in the front seat considered that. "Area 51 is already on the radar. The whispers are out. We've got an excellent cover story for it." He fell silent once more, and Lansale waited in the backseat. "But the Citadel. That we cannot even allow whispers about."

Lansale leaned forward. "The plan was always to make the Citadel 'disappear.'"

"Yes," the man agreed, "but the plan was for that to happen six months from now."

"I will accelerate the plan," Lansale said. "All links to the Citadel will be severed within seven days. I'll personally take care of it."

Antarctica, Approximately 575 Miles East of High Jump Station 28 May 1949

"The last load," the young captain in the gray parka remarked.

"Amen to that," Captain Vannet muttered. Through the scratched Plexiglas windshield, he glanced at the frozen runway splayed out in front of his plane. To his left rear, a staircase descended into the cargo bay of the massive Martin JRM-Mars transport, where his loadmaster was securing the few pallets of luggage the passengers had carried on board. Along the walls, soldiers bundled up in cold weather gear were seated on red web seats, ready to get started on the long journey out of here in the world's largest seaplane, which had

been converted for use in the Antarctic by replacing the
pontoons on each wing with large skis.

Capable of carrying over sixteen tons of cargo or
133 people, and with a wingspan over two hundred feet
wide, the JRM-Mars was a workhouse that had allowed
them to haul more cargo back and forth to this spot
than a squadron of smaller planes.

Vannet couldn't blame the soldiers crowded in the
cargo bay. He'd brought them here four months ago via
High Jump Station set up near the Ross Ice Shelf, then
spent the intervening time flying back from the station
every opportunity the weather gave, bringing in equipment and supplies to these men for whatever they were
building here in the frozen wasteland of the Antarctic. A
week ago that process had hurriedly been reversed with
an emergency order, and he started bringing equipment
and people out. The outflow in equipment and supplies
had been considerably less than the inflow.

The sky was clear and the wind had died down. The
weather report from High Jump Station written down
by his copilot looked good, but Vannet had long ago
learned that the Antarctic was one place where weather
reports could be counted on about as far as the report
itself could be folded into a paper airplane and thrown.
The only constant in the weather here was change—
and the change was usually for the worse.

Vannet wasn't sure who the captain—Whitaker
was his name—worked for. All he knew was that four
months ago he had been ordered to do whatever the
man said. Captain Whitaker had been here waiting to
receive their cargo every time they'd landed at the Citadel—the code name they knew for this unmarked location. Today even Whitaker was going out with them.
If anyone was remaining behind, Vannet knew not and

cared even less. It was their last flight from the Citadel, and successfully completing it was his only concern.

Vannet shifted his gaze back to the "airstrip." The plane sat in a large bowl of ice surrounded on three sides by ice ridges and intermittent, towering mountains punching through the thick polar cap; the strip pointed toward the one open side. The bulky MARS with four turboprop engines mounted on its wings was a powerful aircraft, and Vannet felt confident in its abilities. Bracketed over the plane's pontoons were sets of skis that allowed them to negotiate the 2,000 meters of relatively level ice and snow that these people called a runway. He would be damn glad to never see this place again.

"Closing the ramp," the loadmaster announced in Vannet's headset. In the rear of the plane the back ramp lifted from the thin, powdery snow as hydraulic arms pulled it up. Descending from the top of the cargo bay came the top section of the ramp. Like jaws closing, the two shut against the swirling frozen air outside. The heaters fought a losing battle against the cold as they pumped hot air out of pipes in the ceiling of the cargo bay, ten feet overhead.

Vannet turned to Captain Whitaker. "We're all set, sir."

Whitaker simply nodded and clambered down the steps to take his seat in the rear.

"Let's do it," Vannet told the copilot. Carefully, they turned the nose straight on line, due south. As Vannet increased throttle, the plane moved, slowly gathering momentum as the propellers and skis threw up a plume of snow behind.

Vannet waited until he was satisfied they had enough speed, and then pulled in the yoke. The nose of the MARS lifted, and the plane crawled into the air. Once he reached sufficient altitude to clear the mountains, Vannet banked hard right and headed west. In the distance, out the right window, the ice pack that hugged the shore of Antarctica could be seen as a tumbled mass of broken sea ice that extended to the horizon.

Vannet turned the controls over to his copilot. Four hours and they'd be at High Jump Station, the temporary sprawling base established under the auspices of exploring Antarctica; they would refuel, and then he and his crew and passengers could begin the long stop-filled flight back to their home base in Hawaii. After four months down here they were more than ready to see loved ones and bask in the sun.

The whole mission had turned strange after the initial order to support Operation High Jump, a massive exploration of Antarctica by the military. Almost their entire squadron had received the tasking and deployed south. But on arrival at High Jump Station, a cluster of Quonset huts set next to another ice runway on the shore of a large ice-covered bay, their plane had been detached from the others and given this strange mission to support Captain Whitaker and the Citadel. They'd been warned, in no uncertain terms, that they were not to discuss the mission with anyone.

"I've got the beacon clear," the copilot informed Vannet.

As long as they kept the needle on the direction finder centered, they'd come in right on top of High Jump Station. That was another odd thing. They'd flown every mission on instruments in both directions, never once using a map, not that there were any maps available. As any good pilot would, Vannet had a rough idea where the Citadel was located, using both flight time and azimuth, but he certainly couldn't pinpoint it, and if it weren't for the radio beacons, they could easily become lost.

Satisfied all was going well, he kicked back in his chair to take a quick nap. He was going to need the rest since he was the primary pilot for the longer ten-hour leg from High Jump Station to New Zealand.

Three hours later he was awakened by the copilot. He could feel the plane descending, and looking out of the cockpit, saw the cluster of huts and tents and mounds of supplies that was the land-based hub of the Antarctic High Jump Expedition. Out the right window he could see the massive form of Mount Erebus, an active volcano dominating the horizon. Below lay the Ross Ice Shelf, the edge more than five hundred miles from its origin at the foot of the Queen Maud Mountains.

The copilot swung them around on approach. As soon as the skis touched the ice runway, he reduced throttle and used the flaps to break the plane. It was a long slow process as they slid down the strip, and Vannet watched carefully as his copilot struggled to keep them on a straight line. They finally slowed enough so the copilot could taxi the plane over to where several other smaller C-119 aircraft were parked along with a cluster of fuel trucks.

As they came to a halt, the copilot kept the engines running, which was against normal regulations during refueling, but they had all learned that regulations developed outside of Antarctica rarely worked well in this forbidding climate. They needed to keep the engines running to keep heat flowing to the cargo bay, and more important, to prevent them from seizing up if allowed to cool too much.

Vannet looked out the window as anonymous fig-

ures in bulky cold-weather clothing hooked hoses up
to the fuel points and began pumping the precious liquid in.

He noted a man dressed in a red parka standing in the
shadow of a parked C-119, simply staring at the plane.
For some reason, Vannet felt uncomfortable with that.
He turned his head upon hearing a tap at the cockpit
door. Captain Whitaker stuck his head in.

"Anxious to get home, I suppose?" he asked.

"Damn right," Vannet replied. "In two days we'll be
back in the sun and surf."

Whitaker nodded. "Have a safe flight. You and your
men did a great job. My superiors will be forwarding
letters of commendation for you and your crew to your
headquarters."

That was the least they could do, Vannet thought, to
pay them back for spending four months living isolated
in a damn Quonset hut buried under the snow at High
Jump Station and flying a load every time the weather
cleared. "I appreciate that."

Captain Whitaker disappeared down the stairwell,
and the loadmaster slammed shut the personnel door
behind him. Vannet looked out the window. The man in
the red parka was gone. He looked about and then spotted the man walking next to Whitaker, heading toward
a C-119 whose engines were also running.

Vannet turned to his copilot and navigator. "Do we
have clearance to go?"

The navigator's face split in a wide grin. "We have
clearance, and the weather looks good all the way to
New Zealand, sir."

"All right. Let's go home."

They turned their nose into the wind and powered
up. Soon the seaplane was in the air and over the ice-

covered Ross Sea. New Zealand was ten hours away, due north.

Vannet piloted the first three hours, as they slowly left the white ice behind and finally made it over clear ocean, specked with small white dots far below, indicating icebergs. At that point, Vannet turned the controls over to his copilot and got out of his seat. "I'm going to take a walk in back and get stretched out."

Vannet climbed down the stairs. The loadmaster and his assistant were lying on the web seats strung along the side of the plane, sleeping. The eighty engineers that they had supplied for four months were stretched out in every available spot, everyone trying to catch some sleep.

Vannet walked all the way to the rear, where the ramp doors met, rolling his head on his shoulders, shaking off the strain of three straight hours in the pilot's seat and carefully stepping over slumbering bodies.

His mind was on his wife and young daughter waiting for him in Honolulu, when the number two engine exploded with enough force to shear the right wing at the engine juncture.

The MARS immediately adopted the aerodynamics of a rock, rolling over onto its right side. Vannet was thrown up in the farthest reaches of the tail as the plane plummeted for the ocean from 25,000 feet. He blinked blood out of his eyes from a cut in his forehead and tried to orient himself. Men were screaming and there were jumbled bodies everywhere.

Vannet's primary thought was to try and crawl back up to the cockpit, but his legs wouldn't obey his mind. There was a dull ache in his lower back and no feeling below his waist. He scrambled at the cross beams along the roof of the aircraft with his hands, trying to pull himself forward, climbing over other men at times.

Vannet was twenty feet from the front of the plane when the surface of the water met the aircraft with the effect of a sledgehammer slamming into a tin can. Vannet was crushed into the floor, and was dead well before the remains of the aircraft began sinking under the dark waves.

Area 51, Nevada
28 May 1949

The man who had been in the front seat of the car outside of Bethesda Naval Hospital picked up the phone on the first ring. "Vandenberg here."

The voice on the other end was distorted by both distance and scrambler. "This is Lansale. The final link has been severed. The Citadel is secure."

"Did you receive the last package?"

"Yes, sir. A ground convoy brought them in, but I don't understand why—"

The man cut him off. "It's not your place to understand. Did you secure them?"

"Yes, sir. They're in the base."

"The men in the convoy?"

"Taken care of."

"Excellent."

CHAPTER 1

Oahu, Hawaii
The Present

The woman gasped and the man stopped what he was doing.

"You don't like it?" he asked.

"Like it?" Tai reached down and unstrapped her leg from the weight he had attached to her ankle. "It's killing me." She slowly stretched out the bandaged limb. She looked at the Velcro strap with the two weights attached and then added a third. She strapped it back on her ankle.

"I thought it was killing you," Vaughn noted.

"No pain, no gain," Tai said as she got to her feet and looked down the beach. Vaughn stared with respect at the slender woman of Japanese descent. Her short dark hair was plastered to her head with the sweat from her efforts. They were on the north shore of Oahu, far from the tourists in Waikiki. The first day Tai had been released from the hospital she insisted on hitting the beach, managing to walk about twenty yards in her casts before collapsing. Now she was running five miles. With weights on her ankles. They had just come one way over three miles, so he knew it was going to be even farther today as they turned to head back. She had switched the weights from her hands to her ankles, as was her routine.

With a sigh, Vaughn set out after her as she began to lope down the beach. Three inches taller than her, at slightly over six feet, Vaughn also had a slender build. His hair was beginning to turn prematurely gray, flecks appearing here and there, the result of living in the covert world for too many years.

Now he and Tai were so deep under, he wasn't sure where they were. Their handler, Royce, wasn't even sure who *he* worked for. He'd reported them killed in action three months ago when they'd stopped the Abu Sayif terrorist group in its attempt to attack Oahu with nerve gas sprayed from the deck of an old World War II submarine.

Vaughn kept pace with Tai, but when they got within a half mile of the bungalow they were living in, he picked up the pace. She spared him a glance as he went by, then lowered her head and churned her legs harder. Vaughn felt slightly guilty for passing a woman who was only three months removed from intensive care, but over the time they had spent together, he'd learned she wanted no slack cut, nothing but his best effort. He saw the small path through the jungle that led up to the bungalow Royce had gotten for them and turned onto it. He came to an abrupt halt as soon as he saw Royce

standing there, waiting, leaning against his old Land
Rover with a battered leather briefcase in his hand.

"Been a while," Vaughn said.

"Where's Tai?" Royce asked.

Vaughn jerked a thumb over his shoulder. "She'll be
along in a second."

"So you two are bonding?"

Vaughn wasn't sure how to take that, given the dead-
pan way Royce said it. "We're getting back in shape."

"Good. Because something just happened."

Vaughn turned and looked over his shoulder as he
heard Tai coming down the path. She slowed to a walk
when she saw Royce. He'd only stopped by a couple
of times in the three months, judging their improving
condition but not saying anything.

Neither Tai nor Vaughn had been anxious to press
Royce for more information about the mysterious Organization he worked for, not after it had tried to kill
them several times after using them on a covert mission
against the Abu Sayif terrorists. They didn't know if the
Organization was working for the U.S. government, as
they were told when initially recruited, or some other
government or entity. The real problem had been learning that Royce didn't know either. He worked through
cutouts, a link that only knew the links on either side
but nothing further. And Royce was now their cutout.

"So what happened?" Vaughn asked, now that Tai
was present.

"I just received a letter from a dead man," Royce
said, holding up the briefcase. "Actually a letter from a
man who was murdered by the Organization. The letter
directed me to a package. And there was more than just
a letter in the package." Royce nodded toward the cottage. "Come inside. I'll explain and show you."

They followed him in. Royce placed the briefcase on the small kitchen table. Through the surrounding trees, one could catch glimpses of the ocean and the surf pounding the north shore. "The man who sent me the letter—he used to live here," Royce said. "For many, many years. Although he was traveling most of the time. Doing Organization business."

"He was your Hawaiian cutout," Tai said. A statement, not a question.

Royce nodded. "His name was David Lansale. He'd been in the OSS in World War II. He recruited me into the Organization. I worked for him along the Pacific Rim for many, many years. Then he decided it was time to retire."

Vaughn glanced at Tai. He sensed what was coming. He could tell by her face that she could too. And Royce noted the exchange. He smiled wanly "Yes, I know. A bit foolish to think one could retire from this life. But you do it long enough, get burnt-out enough, when someone dangles a carrot in front of you, you just might jump for it, even though you know better."

"Lansale jumped?" Vaughn asked.

Royce shrugged. "Jumped might be a bit strong of a word. I think he knew his time was up and he took the chance that maybe, just maybe, what the Organization was offering was real." Royce reached out and tapped the briefcase. "But obviously he also had strong doubts or he wouldn't have led me to this."

"Tell us what happened to him," Tai said as she wiped the sweat off her face with a towel.

"Short version," Royce said. "Three months ago—while we were in the midst of our little operation against the Abu Sayif—David 'retired.' He got on a private, unmarked jet with a group of other 'retirees' out at Kaneohe Marine Air Station. The jet took off heading west, for their island paradise retirement. It went down in the ocean, no survivors. No one was supposed to know about it, but I managed to track it through Space Command's eyes in the sky."

"Some retirement your group has," Vaughn said. He stared at Royce. "No wonder you got us on your side. You don't have much to look forward to, do you?"

"I suspected as much," Royce said. "Neither of you have much to look forward to either, especially considering you should be dead."

"Was he your friend?" Tai asked, which earned her a surprised look from both Royce and Vaughn.

After a moment's reflection, Royce nodded. "Yes."

Tai continued. "And his death was part of the reason you kept us alive and want to use us to find out what the Organization really is."

Royce nodded once. "Yes. That's partly it. It was probably the thing that pushed me over the edge. But there have been many things over the years that just haven't added up. And even David was suspicious of it all. Most of the time we seemed to be doing the right thing, but once in a while … " Royce's voice trailed off.

Vaughn had been recruited by Royce right after he led a disastrous hostage rescue mission with his Delta Force team in the Philippines. A mission where his brother-in-law was killed under his command. Tai had also been recruited in a similar manner—except she'd been sent undercover by the Defense Intelligence Agency to try to infiltrate the Organization to learn more about it, a move that had almost cost Tai her life when she was uncovered. Both of them now existed in a void. Thought to be dead by all except Royce.

"The letter?" Vaughn asked, trying to get him back on task.

"It was sent FedEx, but apparently held by a bank until yesterday to be delivered today," Royce said.

"Why the delay?" Tai asked.

Royce sighed. "I think David had it delayed in case he really did end up on that island. To give him time to cancel it being sent and cover his ass." He tapped the briefcase. "The letter directed me to a safety deposit box at the same bank where I found this." He opened the top of the case and pulled out several folders. Royce shook his head as he placed them on the table. "The funny thing is, I got most of this material for him. He sent me to St. Louis, to the National Personnel Records Center, a couple of years ago to do some digging. He didn't tell me what he was really looking for, just the bits and pieces." He indicated the table. "Which we now have here. A puzzle that I think we should solve to get a better idea of who and what the Organization is."

Vaughn sat on the open windowsill, feeling the slight ocean breeze stir.

"It's a strange place," Royce said absently as he stared at the material on the tabletop.

"What is?" Tai asked, confused by the sudden shift.

"The Records Center," Royce said. "Did you know they had a fire there in 1973 that destroyed the top two floors of the old Records Center? Which also conveniently destroyed the personnel records for those men involved in the government's nuclear testing in the late forties and the fifties, and also the records for those troops that had been exposed to Agent Orange in Vietnam.

"Sort of put the crimp in all those lawsuits the government faced from all those same personnel who had come down with various ailments they claimed were a result of those two government actions."

"Convenient indeed," Tai said.

"I got a crash course in the place when I went," Royce said. "I naturally had the highest clearance, and they assigned me a full-time research archivist. In the new archives, you have seventeen acres of paper hidden underground with an eight-story office building housing other federal agencies above it. Papers tucked away in the building run from old social security records to the original plans for Fat Man, the first nuclear bomb. As both of you know, the U.S. government runs on paper, and the National Personnel Records Center is the temporary storage place and clearinghouse for every imaginable type of government record. Even the Organization can't keep a lid on everything."

Vaughn was growing a bit impatient with Royce's recollections, but Tai gave him a look that indicated he needed to listen, so he forced himself to say nothing.

Royce continued. "Unclassified records are in folders placed inside cardboard boxes, which are stacked on rows and rows of shelves. The secure 'vault' contains all the classified records. Every scrap of paper produced by the numerous organizations, and every piece of paper relating to any person that ever worked for the government, are all kept in the Records Center."

"So there's a lot stuff there," Vaughn said, unable to hold back.

"Yeah," Royce agreed, "a lot of stuff, including this." He indicated the desk.

"And that stuff is?"

Royce picked up a folder on top. "Organizational record. Every Army unit keeps them. Regulation. Most are just boring recitations of facts filled out by some second lieutenant as an extra duty." He held up the folder. "But this one—Lansale sent me looking for a specific type of unit. Engineer units, 1949. That served in a cold weather climate. And this one fit the bill: it had photos in it."

He opened it and spread out twelve photos showing a desolate winter landscape and bundled-up men working on some sort of structure dug deep into the snow. Several of the photos were obviously posed, the men aware of the camera, but others showed them hard at work. One photo caught Vaughn's attention and he picked it up. About fifty men were gathered around a crude, hand-lettered sign that read : A COMPANY: THE CITADEL.

"That's doesn't make sense," Vaughn said.

Tai looked at the photo. "What?"

"The Citadel is the military college of South Carolina in Charleston. That sure isn't Charleston."

"I think they're referring to something besides a military college," Royce said.

Vaughn looked closer. Right behind the men was a metal shaft with a hatch on the side. In the faint distance were three massive mountains looming out of the snow-covered landscape. He turned the picture over. Printed in neat lettering was: 12 MARCH 1949. 48TH ENGINEERS. LIEUTENANT MACINTOSH.

"I asked the archivist who was helping me," Royce said, "about what that Citadel thing could refer to. She said it was probably some unit nickname."

Vaughn shook his head. "A company wouldn't be called the Citadel."

"That's what I thought," Royce said. "They've been trying to put as much as possible into digital form at the Records Center, so I had her do a search for the term in the unclassified data base, accessing armed forces installations. We started with the Army. It didn't take us long to learn there were no listings for Citadel. We then moved on to the Air Force and then the Navy with the same negative results. We even checked the Marines. Nothing. What that meant was that this one file folder of photos was the only record in the entire Records Center of such an installation. Or at least in the unclassified records."

Tai frowned. "Why did Lansale send you after this?"

"There's more," Royce said. "This unit history was just the start of what I dug up there. The photos there cover a four-month time period from February through May 1949. It's obvious they were taken in a very cold place, so we checked Alaska. Nothing. Greenland. Nothing. Iceland. Nothing.

"So we checked the unit, the 48th Engineers. Went into the stacks where every unit in the military has their records shipped eventually. We found a box from the 48th Engineers from 1949 through 1950. It was full of the usual stuff: copies of orders, promotions, citations, operations plans, and the various other forms of paperwork that Army units churn out in the course of business. I learned right away that the unit had been stationed right here in Hawaii at Schofield Barracks."

"That isn't Hawaii," Tai said.

"No shit," Royce said. "I found orders detailing two platoons, heavy construction, from the battalion to support Operation High Jump in late 1948."

"What was High Jump?" Vaughn asked.

"We'll get to that," Royce said.

"And what does this have to do with the Organization?" Tai asked. "Besides the fact Lansale sent you after this stuff and then put it together for you to get three months after his death?"

"Have either of you ever heard of Majestic-12?" Royce asked, instead of answering the questions they'd posed.

Vaughn shook his head, but Tai spoke up. "Something to do with aliens and Area 51?"

"That's the cover story," Royce said. "It's also sometimes called Majic-12." Royce spelled it out. "Majestic-12 was formed by presidential decree, this one"— he pulled out a copy—"which was buried deep in the archives among Truman's materials that weren't sent to his presidential library. He signed it into existence in 1947. When he did, he also authorized the building of two classified installations. One at Area 51. The other was called the Citadel.

"Majestic remains one of the most highly classified groups in the United States for the past sixty years." Royce picked up another piece of paper. "The original roster consisted of the first Director of Central Intelligence; the Chairman of the Joint Research Board, Dr. Vannevar Bush; the first Secretary of Defense, James Forrestal; the chairman of the precursor to NASA, and others. A lot of the power of the military-industrial complex was wrapped up in Majestic."

"What does Majestic have to do with the Citadel, whatever it is, and the Organization?" Vaughn asked. "Are you saying Majestic-12 is the Organization?"

"I think Majestic was either part of the Organization or used by the Organization," Royce said. "Majestic actually had a previous operation several of its members were part of. One that was formed as World War II wound down."

Royce paused and then pulled out a chair and sat

down at the table. He stared at the folders from the case. "It's a tenuous thread I'm weaving for you right now, but David wouldn't have made me get all this, then put it together and send it back to me like this, knowing I would get it if he'd been killed, unless there was some validity to it."

"All right," Vaughn allowed. "Weave it for us."

"Operation Paper Clip," Royce said. "A rather innocuous name for a very deceitful operation. As the Second World War was ending, the United States government was already looking ahead. There was a treasure trove of German scientists waiting to be plundered in the ashes of the Third Reich. That most of those scientists were Nazis mattered little to those who invented Paper Clip.

"Paper Clip used OSS operatives along with Intelligence officers from the Joint Intelligence Objectives Agency to go after what they wanted. In some cases they were actually snatching Nazi scientists away from Army war crimes units. Both groups were hunting the same men, but with very different goals in mind. This happened despite the fact that President Truman had signed an executive order banning the immigration of Nazis into the United States.

"Paper Clip brought in a lot of German physicists and rocket experts—the V-1 and V-2 men. NASA got its start through them. Also brought in were those most haven't heard about—the biological and chemical warfare specialists. With plenty of human beings to experiment on, the Germans had gone far beyond what the Allies had even begun to fear. While the Americans were still stockpiling mustard gas as their primary chemical weapon, the Germans had three much more efficient and deadly gases by war's end: Tabun, Soman, and sarin—the last of which the American military immediately appropriated for its own use after the war."

"And the Black Eagle Trust?" Tai asked.

Royce nodded. "Paper Clip did more than just gather scientists. They grabbed a lot of loot. Everything the Germans and Japanese had plundered, Paper Clip went after. When Majestic was formed, Paper Clip came under its control."

"Wealth and knowledge," Tai said. "That's what Majestic-12 went after and controlled."

"And they appeared to have been headquartered in Area 51, on the Nellis Air Force range," Royce said.

"The alien place," Vaughn said.

"Good misdirection cover story," Royce said.

"What the hell does that have to do with these guys standing in the snow?" Vaughn held the original photo in his hand.

"Because Majestic sent them there," Royce said simply.

"To do what?" Vaughn asked.

"That's the critical question, isn't it?" Royce asked in turn.

"To find something?" Tai wondered.

Vaughn was still staring at the photo. "Maybe to build something—they were engineers after all."

"That isn't all that was in the packet," Royce said. He pulled out a folder with TOP SECRET stamped in red letters across the cover. "The U.S. military ran another operation in Antarctica from 1955 to 1956. Called Operation Deep Freeze. They went back to the site of the original base camps that supported High Jump and found most had been destroyed by the weather. Once again they established a main base at McMurdo Sound—which has remained to this day the primary research facility in Antarctica. Again, I believe Deep Freeze was a cover for the Organization to go back to the Citadel."

"And do what?" Tai asked.

Royce opened the folder. "I don't know what was put in the Citadel in the forties during High Jump, if anything. But this is some of what was put in it during Deep Freeze." He slid photos across one at a time.

Vaughn stared for several seconds at the bulky object set on a trailer behind a large snow cat. "A big bomb?"

"Literally and figuratively," Royce said. "You're looking at a Mark-17 thermonuclear weapon. After the first Soviet nuclear test in August 1949, President Truman authorized the development of bigger thermonuclear yield bombs than had previously been contemplated."

"Bigger is better, right?" Tai said with sarcasm.

"Back then it was," Royce said as he looked at a piece of paper in the folder. "The scientists had several problems back then. The first, as you can see, was indeed the large size. But as difficult, if not more so, was that the first types they designed used liquid deuterium as the fusion fuel, which needs to be kept at a constant freezing temperature to remain viable. Ivy Mike, the first one they built, in 1952, was so big it filled an entire warehouse, weighing over seventy-four metric tons, and the entire warehouse had to be kept freezing. Its yield, though, was large: ten point four megatons."

"What good is a warehouse-sized nuclear weapon?" Tai asked.

Royce continued. "They worked on making it smaller and lighter, and eventually they ended up with the Mark-17, which to this date remains the most powerful nuclear weapon ever built by the United States. Even in the classified documents David uncovered, the yield wasn't quite certain, as none of them were ever tested—they were just too powerful. Estimates range around twenty-five to thirty megatons of blast."

"Damn," Vaughn whispered. "That would take out an entire city."

"Yeah," Royce said dryly. He glanced at the old paper. "The Mark-17 was rushed into production as 'emergency capable' weapons in 1954. Each weighed eighteen point nine metric tons and was over twenty-five feet long. Officially, all the Mark-17s were retired in 1957 in favor of smaller, lower-yield bombs that could be carried by a variety of airborne platforms."

"'Officially'?" Tai noted.

"According to these documents David sent me, four Mark-17s were unaccounted for in the final decommissioning tally. A fact that was made highly classified and swept under the rug."

Vaughn looked at the photo of the massive bomb on the trailer. "So they were sent to the Citadel."

"I believe so," Royce said.

"That's a long time ago," Tai said. "Surely the weapons can't be viable anymore?"

"They're cryogenic," Royce said. "As long as the bomb is kept below freezing, it could still be viable. What was a design flaw could turn out to be a design strength if the bombs have been sitting in Antarctica all these years."

"*Okay.*" Vaughn said the word slowly. "But why is this an issue now, today?"

"Because of something I noted on the FedEx form when I received it."

"And that is?" Vaughn asked.

"I'm not the only person David Lansale sent this information to."

Hong Kong

The penthouse suite commanded one of the best views of Hong Kong's harbor and was empty most of the year. Only when a member of the elite group that owned the building was in town were the rooms occupied. The present occupant had been there for what was a record: three months. She was a middle-aged Japanese woman with a slender build. She always dressed in black pants and turtleneck and often wore a long black leather coat.

She was always accompanied by two hard-looking men who never spoke and whose eyes were hidden behind wraparound sunglasses. The bulges under their coats indicated they carried heavy weaponry. The fact it was so obvious also meant they did so with the tacit support of the government, which meant this woman was not only rich, but carried considerable political clout.

For Fatima, these things only confirmed what she had come to Hong Kong suspecting: the Japanese woman, who went only by the name Kaito, was an emissary of the Organization. Fatima was a slight Filipino woman with long flowing hair that she kept bound in a ponytail that stretched down her back. She moved softly and quietly, so much so that the old couple from whom she was renting a room across the street from the office tower rarely knew when she came and went.

They also would never have guessed that she was now the head of one of the most infamous terrorist groups in the world—the Abu Sayif. She had assumed that mantle upon the death of her "uncle," Rogelio Abayon, three months ago. Which had coincided with the death of her father during the failed attack on Oahu.

While it appeared those deaths could be laid at the feet of the United States, Fatima did not buy into such an easy explanation. Abayon had always suspected that there was something darker and deeper at work in the world. Something that was even bigger than the United States. Some force that sought to oppress the majority of people while benefiting its own members.

And Fatima believed this woman she had been watching for a week was one of those on the other side. Abayon had sent a trusted lieutenant here to Hong Kong three months ago with orders to sell a treasure. Part of the Golden Lily. A slice of the plundered wealth the Empire of the Rising Sun had devoured during its expansion across the Pacific Rim during World War II.

Her organization still had the gold hidden in various places. But her "uncle" had sent Ruiz here to sell off much of the art. He had been half successful. The first night's auction was a rousing success, bringing in many millions of dollars to the hidden accounts of various organizations the Abu Sayif was allied with. But there had been no second night as planned.

Ruiz had disappeared. Along with the rest of the art he planned to sell.

And Fatima knew this woman had been the cause of the disappearance and the theft. Her contacts had traced the sale of some of the objects set for the second night's auction back to her.

Abayon had believed that the Golden Lily had been a cover for the Organization's own desires. That the Japanese looting had been sanctioned internationally. And that all those other slices of the Golden Lily that the Abu Sayif had not taken during the war had been coopted by the Americans and others, all still stooges for this Organization.

Today, she planned to learn more about the Organization, if she could. If she couldn't achieve that, at the very least she could achieve revenge for Ruiz. She had thousands of men and women under her command. Many ready to die for her. Yet she was here alone.

She knew Abayon would have approved. To those thousands, she had to prove her ability to command. In the week she had been watching, Fatima had picked up only one pattern to Kaito's day: she went to a local dojo to work out at the same time every morning. It was commendable discipline but bad for security. This morning, Fatima was already at the dojo, waiting. Kaito worked out in a private room set off to the rear, the outer door protected by her guards.

Fatima checked her watch. Kaito had been in there thirty minutes; she usually worked out for forty-five. Fatima walked in the front door of the gym, flashing the membership card she'd paid for with cash three days earlier. She turned down the corridor leading to the private workout rooms, shutting the double doors behind her and sliding the bolt. The two guards watched her approach without much concern considering that combined, they were over four times her weight. She wore loose pants, a sweatshirt, and carried a towel in her hands.

When she was within six feet of the door, one of them held up his hand and spoke in Chinese: "Private."

"Yes," Fatima replied in the same language without halting.

As the men were exchanging confused glances, Fatima fired, the suppressor on the gun making a slight puff as the first round left the barrel. It hit the left guard directly between the eyes. She fired again as the second guard was reaching for his own weapon. Again the shot was straight on, right between the eyes. Both men slid to the floor, dead before they were down.

Fatima pulled the door to the private room open and stepped inside, closing the door behind her. Kaito was in the midst of a *kata*—the formalized movement of a martial art exercise. She didn't even pause, continuing through to the end, bringing her fists slowly together in front of her, breathing out, then turning to face Fatima.

"Are you the masseuse?" Kaito asked.

Fatima dropped the towel, revealing the gun. "No."

Kaito stared at her. "Do you know who I am?"

"I know your name," Fatima said. "I know where you live. I know you killed one of my men, Ruiz."

A lifted eyebrow was the only reaction. "You are Abu Sayif." It was not a question.

"Yes. Where is the rest of the Golden Lily? I believe you owe us payment."

Kaito shook her head. "You received payment enough, especially considering the Golden Lily was ours to begin with."

"There you are wrong," Fatima replied. "The original owners of everything in it would disagree with you on that."

Kaito shrugged. "It is not even worth discussing." She pointed at a towel and indicated the sweat on her brow. "Might I?"

Fatima nodded. Kaito walked to the rack and took the towel.

"You haven't asked about your guards," Fatima noted.

"I assume they are dead. If they are merely incapacitated, they will be dead shortly for failing." Kaito looked at her. "It was a nice attempt by Abayon to try to attack Hawaii, but he failed. As you will fail in whatever foolish thing you are trying now."

"The Golden Lily," Fatima said.

"What of it?"

"There is still much that is missing."

"So?"

Fatima noted that Kaito was slowly moving, taking small steps while talking, getting closer to the wall where various swords and spears were racked. Fatima reached inside her sweatshirt pocket and pulled out a picture. She held it up. As Kaito paused to peer at it, Fatima lowered the barrel of the gun and fired.

Kaito cursed as the round tore into her thigh, knocking her to the ground. She put both hands on the wound, trying to stop the bleeding. "You bitch!"

Fatima tossed the picture toward Kaito. It showed a group of men in winter gear standing in front of a sign: A COMPANY: THE CITADEL.

"I received that from an anonymous source," Fatima said. "Along with other information. There was a note in the packet. It said this Citadel was connected to the Golden Lily. That important pieces of the Golden Lily are hidden there. Where is the Citadel?"

"I will never—" Kaito began, but her words changed to a hiss of pain as Fatima fired a round into her other thigh.

"I will see you dead for this," Kaito said between clenched teeth.

"Where is the Citadel?" Fatima demanded. She aimed the gun at Kaito's stomach.

Kaito stared at the barrel. "I have never heard of this place."

Fatima was tempted to pull the trigger, but held back. "Who would have heard of it? Who exactly do you work for?"

Even in her pain, Kaito smiled. "You would not survive five minutes going up against them."

"I'm standing here with a gun and you're lying there bleeding," Fatima noted. She inwardly sighed, knowing that Kaito actually knew very little. It was the same pattern that Abayon had faced over the decades as he tried to penetrate the Organization. She had received the package from FedEx through one of her cutouts in Manila. Who sent the package was unknown. How that unknown had also known the Abu Sayif cutout was also troubling, as it indicated a high level of access to intelligence information in both directions: about her own group, the Abu Sayif, and about the Organization.

"Who do you report to?"

"I will never—" Once more Fatima fired, the round hitting Kaito in the elbow, tearing the bone and nerve junctions. The Japanese woman screamed in pain, the sound echoing off the padded walls. Fatima went over to Kaito and ripped off her training *gi,* leaving the woman naked and bleeding on the floor. Fatima's focus was on the tattoo in the middle of Kaito's back. It was an intricate design of an octopus centered at the base of her spine, the tentacles spread across her back, two of them trailing down her buttocks and one even between her legs, indicating complete dominance. Fatima had seen it before and knew what group it represented, so she had the next step in her quest.

"I gave Ruiz an honorable death," Kaito hissed through her pain. "He died with a sword in his hand. I request the same."

"Ruiz, who probably had a hard time figuring out

which end of the sword he was supposed to hold?" Fatima asked. "I'm sure fighting against you was most fair." She walked over to the weapons rack and withdrew a samurai sword. She tossed it to the bleeding, naked woman, who caught it in her one good hand.

Then Fatima fired once, the round hitting Kaito in the left eye. The small bullet shattered inside her skull, tearing her brain up and killing her. She slapped back on the mat, a small trickle of blood seeping out of the socket.

Fatima pocketed the gun and left the room.

CHAPTER 2

Oahu, Hawaii

"The Citadel is in Antarctica, as you can tell from Truman's document, which David included in the packet," Royce said. "Where, exactly, though, is the problem. Antarctica is a very large place."

"Why is this Citadel so important?" Vaughn asked. "Besides the fact it might hold four hydrogen bombs, each capable of destroying a major city?"

Royce stared at him. "Majestic-12 built two bases when they were established. One was Area 51. Do you want to try to infiltrate it?"

Vaughn shook his head.

"And the other," Royce continued, "is the Citadel. Since no one has heard of it, perhaps it might be a little easier to approach, at least in terms of security. I'll grant you the terrain and weather are probably the most brutal in the world." He paused. "But the main reason is that David Lansale sent me—and someone else—this information. From the equivalent of his death bed. Actually from beyond his death. So I'm going to take a leap of faith and think it's important, very important. And that David wanted to poke a stick into the ant's nest that the Organization is and see what happens."

Poke a stick? Vaughn stirred irritably, not thrilled with being the stick.

Tai reached up and put a hand on Vaughn's arm. "Let's hear him out."

"Antarctica is ice-covered," Royce said. "The actual extent of the land underneath the ice is a best guess to a certain extent. A lot of people don't realize it, but the North Pole is ice on top of the Arctic Ocean—not a landmass. Antarctica is a true landmass, and it holds ninety percent of the world's ice and snow. And, interestingly enough, it is the only continent not to have its own native population."

Vaughn looked at the picture once more and the mountains in the background. "How well-mapped is Antarctica? I mean how could this Citadel, if it's there, have remained hidden for all these decades?"

Royce didn't seem to appreciate the "if it's there" qualifier. "If you wanted to hide something, the best place in the world would be Antarctica. Plus, according to the photos, it was built under the ice and buried. Although Antarctica is the size of Europe and the United States combined, less than one percent of it has been seen by man."

Vaughn was skeptical. "Even with overflights?"

"Even with overflights. From 1946 through '47 the U.S. Navy ran a mission called Operation High Jump using over five thousand men, thirteen ships, and numerous planes and helicopters. They took so many pictures that some of them haven't even been developed yet. Despite all that equipment and manpower, their coverage of the interior was very limited. With all that manpower, they managed to photograph about sixty percent of just the coastline."

"And build the Citadel," Tai said.

Royce nodded. "I think High Jump was just a cover to put the Citadel in place in Antarctica or it was used as a convenient cover once the exercise was planned. And it looks like they put it under the ice. The war was just over and the material and men were available. The government made no secret of the operation. You can look the mission up. It was well-documented. However, what no one seemed to wonder was why the government was so interested in Antarctica. And why did they dispatch dozens of ships and airplanes to the southernmost continent so quickly after the end of the war?"

"To hide things," Tai said. "So much of what was plundered by the Japanese and the Germans during the war has still never been found. Maybe that's where some of it went."

"It's likely," Royce said. "High Jump was a very extensive operation. The largest exploration operation launched in the history of mankind up to that point. The official expedition took so many pictures of Antarctica that they all haven't even been looked at to this date. Like I said before, the expedition surveyed over sixty percent of the coastline and looked at over half a million square miles of land that had never before been seen by man. I found boxes and boxes of reports and pictures from High Jump in the archives.

"Antarctica is a pretty amazing place. The ice cap is three miles thick in places. The current altitude of the land underneath the ice is actually *below* sea level in many places, but that's only because the weight of the ice on top depresses the continent. If the ice were removed, the land would rise up. Even today with all the subsequent explorations, only about one percent of the surface area of Antarctica has been traversed by man."

"What about satellites?" Vaughn asked. "They should have complete coverage."

Royce shook his head. "Satellites are either in synchronous orbits, which means they move at the same speed as the rotation of the earth, thus staying relative over the same spot, or they have their own orbits. As far as I know, there are none in a synchronous orbit above Antarctica—no reason for one to be. There are no weapons allowed down there by international treaty, thus no military presence."

"No weapons at all?" Vaughn asked.

"None," Royce said. "Some satellites run the north-south route and cross the poles, but two factors work against their picking up much. First, quite simply, no one has been that interested in Antarctica, so they simply aren't looking as they pass over that part of their orbit. Secondly, the weather is terrible down there, and it's rare that the sky is clear enough to get a good shot of the ground."

"You just said there are no weapons allowed down there," Tai noted. "So, I assume four big nukes would be a bit of a violation?"

"A bit," Royce allowed.

Vaughn had some experience working in cold weather climates during his time in Special Forces. He was beginning to get a strong sense of where this was heading. "What's the weather like down there, besides cold?"

"Bad," Royce said. "Usually very bad. Antarctica is

the highest, driest, coldest, windiest continent. Wind gusts of a hundred and fifty miles an hour are not un- usual."

"What do you mean driest?" Tai asked. "It's covered in snow."

"That's a misconception," Royce said. "It hardly ever snows or rains there. But you do have a layer of snow covering the ice that gets blown about a lot, causing whiteouts and blizzards. But there's very little actual precipitation."

"All this is fine and well," Vaughn said, "but as you've made abundantly clear, Antarctica is a large place. How do you propose we find this Citadel down there?"

Royce held up the picture of the men holding the sign. "You ask the man who took this picture."

Manila, Philippines

As she got closer to the designated place, Fatima felt more and more as if she were back in Japan. Very strange, considering she was less than two miles from her new headquarters hidden in the heart of the Filipino capital city.

It was a section of Manila, approximately ten blocks, with a concentration of Japanese who lived there, along with all the trappings for tourists to get a taste of the Asian homeland. It was bordered on the south by a five-acre mall that contained various shops, restau- rants, galleries, and Japanese gardens. At this time on a Friday night it was well lit and packed with people. Not exactly what Fatima desired in a covert meeting place, but she had no other choice.

She checked the directory for the center and found her destination. The Sensei Bookstore contained the city's largest collection of books in Japanese, so it was not strange at all when she walked up to the register and made her request in Japanese, naming a specific book she was looking for.

The response of the young woman standing behind the counter, however, was not normal. Her eyes flickered back and forth, then she lowered them.

"You must go to the Kawasan restaurant," she said in a low voice. "Down the stairs directly across from the door you came in. Turn right. One hundred meters. On the right. They will expect you."

Fatima turned and departed, glancing over her shoulder as she pushed open the door. The woman was on the phone, but still avoided looking at her. This piece of information had cost Fatima over $25,000.

She followed the instructions. The Kawasan was darker than the bookstore, and there was a queue of people outside. Fatima bypassed the line. A thin Japanese man in a very expensive suit stood next to the maitre d', watching Fatima approach. He took her right elbow in his hand. "This way," he said in Japanese.

Fatima felt the man's thumb press into the nerve junction on the inside of her elbow, effectively paralyzing her right hand. They wove their way through the darkly lit bar, then through a swinging door. Another man sat on a stool in the small corridor, a raincoat folded over his lap. The two men nodded. Fatima heard a distinct click, a door unlocking. They passed the second man, going through another door. It swung shut behind them with another click. Two men stepped forward, and Fatima's guide let go of her arm. They were in a short corridor with walls of some dark material that Fatima couldn't quite make out. The lighting was also strange.

"Hands out."

One of the men ran a metal detector carefully around Fatima's body. The other man then patted her down, double-checking, doing nothing sexual at all as he ran his hands over her breasts and between her legs. Then, with one on either side, they escorted her to a set of metal stairs. Their shoes clattered on the steel as they went up. A door opened, and Fatima blinked. They were on the top of the mall in a glass-enclosed room about sixty feet long by thirty wide. It was dimly lit by the reflected light from the surrounding city and the sky overhead. A dozen tables were spread out on the roof, and the two men led her to one separate from the rest, where several men dined.

Fatima was brought to a halt facing an older Japanese man who sat at the head of the table. She could see that the man's skin was covered in various tattoos, the signs of his Yakuza clan. Serpents disappeared into the collar of his gray silk shirt and dragons peeked out from his shirtsleeves. His fingers were covered with gaudy gold rings, jewels sparkling in the streetlights. Fatima shifted her gaze, checking out the roof.

The old man laughed. "The glass is specially made. It can take up to a fifty-caliber bullet. If my enemies wish to use something larger than that, then nothing much will stop them. It is also one-way. We can see out. Those on the outside see only black, making it also rather difficult for a sniper."

Fatima turned her eyes forward and waited.

"I am Takase, Oyabun of all that you see. I received a message from your servant," the old man said.

"I have no servants," Fatima said. "Only comrades in arms."

"Noble," Takase said with a sneer. "I understand you had a meeting with Ms. Kaito."

"Yes."

The old man ran a hand across his chin, stroking his thin beard. "She did not come out of the meeting feeling very well."

"She did not."

"There is no love lost between my clan and the Black Tentacle clan."

"That is why I am here."

Takase leaned back in his seat. "What do you need?"

"Information."

Takase's hand slapped the tabletop. "This is *my* part of the city. You show me respect."

Fatima stood still.

"I could have you killed and no one would ever hear from you again." The old man gestured, and the guards grabbed her arms.

"I would very much appreciate your assistance ... Oyabun," Fatima said as one of the guards placed a blade across her neck. The last word rolled off her tongue with difficulty. Showing any sign of respect for such a man distressed Fatima. But she needed him now.

He smiled as he dug his chopsticks into his food. "The great leader of the feared Abu Sayif. Except Abayon failed and is dead. And now a girl takes his place."

"I am no girl," Fatima said. "If I do not leave here unharmed in thirty minutes, this entire block will be destroyed. You are in *my* country. Oyabun."

"You attack me," Takase said, "then there will be war between our groups."

"A war you will lose in *my* country," Fatima said.

The sticks poised. "What do you want to know?"

"Kaito was Black Tentacle. Who does the Black Tentacle work for?"

"No Yakuza works for—" Takase began, but Fatima cut him off.

"Have your man remove the knife from my neck and have the others release me."

Takase gestured, and the guards backed off.

Fatima continued. "You are not a stupid man or else you would not be alive. You know there is an Organization out there that is bigger than the Yakuza. Bigger than any government. That uses others. That has been around for a very long time."

Fatima waited. Takase put down the chopsticks. He gestured, and those at the table with him left. The guards backed up out of hearing distance. "And if I knew of such a thing?" he asked, although he did not wait for an answer. "If such an Organization existed it would be so powerful I would not want to do anything to incur its wrath."

"That is indeed smart," Fatima said. "But I just want to cut a tentacle off, not take on the entire Organization. To do so, I must know where to find this tentacle. And as you indicated, this tentacle is something that is not friendly to you."

Takase considered this. "Why are you so concerned about this Organization? You fight the Christians, the Americans. Are they one and the same?"

"We fight the rich, who are gluttons," Fatima said. "Those few who keep the majority of the world's wealth and resources to themselves while millions starve and die of disease."

Takase laughed. "Such nobility from terrorists. The

dog is chasing its own tail. Political games don't interest me." He stuffed food in his mouth and chewed. "I will inform you when I have something to inform you of. My men will find you. Do not come back here."

Fatima turned and followed the two guards back to the stairs.

Behind Fatima, Takase waited until the woman was gone, then the old man stood. He quickly walked to an elevator, a pair of guards surrounding him as he moved. He stepped in, leaving the guards behind. It whisked him down over 150 feet, through the Japan center to a level four floors belowground. When the door opened again, Takase stepped forward into a large room, then bowed toward a figure behind a desk twenty feet in front of him, hidden in the shadows cast by large halogen lamps on the far wall. Takase spoke, while bowing, his words echoing off the heavily carpeted floor. "The new head of the Abu Sayif was here. She has asked for information about the Black Tentacle. It goes as you said it would, Oyabun. What should I do?"

The man seated behind the desk lifted a wrinkled and liver-spotted hand. When he spoke, his voice was so low, Takase had to strain to hear him. "She is reaching out into darkness. It is a dangerous thing to do, but Abayon would not have picked her if she were not special."

"She did kill Kaito," Takase noted.

There was only the sound of a machine pushing oxygen into the old man's lungs for several moments before he spoke again. "Let her know about the Black Tentacle and the I-401 submarine. That should keep her occupied and cause both the Black Tentacle and the Organization to remain busy."

Takase bowed his head in compliance. "Yes, Oyabun."

* * *

Two blocks away a man on a dark rooftop fiddled with
the controls on a small laptop computer and listened
to the voices from the top of the building through the
headphones he wore. In front of him a black aluminum
tripod held what looked like a camera. Actually, it was
a laser resonator. It shot out a laser beam that hit the
black glass on the top of the Japan center. The beam
was so delicate that it picked up the slightest vibration
in the glass. Reflecting back to a receiver just below
the transmitter, a computer inside interpreted the sound
vibrations into the words that caused them.

It had not taken the man long to tune out the background noise and get the computer to pick up the voices
inside. He'd heard the entire exchange between Fatima
and Takase. Satisfied that Fatima had left the room, he
quickly broke down the laser and placed it into a backpack along with the computer. Within thirty seconds he
was gone from his perch.

The room Fatima was renting was on the second floor
of a six-story hotel. She had picked it, as she'd been
taught in the terrorist camp in the Middle East so many
years ago, for its transient and illicit clientele, mostly
prostitutes and drug addicts. She hadn't even had to say
a word when getting the room. She'd shoved two hun-
dred-dollar bills at the clerk and received a key in return. Very convenient and inconspicuous, just as she'd
expected.

Abayon had been her godfather, and his best friend,
Moreno, her grandfather. Abayon had died in the explosion of his Jolo Island mountain lair at the hands of
the Americans, and Moreno had gone down with his
submarine during the failed nerve gas attack on Oahu.

She had thousands of loyal "soldiers" ready to do her bidding, but felt completely isolated with the passing of the two old men who had taught her so much.

Fatima unrolled her prayer mat and then knelt on it. She faced toward Mecca and began her prayers, but her mind kept sliding among the various issues confronting her. Her body was still tense from the encounter with the local Yakuza warlord.

These were the times she had doubts. When she wondered if this Organization her godfather had fought against was nothing more than the shadow of the western world looming over the third world, or even a religious schism: the Vatican had wielded tremendous power and controlled great riches for many hundreds of years. Although Abayon had tried hard not to make the Abu Sayif's battle to be against Christians, it seemed inevitable at times. Surely there were many in the western world who viewed Islam as the equivalent of terrorism.

Even as she prayed, she continued to consider the factor religion played in all the divisiveness. There were many of her followers who believed their battle, as devout Muslims, was against Christians. And they believed that battle had been forced on them by the western world through various actions, most particularly the unprovoked invasion of Iraq by the United States and its cronies. But in private, Abayon had always tried to steer her away from seeing things in that manner.

Abayon had fought beside Christians in World War II to free the Philippines from the hold of the Japanese. In fact, he believed that Christians and Muslims shared a common path and should be *closer* to each other rather than fighting. It was an opinion he had not shared loudly, particularly when dealing with other Islamic groups the Abu Sayif was loosely affiliated with.

For Abayon, and now for Fatima, it was a war between the haves and the have-nots. Between those who controlled the world's economy to further their own aims and those who suffered because of that. Fatima had no doubts that the large gap existed, she just wondered if it was being controlled by one organization, as her great-uncle had claimed, or simply the result of capitalism run amuck.

Fatima had to admit that Abayon had had solid reasons for his suspicion that this international Organization existed. He had become aware during the early years of World War II that as the Japanese expanded their empire around the Pacific Rim, their front-line troops were followed closely by elements of their secret police, the Kempetai, which began the systematic looting of the lands they conquered. The spoils were given the innocuous code name Golden Lily.

While fighting with the guerrillas, Abayon was captured along with his wife and sent to the infamous Unit 731 concentration camp in Manchuria. It was a horrible place where the Japanese tested chemical and biological weapons on living prisoners. Surprisingly enough, in this place of death, Abayon ran into an American, a man who had been part of a secret mission into Japan using Doolittle's raid as the cover for their parachute infiltration near Tokyo.

The American had been briefed that his three-man team's mission as part of the OSS—Office of Strategic Services, the American precursor to the CIA—was to parachute into Japan and make their way to a university where Japan's only cyclotron was located. He thought they were going to help destroy Japan's nascent nuclear weapons capability.

But the American had been shocked to be met at the drop zone by members of the Kempetei. One of the three was executed on the spot. The true surprise for the captured American who told this story to Abayon was that the third American, a man named David Lansale, was greeted by the Kempetei not only as if they expected him, but as if he were a guest.

All this Abayon had told her at her last meeting with him, before he sent her away, as if he were anticipating his coming death. After his escape from Unit 731 and the end of the war, Abayon tried to find out who this David Lansale was, who was greeted by the Japanese while the two countries were locked in a life and death struggle.

Supposedly he was an operative of the OSS, but Abayon found out that was just a cover. Abayon found information suggesting that Lansale was an envoy sent from the Organization's American branch to the Japanese representatives of the Organization, to coordinate the course of the war and the disbursement of the Golden Lily when the war was over. He found out that Lansale met with Emperor Hirohito's brother, Prince Chichibu, to coordinate the Golden Lily project. The deal made was that the Japanese could continue the Golden Lily, unopposed by the Allies, but that none of the loot was to be sent back to Japan proper.

Most of the riches were sent to the Philippines, some to other places, but none to Japan. It was a trade, Abayon had explained to her: by putting the Golden Lily in places where the Allies, particularly the United States, could recover it easily after the war, the Allies agreed to leave the Japanese Emperor in position after the war, a rather remarkable thing in hindsight.

As he finished telling her this, Abayon had laid on her another piece of startling information, this in regard to the agent David Lansale: that he was photographed in Dallas on November 22, 1963, the day President Kennedy was assassinated.

And now Lansale had risen once more, a specter in her life, in the form of the FedEx package she had received just the other day, containing the information about the Citadel.

Fatima believed that Kaito—and the Black Tentacle—were just an outer ring of the Japanese representatives of the Organization. And now she waited to find out if she could delve deeper.

At a knock at the door, Fatima turned her head. She drew the silenced pistol and stood in the corner, in the shadows. "Come in," she called out.

A man entered, just a dark figure. He took two steps and halted, hands well away from his sides. "I bring a message from the Oyabun. He says you look in the wrong direction. Japan is not where you want to go. The Black Tentacle is significant in its dealings with this Organization for the things they do for it. For one of those things that connects with what you seek, you want to follow the path of I-401."

Fatima was confused. "What is I-401?"

"A World War II Japanese submarine," the man said. "You can learn about it easily enough doing basic research. What you cannot learn easily enough is its last mission. And where it ended up. Even we do not know that. But if you do, then you will learn of this Citadel you seek."

"Who would know?" Fatima asked.

"Someone at the docks in the old American naval base. There is an old tug captain named Shibimi. He is a member of the Black Tentacle. We will let you know where and when you can meet him."

With that the man turned and was gone, shutting the door behind him.

Fatima slowly lowered her pistol. Her grandfather had just died on board a World War II era submarine. And now she must find the whereabouts of another one. This did not bode well.

A block away, the man who had been listening to Fatima's Yakuza meeting lowered the lid on the metal case that held the laptop computer. He had picked up the conversation in Fatima's room quite easily from his position in the windowless rear of a black van. He slid through a curtain to the front of the rental van and drove to the hotel where he was staying. It was much nicer than Fatima's. He parked in the garage and retired to his room.

Then he opened up a state of the art satellite radio and sent a coded message.

CHAPTER 3

Switzerland

Lake Geneva, or Lac Léman, as it is locally known, stretches in a northward arc from Geneva at one end, in the west, to Montreux at the other end, in the east. Built atop a rocky outcrop on the shore of the lake is Chillon Castle, just south of Montreux.

As castles should be and usually are, Chillon is located at a strategic point, controlling the narrow road that ran between the lake and adjacent mountains. This road had been a major north-south thoroughfare dating back at least to the days of the Roman Empire. It led to the Great St. Bernard Pass, the only connection between northern and southern Europe for hundreds of miles in either direction, east or west.

On top of the original Roman outpost, a castle had been built in the ninth century A.D. to guard the road.

The counts of Savoy razed that rudimentary structure and began building the current castle in the middle of the twelfth century. It was modified and rebuilt numerous times over the centuries that followed.

The castle has a unique design because of the spot on which it sits. The side facing the road and landward is a typical fortress wall, designed for military purposes. The side facing the lake, however, has the air of a summer residence for very rich people, which it has been over the centuries. It was very unlikely that an enemy would come over the Great St. Bernard Pass hauling boats with them, which determined the unique construction of the castle complex.

During the Romantic Era of the nineteenth century, the castle gained fame throughout the world in narratives by writers and poets such as Victor Hugo, Rousseau, Shelley, Dumas, and most notably, Lord Byron. *The Prisoner of Chillon* by Byron revolved around the legend of the imprisonment of Bonivard in the castle's dungeon in the sixteenth century.

All this is the known history of the castle.

The unknown history is much more interesting, for it was here that the Organization, whose name was always kept secret, established their headquarters in the Year of our Lord 1289. It was from Chillon that the High Counsel who oversaw the destruction of the Knights Templar and the burning of Jacques De Molay at the stake in 1314 rode forth, and it was to Chillon that he returned from Paris.

The Organization understood the concept that their headquarters had to be both secure and accessible, as they had dealings around the world. Long before *The Purloined Letter* was written, the Organization decided that the best place to hide their headquarters was in plain sight. At that time Switzerland was in the center of the known civilized world. The lords of Savoy owed their good fortune—as did almost all the great families in Europe—to the Organization, so it was not difficult to have two parts to the castle: the part that even today a tourist can go and see, and the part that no one except those who are part of the Organization's highest ranks can enter or even know exists.

It is not by chance that Switzerland has gone to extreme lengths to maintain its neutrality through numerous wars, including both world wars, an amazing feat considering its central location in Europe. It is also not by chance that Switzerland is the banking center of the world. The Organization did not deal in chance. They dealt in logic, power, and control. In essence, much like Vatican City is run by the Pope and Church, Switzerland has been controlled by the Organization for centuries.

In the early days of the castle, the Organization met in a secret room adjacent to the dungeon, where the sound of the waves of Lake Geneva lapping against the stone walls could be heard intermingled with the moans and cries of the prisoners, a mixture that seemed to be indicative of the way the group conducted itself.

As time went on and technology improved, the Organization dug deeper into the granite below the castle. Today it is not a large complex, but contains perhaps the most sophisticated computer and intelligence center in the world, rivaling anything in the Pentagon or at Microsoft.

The center of the complex is known simply as the Intelligence Center, or I.C. It is a circular chamber, exactly ten meters across. The walls are lined with the largest flat-screen displays available, all of which are hooked into the main computer. In the center of the I.C., on a series of four progressively raised platforms, much like a large wedding cake, sat four men. Each level could rotate at the man's command who occupied it, allowing each a 360-degree view of the displays.

The seating arrangement also reflected pecking order in the four levels, with the man at the bottom being senior. The four men, called "Assessors," work six-hour shifts, which can be extended indefinitely during periods of crisis to allow someone who was on duty during the initiation of the crisis to always be present until the crisis is resolved.

The Assessors sat in comfortable chairs, with a keyboard extended across their laps. They didn't use a mouse, but rather, wore gloves that had photo-optic leads attached with which they could interact with whatever data came up on the screens by pointing and bending their fingers. It was a complicated system that required six months of full-time equipment training before a new Assessor was allowed into the I.C. for his or her first shift.

While sophisticated and cutting edge, the true genius of the I.C. was buried one level below: the computer that ran the system. It was the most powerful mainframe in the world. The Organization could afford it. As important as the hardware was the software. The Organization had its own software company located in Geneva that worked only on its projects, the primary one called the COAP: Course of Action Projector.

Understanding that human beings were flawed in the analysis of information and intelligence, the Organization was trying to develop a software program to do it more efficiently. At present, version 3.2 was loaded into the mainframe below the I.C., while the programmers in Geneva labored on 3.3. The COAP took in all the data it could gather—a staggering amount, given the capabilities of the Internet—and tried to project what was going to happen based on probabilities. It was cold, it was logical, and it worked 72.3 percent of the time, at least based on results for the past five years. With 3.3, the Organization was hoping to get that rating up over 80 percent.

The machine, however, never had the final word. That was left to the High Counsel, who had his office in a chamber forty-two meters from the center of the I.C. He communicated via secure intercom with the Assessors and had no direct access to COAP, an interesting arrangement, in that it meant the computer's projections came to the High Counsel through humans.

A problem now on the screens and being considered by the Assessors was the disturbing information being forwarded from the Philippines. The intercepted conversations between Fatima and Takase, and then Fatima and Takase's representative, had just been played, and all four Assessors were lined up, like blocks ready to tumble over each other, listening to it.

As the tape came to a close, the High Counsel's voice echoed out of the speakers in the I.C. ceiling: "Do we know for sure it was Lansale who sent the information to Fatima?"

COAP had been analyzing intelligence concerning this for over twelve minutes now, an eternity for the machine. One of the Assessors shifted his ring and seat slightly to the left to look at the results to answer the High Counsel.

"Eighty-two percent probability that Lansale was behind it."   ·

"And the probability that Fatima can track I-401?"

A different Assessor had been working on that. "That's difficult to figure because we don't know what exactly was in the packet that Lansale sent her."

"Do *we* know where I-401 went?"

"No, sir. That was a joint Far East and North American Table operation at the end of World War II."

"Why would Lansale send the Abu Sayif this information?" the High Counsel wondered out loud.

To that, no one had an answer, as no one dared point out the fact that the Organization had just recently "retired" Lansale with extreme prejudice after over half a century of faithful service. A man who knew so many secrets was a dangerous man. Even now in death.

The High Counsel had not expected an answer. "Has Royce reported?"

"Yes, sir. He says he can bring a team together to deal with Fatima."

"Authorized and execute," the High Counsel ordered. There was a short pause. "And what of the Citadel?"

Another awkward silence descended.

"I want an answer," the High Counsel demanded.

The Senior Assessor cleared his throat. "Sir. The Citadel was apparently part of the North American Table and is somehow connected with this submarine I-401, which means the Far East Table was also involved. It explains why Fatima went after Kaito. She was the most junior member of the Far East Table."

One of the other Assessors spoke up. "Fatima going after Kaito might have been revenge over the Golden Lily, Hong Kong auction that Kaito ran. She betrayed the Abu Sayif."

The Senior Assessor shook his head. "I would think that also, except for the information we just received from our agent that she was given information. And the computer agrees with me."

"I know Royce will be on it," the High Counsel said, "but to expedite things, give our agent in the Philippines the authorization to take direct action to stop this line of inquiry by Fatima. Whatever Lansale sent to Fatima, it had to be something very important. He wasn't a stupid man by any stretch."

The Senior Assessor blinked. "Sir, doing that before we have complete data might not be the best move. I recommend—"

"Action in the Philippines," the High Counsel ordered. "We will wait on more information to determine what else to do. But right now, Fatima and those she is trying to contact is a problem that needs to be eradicated."

"Yes, sir."

"Back to the Citadel," the High Counsel said. "What do we know about it?"

The Senior Assessor answered. "It appears when they formed Majestic-12 they not only established Area 51, which they still use, but the Citadel."

"'Apparently'? 'Appears'?" The High Counsel turned in his chair and faced his Assessors on screen. "Does this place exist?"

"Not in our computers," the Senior Assessor admitted. "The formation of Majestic in 1947 naturally predates the use of computers and—"

"The vast majority of our history predates the use of computers," the High Counsel interrupted.

"Yes, sir. But we can only process information the North American Table sent us. And apparently, we never received any data from the North American Table about it."

The High Counsel leaned back in his chair, considering this. "So there are two possibilities. The Americans withheld the information. Or they lost it."

"Sir, there is a third possibility," the Senior Assessor said. "Lansale was the man who sent the packet to Fatima and the Abu Sayif. Lansale was one of the senior—if not the senior—field operative for the North American Table for half a century. The things he did and was involved in, well—there is no need to say there are far more significant things than this Citadel and a lost World War II submarine."

"As noted, Lansale wasn't stupid," the High Counsel said. "He picked this one thing to send to Fatima in case of his death. Summon the head of the North American Table. Tell him to bring everything they have on this Citadel. Inform the Far East Table of our concerns and find out what they know about this I-401 submarine."

Oahu, Hawaii

"That's him," Tai said.

Vaughn stared at the bent-over old man who was slowly walking down the street, a plastic bag dangling from one hand. Royce had tracked down former First Lieutenant MacIntosh using his Organization resources without much trouble. MacIntosh had retired as a lieutenant colonel from the Army right here on Hawaii after putting in thirty years of service. According to the file, his wife had died eight years ago and he lived alone in the small bungalow.

"Let's hope he doesn't have Alzheimer's," Vaughn said as he opened his car door.

They walked down the sidewalk and came up on MacIntosh, one on either side. He didn't notice their presence until he turned for the walkway to his small house.

"Who the hell are you?" he demanded as Vaughn blocked his path. Then he noticed Tai and his demeanor changed. "And who are you?" he added with a smile.

Tai shot Vaughn a look, and he knew what she was thinking.

"We have some questions, Colonel MacIntosh," Tai said.

He looked her up and down. "You still haven't said who you are."

"I'm a reporter with CNN," she replied.

"And him?" MacIntosh jerked his head at Vaughn.

"My assistant," Tai said. Vaughn rolled his eyes but didn't say anything.

"And why would a beautiful young woman like you want to talk to me?" MacIntosh asked. "Not that I object," he hastily added.

Tai smiled. "It has to do with when you were in the Army."

"I assumed that when you called me 'Colonel,'" Mac-Intosh said. "And to be precise, I retired as a lieutenant colonel." He nodded toward his bungalow. "Why don't you come inside and sit down."

They followed him in. Vaughn glanced at Tai as Mac-Intosh pulled a bottle of vodka out of the plastic bag. He made no attempt to hide it, indeed, he offered some to them. "A glass?"

Both Tai and Vaughn politely declined. MacIntosh poured himself a glassful over the rocks and then lowered himself into a chair around an old wooden kitchen table. Tai and Vaughn flanked him, Tai pulling out an iPod with an iTalk recorder on top. "Do you mind if I record this?"

MacIntosh shrugged. "I'm not supposed to talk about what I did in the military. Secrets and all that good horseshit. But, hell, I retired a long time ago. And I'm dying." He said it matter-of-factly. He held up the glass. "Yeah, I drink all the time. Why the hell not? Doc said I got about six months. Fuck it. Nothing's been worth it since Meg died." He took a drink. "So what do you want to know?"

Tai leaned forward. "We've learned that the Army built a secret installation, called Citadel, in Antarctica in 1948-49."

MacIntosh frowned. "What kind of secret base?"

"We don't know," Tai said. "That's why we're asking you."

MacIntosh gave a sly smile. "Why are you asking me specifically?"

Vaughn pulled out the black and white photo and laid it on the table. "Because you took this picture. And others."

The smile was gone from MacIntosh's face as he looked at the picture. "Yeah, I took that." His voice sharpened. "Listen, we were told everything about that place was classified. I mean, it was a long time ago and all that, but still, a guy can get in trouble."

Tai leaned forward in her seat once more and flipped the picture over. "They have your name on the back."

There was a long pause, and finally MacIntosh spoke, his voice resigned. "Yeah, I took those damn pictures. At first I didn't see what the big deal about the whole thing was anyway. It was an additional duty I was assigned: battalion historian. But they told us not to talk about it— national security and all that."

"Who are 'they'?" Tai asked.

"The big shots. High-ranking officers. Except I could tell they didn't know shit either."

Tai leaned back. "What about the air crews that flew you in there? Do you know where they were from?"

"There was only one air crew that did all the flights. I think they were home-based out of here—Hawaii. They sure didn't like the cold. Flew a big-ass seaplane that had been modified to land on ice." His eyes got a distant look. "No one liked the cold."

"You were with the 48th Engineers," Vaughn said.

"Yes."

"A company?" Vaughn added.

MacIntosh shook his head. "No. I was with Battalion staff. If I'd been with A Company, then ... " His voice trailed off.

"Then what?" Tai pressed.

"Then I wouldn't be here. They all died."

"How?"

"Plane went down on the way back," MacIntosh said. "No survivors. Hell, they never found the plane or the bodies. Went down in the ocean. And it was a damn floatplane, so it had to have crashed, not made an emergency landing."

Vaughn glanced at Tai. He knew she was thinking the same thing he was—very convenient. And exactly the way Lansale had died.

"Why weren't you on the plane?" Tai asked.

"I should have been," MacIntosh said. "But I got evacuated during one of the supply runs. Actually, the last supply run before they pulled the company out. And since I wasn't on the company roster, I guess no one missed me on the last flight." He held up his left hand. "Frostbite. From taking those damn pictures. I got careless. You'd think I'd have known better after three months, but—anyway, I got the bite bad and needed to be medevacked. I hopped a ride on that plane. Never got listed on the manifest.

"From there they sent me on back here to Hawaii. One plane early. If I hadn't been medevacked ... " MacIntosh fell silent.

"Where was the Citadel?" Tai asked.

"I don't know."

Tai frowned. "What do you mean you don't know? You didn't know where you were?"

MacIntosh tried to explain. "I mean, I knew we were in Antarctica, but I couldn't tell you where. We weren't allowed any maps. When we flew, they blacked out the windows in the hold of the MARS. No one in that company knew where the hell they were the entire time they were there."

"You had to have some idea," Tai pressed. "What direction from High Jump Station?"

"You ever been to Antarctica?" MacIntosh didn't wait for an answer. "The goddamn place is one big jumbled-up mass of ice and mountains. North or south?" MacIntosh laughed. "Compasses don't work too well down there. Do you know that the magnetic pole is farther north of the true South Pole than where they had High Jump Station? In fact, magnetic south from High Jump Station, which is now where McMurdo Station is located, is actually west if you look at a map. That was the most screwed-up place I've ever been. All I know is that the site was a little less than a four-hour flight by MARS seaplane from High Jump Station. You look at the pictures and you got as good an idea of where that place was as I do."

"What did the engineers build there?" Tai asked.

"They didn't really 'build' anything per se," MacIntosh said. "They put together a Tinkertoy set. It was all prefab," he explained. "They flew this thing in by sections, and the MARS was the only plane big enough to fit them inside of. Someone with a lot more brains than we had in our outfit designed that thing. Each piece could just fit inside the plane, yet when they put it all together it was surprisingly big. Of course, there was a shitload of cargo coming in. Hell, they spent almost an entire week just bringing in fuel bladders. That plane flew every moment the weather allowed. Must have made over a hundred trips at least. That I know of. And I heard whispers that other stuff was brought in over land by those big snow cats they—huge tractors with treads."

"Whispers from who?" Vaughn asked.

"Some of the guys," MacIntosh said vaguely. "We weren't supposed to talk about anything. But you know how the Army is."

"Yeah," Vaughn agreed.

MacIntosh smiled. "You had the look. Can't ever get rid of it." He looked at Tai. "You too. You were military, weren't you?"

Tai nodded. "Yes. I was." She tapped the photo. "What was it that A Company put together?"

"They put it under the ice." MacIntosh shrugged. "My best guess is that it was some sort of C and C structure—Command and Control. They blasted out deep holes in the ice, then used 'dozers to clear it. Then just put the buildings together in the holes. Then the bulldozers and weather would cover them up fast. Ice would seal in around the walls. Before we were even done, they brought in other guys to put in other stuff. I remember a lot of commo equipment. They sealed off sections of the place as we finished, so I really couldn't tell you what it looked like on the inside when it was completed. None of the other specialists they brought in had a clue where the hell they were or what they were working on.

"The guys in the 48th stayed in several prefab Quonset huts on the surface, and we broke those down and took them back out with us when we left. All that you could see when we took that last flight out was the entry and ventilation shafts. Everything else was underground."

"What did it look like underground?" Vaughn asked.

"There were twelve of the prefab units."

"How were the units laid out?"

"We set them up in three rows of four, about eight to ten feet apart, and roofed over the space between, which just about doubled the underground area of the main base."

"That took four months?"

"What took the most time was blasting out that much ice and snow even before they brought in the first unit. They also dug two really big tunnels on either side for storage and two areas for fuel. Plus the long tunnel and area for the power station."

"Do you have any idea who was stationed there?"

"You know, that was the funny thing. When I flew out, I really don't think there was anybody left behind besides Alpha Company, and they were all on that last plane out."

Vaughn sat back in his chair and stared out at MacIntosh's small backyard. It seemed strange to be talking about this, looking at the bright Hawaiian sunshine.

"I don't get it," Vaughn said, trying to process everything. "Why go through all that trouble to build something if no one was going to use it?"

"Hey, you got me." MacIntosh snorted. "I'm just a poor taxpaying schmuck like everyone else. I don't know why the government spends money like it does."

"What about nuclear weapons?" Tai threw in.

MacIntosh was startled. "What?"

"Mark-17 nuclear bombs," Tai said. "You can't miss them. Big suckers."

"I don't know what the hell you're talking about, miss. I didn't see no bombs, that's for sure." He paused in thought. "But then again, I didn't see everything in that place. I don't think anyone from the 48th saw the entire thing. Everyone's job was very compartmentalized."

Vaughn tapped the photo. "So you have no clue what this base was built for? Who it was built for?"

"We followed orders," MacIntosh said.

"Ever occur to you that the people issuing the orders were ... " Vaughn tried to figure out how to phrase it and then simply gave up, knowing it didn't matter.

MacIntosh stirred. "There was this guy who came out every so often on the MARS. He was a real strange fellow. Spooky."

"Military?" Vaughn asked.

"He didn't wear a uniform," MacIntosh replied.

"Why was he spooky?" Tai asked.

"Just was. Cold eyes."

"Did he have a name?"

"David Lansale."

Vaughn took a deep breath and glanced at Tai. They both stood.

"Thank you for your time," Tai said as she turned off the iPod and put it in her pocket.

MacIntosh took another deep drink of vodka. "Come back any time. I don't get many visitors."

Manila, Philippines

Fatima watched her figure in the mirror. Muscles flowed as her legs and arms performed one of the required movements of a fifth-degree tae kwon do black belt.

"Hai!" she shouted, her fist halting a millimeter from its reverse image. She slowly pulled the fist back as she returned to the beginning stance. The windows in the one room motel room were open, and the chill night air hit the sweat pouring off her skin, creating a thin layer of steam. She wore only a pair of cutoff white shorts and a sports bra. Her feet slid across the floor as she began another formalized *kata*. The calluses that years of working out had built up made her hardly notice the rough wood floor.

The room was empty except for the rest of her clothes hung and stacked in the closet. A bed sat near the window, but Fatima had not used it. If she had to rest, she slept on a thin mat, moving its location on the floor every night. Sometimes she slept right under the window; sometimes just behind the door; sometimes she folded her body into the scant space in the bathroom, a gun always close at hand.

Fatima's leg snapped up high: front kick to the face. She froze for a second, then slowly lowered the leg, her head canted to one side. Her cell phone was vibrating. She went over and picked it up. "Yes?"

"Shibimi's tug is docking at Pier 23 in an hour. He thinks you are an arms dealer. Black market. He will talk to you but he wants something in exchange."

"What?"

"Weapons. Ten M-16s. With a thousand rounds of ammunition."

The phone went dead.

Two and a half miles away from Fatima's location, the computer awoke with a chime. The man had been reading a book, and he carefully marked his page before flipping open the computer's lid. The display told him Fatima was moving. He shut the lid and gathered his equipment.

Oahu, Hawaii

"Lieutenant Colonel MacIntosh, retired, United States Army?" Royce asked.

"Yes?" MacIntosh's eyes were blurry and his speech slurred. He stood in the door of his cottage, one hand on the frame to steady himself.

"I have a couple of questions," Royce said as he brushed by the old man.

MacIntosh shut the door and turned. "Are you from Intelligence?"

Royce nodded. "Yes. You talked to that couple that was just here, didn't you?"

MacIntosh sighed. "That was so long ago, who cares now?"

"You told them everything you know about the Citadel?"

MacIntosh went over to the table and picked up his glass. "Yeah. What are you going to do? Court-martial me?"

"I don't have a problem with you talking to them," Royce said. "In fact, I sent them to you."

MacIntosh frowned. "Then what do you want?"

"I want to make sure you don't talk to anyone else." Royce stepped up to the confused old man and lightly slapped him on the back of the neck.

MacIntosh started and reached up to feel where he'd just been touched. "What the hell was that?"

Royce slid off the metal ring he had on his middle finger, carefully avoiding the small barb that protruded from it. He slipped it into a metal box and put it in his pocket. "Good-bye, Colonel."

MacIntosh was still rubbing the back of his neck. "What did you do?" The words came out slowly and even more slurred than before.

"Killed you," Royce said as he turned for the door.

MacIntosh tried to get to his feet but couldn't move. He tried to speak again but the muscles wouldn't respond. Royce paused at the door and looked over his shoulder. MacIntosh's eyes had lost their focus and his chest wasn't moving. His head slumped forward.

Royce pushed open the door and left the dead man behind.

Philippines

An hour was not much time. Fatima made a couple of calls as she gathered her gear and left the room. She knew she would not be coming back to it.

Weapons, especially M-16s, were not hard for her to get her hands on. The Abu Sayif had numerous stores of weapons. She had called to find out the closest location for these specific guns.

The drop site she'd been given was in a storage unit. Fatima unlocked the combination padlock and pulled up the door. Two crates and one small box lay just inside, in front of other boxes containing various equipment. The Abu Sayif was efficient. She didn't know who had put the guns in there, and she was sure that whoever had didn't know she was taking them out. The storage unit was a good cutout between operatives and support personnel. The Filipino government took a hard line with the Abu Sayif, especially right in Manila.

Fatima uncrated the ten M-16s and the ammunition. The M-16s were brand new, probably stolen from a government warehouse or even bought right out of government soldiers' hands.

Fatima worked on one of the M-16s, secreting a small transmitter inside the hollow of the pistol grip; a place no one would have any reason to look. Then she broke each gun open, removed the firing pins and then reassembled them. She tied the guns together, then wrapped plastic bags around them, waterproofing both them and the ammo. The package was bulky, but she managed to stuff it into a large rucksack.

Fatima relocked the door to the bin. She just barely had time to make it to the designated meet site. She put the rucksack on the passenger seat of her old Chevy and began driving through the streets of Manila.

By the time she arrived at the old American naval base in Subic, she was shifting into her action mode. There was some activity, but nothing nearly as it used to be when the Americans ran their fleet out of it. She drove past the empty guard shack and toward the piers.

When she got close to the designated pier, she parked the car and looked around. There was indeed an old, rusting tug moored at the designated pier. But all its lights were off and it looked deserted. To her left there was an old ammunition bunker, built like a small fort, with a gate entry wide enough to take a truck. The steel gates were wide-open, and she could see a light inside with flickers of shadows, which indicated people moving.

Taking the rucksack full of weapons, she left the truck. Fatima felt almost naked walking across the street toward the ammo bunker, and she had a feeling she was being watched. She noted that there were no other vehicles about. As she entered the brick archway, she sensed someone behind and spun around. Two dark figures stood there, blocking her way out.

"Come in!" someone who spoke English said, his voice echoing in the courtyard. Fatima turned and walked forward. The small courtyard was surrounded by the bunker's walls, two stories high on all sides, with brick arches opening to the ammunition mezzanines. She couldn't see who had called out. The voice could have come from one of dozens of arched openings on any side, from any floor.

Fatima walked directly to the middle and put the rucksack down. She folded her arms over her chest and waited. The two men who had followed her were now standing inside the entrance, also waiting.

A shuffling sound drew her attention, and Fatima turned to her right. Two other men were walking out of the shadows from the north wall.

"You have the guns?" one of the men asked, again in English, which most Filipinos knew. As he cleared the shadows, Fatima finally got a good look at his face. Japanese. There was no mistaking the facial features. But too young to have been alive during World War II.

"I have them."

The man gestured, and the man at his side came forward and opened the rucksack, checking the weapons and ammunition.

"Where is Shibimi?" Fatima asked.

The man was breaking down one of the weapons, his hands moving expertly over the metal pieces despite the lack of light.

"It is functional," the man called out to his leader in Japanese. Fatima realized they didn't know she understood their language.

"Where is Shibimi?" Fatima repeated.

"He will be here shortly," the leader said in English. "*Kill her*," he called out in Japanese to his men.

The man with the M-16s near Fatima was sliding a magazine into one of the weapons. Fatima considered it a fundamentally unsound business practice to be killed by her own merchandise. She turn-kicked toward the man with the M-16, only to see him sidestep the strike, grab her leg and twist, dumping her on her back. The Japanese put the stock of the M-16 into his shoulder and aimed down at her. He pulled the trigger, and nothing happened.

In his moment of confusion, Fatima drew her silenced pistol and fired twice, both rounds hitting him in the head and knocking him backward. A second man came running forward, a silenced submachine gun at the ready, and then abruptly halted as sparks flew off the concrete floor near him. Fatima could feel the presence of bullets flying by, although she heard no sound of firing. She rolled and looked up, spotting the muzzle flash of a weapon being fired high up on the south wall. The Japanese who had been about to shoot her jumped right, out of the way of the unexpected firing, grabbing the duffel bag with the other weapons and getting behind the cover of one of the large crates.

Fatima didn't stop to savor her reprieve. She scuttled on her back, the concrete ripping through her shirt, managing to get behind a large pile of boxes. At least she was concealed from the Japanese, she realized. Whoever the gunman on the wall was had a perfect shot at her, but he'd had a perfect shot at her earlier and hadn't taken advantage of it, so she felt she had to take the chance.

The second Japanese man let loose a sustained burst of fire up at the wall, but the man was firing blindly, not sure where his target was. The gun battle was eerie, played out in almost total silence, only the flaming strobe of the muzzle flashes and the sparks of rounds ricocheting giving any hint as to what was happening.

Fatima peered around the crates, keeping low. The Japanese leader had joined the gunman. While the leader provided cover, the other ran with the duffel bag toward the archway where the other two waited. And was cut down in mid-stride by a burst of automatic fire from the unseen gunman. The leader took that as a hint to escape and sprinted for the exit, grabbing the duffel bag as he went by the body. And then he was gone. Fatima twisted toward the entrance where the last two Japanese had been, but there was no sign of them now, and she assumed they were most likely leaving with their leader.

She turned toward the wall behind her, pistol at the ready, and waited, but spotted no movement. "Who is there?" she finally called out in English. Her words echoed off the wall with no reply.

Silence reigned, and Fatima did nothing to break it. She gave the surviving Japanese and unknown gunman plenty of time to escape, then stood. She didn't hear any sirens. Time to be going. First, though, she went to the closest body. She checked for tattoos, and as she had suspected, found the mark of the Black

Tentacle on it. She then cautiously made her way to the entryway and slipped through, ran to her Chevy and jumped in.

As she drove away, she opened up the GPS tracker and turned it on. She drove slowly and carefully, in no rush, wanting the Japanese to think they had escaped her. The unknown gunman bothered her, a wild card, and she had no clue who had played it.

Fatima glanced at her cell phone, considering whether it was time to call in more firepower. That's when she noticed that the bug had stopped moving. It was about two miles ahead of her, still inside the sprawling Subic Bay compound. She cut her lights and drove closer, coming to a halt when she rolled to a stop close to the flashing green dot on her GPS screen.

She looked ahead. A trawler was tied to the pier in front of her. She reached down, retrieved a set of night vision goggles and put them on. Through them she could see the boat clearly.

Two hundred meters away a stranger watched Fatima watch the boat. She sat cross-legged on top of a warehouse, a silenced submachine gun across her knees. She knew who the extra shooter was on the wall during the ambush. So even though her main focus was on Fatima, she also checked out the surrounding area, trying to find if the shooter was still after the same scent.

While she was searching the shadows through a night vision scope, her attention was distracted by movement on the boat.

Through the night vision goggles, Fatima watched four men come down the gangplank. They did not have the duffel bag of weapons with them, but she didn't care about that. What she did care about was the man who appeared to be in charge: he was old, definitely with enough years to have served in World War II. She observed as the Japanese got into an old model Ford LTD and a newer Camaro parked nearby. As they peeled out of the lot, she followed. When they cleared the old Navy base, traffic got heavier. Checking her rearview mirror, she noticed a black van following farther back and made a note to keep an eye on it.

The procession continued until they were heading into the mountainous countryside surrounding Subic Bay. Glancing in her rearview mirror, Fatima could tell that the black van was holding its position. The two cars were ahead in the far right lane and scrupulously staying at the speed limit.

She didn't like her position between the Japanese and whoever was trailing. She was too close to the Japanese Yakuza, and there was a good chance they would detect her presence. She didn't want to take a chance, though, and go behind the van, since she didn't know who was at the wheel of that vehicle. For all she knew, there were other Japanese.

They approached a point where the road cut a tunnel through the knee of a mountain. Fatima was a hundred feet behind the Camaro, which was right on the bumper of the LTD. Both cars slipped into the mouth of the tunnel, and she kept her distance. She glanced in her rearview mirror; the van was also keeping its place.

As Fatima returned her attention to the front, she automatically pulled her foot off the gas pedal. The brake lights on the Camaro were bright red in the tunnel ahead. She heard the squeal of rubber as the Camaro spun about. A car in the other lane narrowly avoided collision, swerving out of the way. Fatima slammed her foot on the brake as the headlights of the Camaro fixed on her windshield.

She halted, but the other car didn't. The front bumper of the Camaro smashed into the left front grill of the Chevy, jolting Fatima forward against her seat belt, then snapping her head back, bouncing it against the headrest. The Camaro pinned the Chevy against the wall of the tunnel, the right front side hitting concrete.

Two men jumped out of the Camaro, M-16s at the ready. Fatima ducked before they fired, the bullets shattering the windshield above her, showering her with broken glass. Either the M-16s weren't those she had given them or the missing firing pins had been replaced.

She unbuckled her seat beat and slithered between the front seats into the back, where the backseat was down. Bullets continued to stream by over her head. She added a few rounds with her pistol, shooting out the right rear window of the car.

Gathering herself, she dove out through the opening she had just created. She bounced off the right wall of the tunnel, grunting as she felt pain jar through her shoulder. Hitting the pavement, she rolled, pistol at the ready, peering underneath her Chevy. She could see the legs of the Japanese on the near side of the Camaro. She fired twice, both rounds hitting the man in the ankle, tearing his leg out from under him. Fatima fired again at the prone figure, this time a head shot, killing the stunned man instantly. All of four seconds had elapsed since the accident, and the only noise had been that of the collision and the bullets shattering glass.

Now there was the sound of another car coming to a hurried halt, and Fatima took a chance, popping her head up over the trunk to see what the tactical situation was. She expected the LTD to be there, disgorging more gunmen, but was surprised instead to see the black van twenty feet away and a man leaning out the passenger's side, a silenced Steyr automatic rifle in his hands. He hosed down the second Japanese, blowing blood and guts all over the right side of the Camaro. Fatima froze an image of the man in her memory: Oriental, mixed, although more Japanese features than Korean, short and thin, and from the way he handled the gun, a professional at the job of killing.

Her visual inventory was brought to an abrupt halt as the man turned the smoking barrel of the Steyr in her direction. For the second time, she dove for cover as bullets tore chips out of the concrete above her head. Fatima fired underneath, but the man was inside the van, and all she could shoot at were the tires.

The firing abruptly ceased, and she heard a vehicle accelerate away. She carefully edged her head around the rear of the Chevy. The van was gone. Two smashed vehicles and two dead bodies. She watched the van disappear down the tunnel to the east.

"Fuck," she said, standing up and dusting off broken glass from her clothes. There was a bottleneck of frightened motorists in their cars to the west, but no sign of police yet. Fatima reached into the front of the Chevy and pulled out her homing device. There was nothing else in the vehicle that could identify her.

She brought the muzzle of her weapon up as a white van wove its way through the halted cars and raced up to her. She had a perfect sight picture on the driver, who leaned over and threw open the passenger door. "Get in!" the woman yelled.

Another Japanese person, Fatima noted, keeping her weapon steady. She heard sirens in the distance.

"Get in!" the woman repeated. The sirens were getting closer.

Fatima hopped in, keeping her weapon trained on the driver. The woman took off, heading west. They passed through the tunnel and out into the night air on the other side of the mountain.

"I don't see them," the driver said, peering ahead.

"And you are?" Fatima asked. The woman appeared young, somewhere in her mid-twenties by Fatima's best guess. She wore gold-rimmed glasses and a very nice dark gray outfit. Fatima pressed the barrel of her pistol into the side of that suit and repeated her question. "Who are you?"

"My name is Araki," the woman replied. She appeared not to notice the gun poking into her side.

Fatima spared a glance out the windshield. There was no sign of either the van or the LTD. "And you are with?" Fatima asked.

"Japanese CPI," the woman said. "I assume you are with a Filipino government agency," she added.

"Why do you assume that?" Fatima asked. She knew what CPI was: Central Political Intelligence, a secret arm of the Japanese government formed after the Tokyo gas attacks a few years back.

"You were following the Japanese Yakuza," Araki said.

"And?"

"Who else would be following them?" Araki asked. "Other than police or other Yakuza. And you do not appear to be Japanese, thus I deduce you are police."

Fatima wasn't sure whether to take Araki for what she claimed to be, but since she had the gun in the woman's side, she wasn't overly concerned at the present moment about the veracity of her claim. If Araki wanted to think she was police, that was fine with her. With her right hand, Fatima flipped open the cover on her direction finder and turned it on.

Araki glanced over as they wound into the jungle between Subic and Manila. "You have a fix on them?"

Fatima nodded. "They're southeast."

Araki accelerated.

"Coming up on due east," Fatima reported.

Araki took a turn onto a dirt road in that direction.

"Do you know of a man named Shibimi?" Fatima asked.

"Yes. He was in the Ford LTD. He is a senior member of the Black Tentacle Yakuza." Araki slowed as the road narrowed. "Do you mind?" she asked, pointing at the gun that Fatima still had poking into her side.

"Actually, I do mind," Fatima replied, keeping it in place. "I have no proof you are who you say you are, and I just had two different groups of people shoot at me for no reason that I know of. So forgive me if I'm not exactly in the most friendly mood."

"I understand your concerns about my identity," Araki said. Her English was precise, and she enunciated each word clearly. "But you must know that I do not carry an identification card. I am working in your country on a mission of deep concern to my own country."

"Pretty weak," Fatima said, checking the direction finder. The small dot indicating the Japanese had stopped less than a kilometer ahead. "Unfortunately, I really don't have the time to have a deep discussion with you about all this. There is someone I have to catch up with."

Araki nodded. "Shibimi. Why are you following him?"

"Why are you?" Fatima asked.

"I am not following Shibimi," Araki said. "I am following a man who is following them."

"The Japanese guy in the black van with the Steyr AUG," Fatima said.

"Correct."

"And who is he?"

"That is my concern," Araki said.

"He tried blowing my head off back there in the tunnel," Fatima said. "That makes it my concern. Also, in case you haven't noticed, you're in the Philippines now. I could have your ass thrown in jail," she bluffed.

"As you threw me in jail, would you also admit to selling the Japanese Yakuza those weapons back at Subic?" Araki asked in a level voice.

Fatima pushed the barrel harder into Araki's side, evoking a surprised grunt of pain. "Do not fuck with me. I could also just make you disappear."

"I imagine you could," Araki said.

Fatima could see her swallow, trying to control her fear. The woman was doing a reasonably good job of remaining calm, but Fatima sensed that Araki wasn't a seasoned agent. She didn't have the hard edge that people in the world of covert operations gained after only a few years in the field—if they survived that long. Of course, she could also be better than most and a good actor. That made Fatima wonder exactly what Araki's role here was.

"We need each other," Araki said.

"Why do I need you?" Fatima asked, checking the direction finder one more time. The dot was still stationery. "They've stopped about five hundred meters in front of us." Looking ahead, she could see that the road descended through the jungle, and there was the glow of lights ahead, indicating some form of civilization.

Araki stopped the van and turned off the lights. She looked at Fatima. "I want the Japanese man," she said. "You want this Yakuza, Shibimi. But I do not think you know what these people are up to. I do not know what Nishin—that is his name—is up to, other than the fact he is following the Yakuza also. There are many unanswered questions. Two minds can answer them better than one. I have access to my agency's resources, which are quite extensive. And as you've noted, this is your country, so you have the local contacts. Remember, the enemy of my enemy is my friend."

Fatima snorted. "You sound like Confucius."

"Confucius was Chinese," Araki began. "I am—"

"Yes, Confucius was Chinese," Fatima interrupted. "Confucius, originally known as Kung Chiu, born 551 B.C., died 479." She removed the gun from Araki's side and holstered it. "Personal virtue, devotion to family, most especially one's ancestors, and to justice—all are tenets of his teachings."

"Very impressive," Araki said.

"Why are you following this Nishin?"

"I cannot tell you that."

"Cannot or won't?"

Araki shifted in her seat uncomfortably. "I am not authorized."

Fatima tapped the direction finder. "In the interests of each of our goals, let's go talk to these people."

"We just drive down there?" Araki asked.

Fatima had the pistol on her lap. "Yes. Do you have any weapons in here?"

Araki nodded. "Behind you. That plastic case."

Fatima twisted in the seat and opened the lid. Set in

foam padding were two MP-5 submachine guns with silencers, along with two dozen loaded magazines. "Very nice," she said as she pulled them out. She passed one to Araki and took the other. They split the ammunition between them, locking and loading the guns.

"This is not much of a plan," Araki said as she started the engine. "We could be driving right into a Yakuza base."

Fatima smiled. "I know where we are, and I know what's down there. And it is a good plan because of that."

"And you are averse to sharing this information?" Araki asked.

"I am not authorized," Fatima said, and laughed. "Don't worry. It is not a Yakuza base. It is a rebel base. A splinter cell of the Abu Sayif. They do business with the Yakuza on occasion."

"That is even worse," Araki said. "The Abu Sayif are terrorists, as bad as the Yakuza."

"I have had dealings with the Abu Sayif," Fatima said. "Do not worry. We will be all right. So drive."

Araki reluctantly put the van in gear, and they rolled forward down the dirt trail. "There is no reason for us to trust each other."

"Were you on the wall in the compound when I switched the weapons?"

"Yes. But I didn't shoot at the Yakuza, that was Nishin."

"Why didn't he shoot me?"

"Because he actually didn't have an angle on you. Also, I think he probably wanted to figure out who was who first. Or perhaps he wanted to speak to you before shooting you. I do not know for certain."

"Close now," Fatima said, checking the display.

They continued down the road until the jungle pulled back on either side and they could see the source of the lights: a ramshackle village of about twenty buildings. "There's the LTD." Fatima pointed. There was no sign of any people around the buildings. The LTD was parked outside of what appeared to be warehouse.

Araki drove farther down the road and parked the van in a position where they could observe the car but be hidden in the shadow of one of the buildings. "Any ideas why they would be here?" she asked.

"They're probably trying to sell the weapons they just purchased to this Abu Sayif group." Fatima was finding the entire thing rather ironic but didn't think this was the appropriate time to mention that. "There's no sign of the black van and your Nishin fellow. Perhaps it might be the time to tell me exactly who he is and why you are after him."

"He is a ronin for a secret organization," Araki said.

"A ronin?"

"A bit more complicated in definition than hit man. Nishin does not work for hire. He is sworn to do his master's bidding."

"And his master is?" Fatima noticed movement by one of the windows of the warehouse the LTD was parked outside of.

"I have only heard it referred to as the Far East Table."

"What the hell is that?"

"That is what I wish to ask Mr. Nishin."

The door to the warehouse slid open, and Shibimi stomped out, followed by his guard.

"Let's go," Fatima said, opening her van door and getting out. "Shit," she cursed as a dark figure with a silenced Steyr automatic stepped out of the shadows twenty meters to the right. The suppressor on the end of the barrel spit silent flame. The guard was slammed back into the metal wall, where he left a trail of blood as he slid to the ground.

Shibimi drew a pistol and ran for cover.

Fatima moved forward, sticking to the shadows of the buildings, getting closer to Shibimi's position, keeping one eye on the ronin, who was slowly moving forward also, focused on the car.

"Do not kill him," Araki hissed, weapon at the ready just behind Fatima's left shoulder.

Fatima had a feeling one of them was going to get their man as Shibimi fired a couple of rounds at Nishin, who then fired back. The crack of Shibimi's pistol going off reverberated through the small village, and people began to spill out of doorways, some of them armed with automatic weapons.

Fatima realized this was going to turn into a disaster, and she needed it to be over quickly. She snapped a shot at Nishin, hitting him in the side. As Shibimi turned in confusion to see who had fired, she sent a three-round burst into the old man's legs.

"Abu Sayif!" Fatima cried out, stepping out of the shadow into the glow of one of the arc lights. "Bind those two men," she ordered as the closest armed villagers recognized her.

Araki turned to her in surprise as a half-dozen men ran to the two wounded men, securing them. "Who are you?"

Fatima turned the smoking muzzle of her weapon toward Araki. "I am the leader of the Abu Sayif. And perhaps now you can tell me who you really are before I kill you. And then I will extract the truth from our two wounded friends over there."

CHAPTER 4

Oahu, Hawaii

"It appears I wasn't the only one to get a packet from David," Royce said.

Vaughn and Tai had been discussing what they had learned from MacIntosh, combining it with the information that Royce had given them earlier, when Royce walked in the door of the bungalow.

"What do you mean?" Tai asked.

"I just received a message from the Organization. The new head of the Abu Sayif, a woman named Fatima Al-Sheef, apparently got either the same or a similar packet from David that we received."

"Why?" Vaughn asked. "Why would he do that?"

"I don't know," Royce said.

"How about venturing a guess," Vaughn prompted.

Tai jumped in. "To put the pressure on. If Lansale

had just sent the information here, then we could sit on it. But by sending it to the Abu Sayif, he's rung the starter's bell from his grave. And it's actually a three-way race because the Organization now knows about the Abu Sayif package."

"Race to where?" Vaughn asked, although he already knew.

"To find the Citadel," Royce said, "and uncover what's in there. And its link to the Organization."

"If it still exists," Vaughn said. "It's been down there a long time."

"I guess you're going to find out," Royce said.

"And what are you going to be doing?" Tai asked.

"I'm going to do what the Organization has ordered me to: try to stop the Abu Sayif before they get too close. So in a way, I'm taking out your competitors."

Vaughn considered that. "But won't the Organization simply send some people down to the Citadel and take care of things?"

Royce smiled. "From the way the message was worded and the way David sent us this information, I have a feeling that the Organization doesn't quite know the location or contents of the Citadel either."

"How can that be?" Tai demanded. "The Organization ordered it built."

"I think *part* of the Organization ordered it built, and David organized it and oversaw it," Royce said, "but I have the feeling the information was never sent all the way up to the top."

"Left hand not knowing what the right is doing," Vaughn said as he considered that. "So there might have been people like Tai and me before, inside of but not part of the Organization who did their own thing."

"I have no doubt David played a very dangerous game," Royce said. "Just as I am."

Tai ran a hand through her short hair. "My big question is: what did they build down there and why? We're talking 1949. Truman is President. The Cold War has just begun. We know about the nukes, but it doesn't make much sense that the only purpose of this base was to store some nuclear weapons in Antarctica with no delivery system."

"Whatever the Citadel is," Vaughn said, "it was important enough to kill a lot of people to cover it up."

"So how do we find it?" Tai asked.

"We need an expert," Vaughn said. "Someone who knows Antarctica." He looked at Royce. "I don't suppose you have one handy?"

"Actually"—Royce drew the word out—"I do. And I already made an initial contact. A man named James Logan. He works for the environmental group Earth First."

"Great," Vaughn said. "A tree hugger."

"There aren't any trees in Antarctica," Tai said.

"Logan has done work for me before," Royce said. "He might love trees but he enjoys money more. Plus we have leverage on him."

"What kind of leverage?" Vaughn asked.

"You don't need to know that," Royce said. "Suffice it to say I have a strong enough carrot and a powerful enough stick that Logan will do whatever you need."

"Where's he now?" Tai asked.

"Australia," Royce said. "Saving kangaroos or something." He reached into his briefcase and pulled out a sleek satellite phone. "You can call him on this." He slid a piece of paper across. "Here's his number."

Royce dialed in the number, then punched the

speaker-phone option and put the phone on the wood table.

"Hello?" a voice with a rich Australian accent answered.

"Is this James Logan?"

"Who are you?"

Royce spoke up. "It's Royce, Mr. Logan. Calling with two friends of mine from Hawaii."

"Fuck. Hawaii. Must be early in the morning there, isn't it?"

Tai rolled her eyes. "It's a little after eleven."

"It's a little after midnight here." The voice waited for an apology, and getting none, moved on with a sigh. "All right. What do you want?"

Tai spoke. "Royce tells us you've been to Antarctica several times."

"Yes. I've been there four times. I also wintered over at the Earth First base there three years ago. Why? What's up?"

"We've received information about something," Tai said, "and we were wondering if you could give us some help."

"'Wondering'? Do I have a choice, Royce?"

"No."

The voice was resigned. "What's the information?"

Tai continued. "We've discovered that the United States military built a secret installation, called the Citadel, in Antarctica in 1949."

"What kind of secret base?"

"We don't know," Tai said.

"Where exactly was the place built in Antarctica?"

"We don't know," Tai repeated. "That's why they call it a secret, Logan."

"Well, I've been down there and I've also talked to

a lot of people stationed down there, especially at Mc-
Murdo, and I've never heard anything about a place
called the Citadel. It would be pretty difficult to cover
something like that up, although 1949 was a very long
time ago."

Tai waited in silence, prompting Logan to speak
again. "Even though it was built in 1949, it would still
have broken the 1959 treaty, as the treaty was retroac-
tive. Any base that is built down there, even if it's temporary, has to be open for inspection by any of the other
signees of the treaty. If a base is hidden, well, then it
certainly isn't open for inspection.

"Second, if the U.S. military built it, then it's probably some sort of military base, and if it still exists, that
would be a gross violation of not only the letter of the
current 1991 accord governing things in Antarctica, but
also the spirit. Tell me what you have on it so far."

Tai gave a quick summary of the engineers, the photos, the planes, but left out the information about the
atomic weapons. When she was done, Logan asked her
to describe the photos carefully. He was silent for a
little while before speaking again.

"Well, High Jump Station evolved into McMurdo
Station, which is the largest base in Antarctica. So we
have a start point. You got this Citadel being a four-
hour flight by MARS Boxcar from there, so we have
a radius. But we don't even know if it's south, east, or
west. Most likely south or east, though."

"Why do you say that?" Tai asked.

"If the U.S. military built this thing and wanted to
keep it a secret, as you've said, then they'd probably
want it to be far away from any other countries' potential stations, based on how Antarctica was sliced up for
research. The Russians eventually had a base in Lenin-

gradskaya, about five hundred miles to the west of Mc-
Murdo, and the French built one farther along the coast
in that direction. South from McMurdo there's nothing
until you hit the South Pole itself. So that would seem
like a good place to hide a base. Maybe in the Transarctic Mountains.

"East from McMurdo is Marie Byrd Land, and there
was nothing permanent out there for almost two thousand miles until '71, when the Russians put a base in,
called Russkaya, right on the coast there to the east.
But if it was 1949 and I was going to put some sort of
secret base in, that might be a direction I'd go."

Vaughn was making notes of all that. "Anything else
you can think of that might help?"

"I'll work on it and check around," Logan said.
"When are you arriving down under?"

Tai looked up at Royce, then back at the phone. "As
soon as possible."

"Fly through Auckland, New Zealand, and I can
meet you there," Logan said. "Then we can take a hop
down to McMurdo, which would be the place to stage
out of."

"We'll touch base once we're en route," Tai said,
shutting off the phone.

"Pretty vague," Vaughn said. "Talk about looking for
a needle in a haystack. And it's a needle buried under
ice. There might not be anything on the surface we can
spot even if we get a good idea of where the base is."

"There is something I could do," Royce said, "but
it's dangerous."

"And that is?" Tai asked.

"Check the Organization's database that I have access to for information on the Citadel. I couldn't do it
before, because I have no doubt such an inquiry would

be flagged. But now that I've been tasked with closing out the Abu Sayif and their interest in the Citadel, I don't think it would be that unusual for me to query the d-base reference. Might fly under the radar as part of the operation with which I've been tasked."

Vaughn shrugged. "Without any more data, we've got no chance of finding this place, so you might as well go for it. We'll be out of here as soon as we have something solid, so you'd have to deal with any fallout."

Royce sat down at the table and opened his laptop. "I have restricted access to the database," he warned as he began typing, "but let's see what I can come up with."

Area 51, Nevada

The flashing light on the secure phone drew the old man's attention away from the computer displays lining the wall of the command center. Despite his years, there was still a bounce to his step as he walked over to his desk. He was tall, with a stomach that was flat as a board. His silver hair framed a distinguished face that attracted women a third his age and made the men around him choose their words with care. A long finger reached out and hit the speaker button. A brief whine and a green light on the phone indicated the line was secure from eavesdroppers.

"This is Dyson."

"This is Analyst Six. I am calling you as per instructions, sir. My people have detected an inquiry into the secure database that you have coded for alert."

Dyson's slate gray eyes focused on the phone as he leaned forward slightly, the muscles in his forearms rippling as he rested them on his desk. "Subject?"

"Citadel."

The old man's eyes closed briefly and then opened. "Source?"

"Our man in Hawaii, Royce."

Dyson considered that. "Royce already has the tasking reference the Abu Sayif, correct?"

"Yes, sir."

"And what has he discovered?

"The name exists in our database. In David Lansale's file."

Dyson bit back a curse as some of the pieces fell into place. "What else?"

"Not much. The original funding for the Citadel fell under Operation High Jump conducted in Antarctica, with additional funding covertly added via the Black Eagle Trust. It's classified as an engineering operation. That's all that is in the Citadel file."

"Did Lansale conduct an unsanctioned mission?" Dyson asked.

"No, sir. There is an official sanction number on the file. I cross-referenced the number and found it linked with two other missions. The first actually predates the Citadel. An American submarine tender was diverted in the South Pacific during the closing days of World War II to refuel a submarine."

"So? What's so special about that?"

"It was a Japanese submarine. And the sub tender went down with all hands a day after making the rendezvous and refuel."

"Not a coincidence," Dyson said.

"I don't know, sir, but it seems unlikely. There is no further information on this or where the submarine was headed."

"The second link?"

"A covert mission in 1956 during Operation Deep

Freeze. A long overland convoy traveled to the Citadel from the coast of Antarctica and made a delivery there. The convoy was never heard from again."

The body count was getting very high, Dyson thought. While the Organization was not averse to whatever cost was necessary to accomplish its goals, this was definitely beginning to look like a very major operation.

"What did the convoy deliver?"

"Among other things, four Mark-17 thermonuclear warheads. The largest yield bombs ever built by the United States."

Dyson closed his eyes briefly. "Have the warheads ever been accounted for?"

"No, sir. The most likely explanation is that they must still be there in the Citadel."

"Anything more?"

"Negative."

"Thank you."

Dyson turned the phone off, then picked up the tersely worded communiqué that had just been decrypted and then delivered to him. It was a directive from the High Counsel in Geneva, head of the North American Table, to present himself in person. And the subject of the meeting was to explain the Citadel and why Geneva had no records of such a place.

Which meant he was going to have to explain the scanty yet startling records that the North American Table had of it.

Philippines

"He will die with twenty-four hours," the medic informed Fatima, pointing at the young Japanese man who had been Araki's target. "And he"—the medic indicated the old man in the bed next to him—"will live if we treat him. If not, he won't last forty-eight hours."

Fatima turned to the Japanese woman who had saved her in the tunnel. Araki was tied to a chair facing the beds the two wounded men occupied. "And you," Fatima said to her, "will die immediately if you lie to me."

Araki glared at her, face flushed in anger. A half-dozen Abu Sayif guerrillas were gathered round, weapons at the ready. Fatima walked up to Araki and drew a knife. She laid the cold flat edge of it against Araki's cheek.

"Perfect skin," Fatima said. "It would be a shame to see it marred. You said you work for CPI—Central Political Intelligence. And you were following this man, Nishin." She removed the knife and pointed it at the young, wounded Japanese man. "Why?"

"To find out who he works for," Araki answered.

"He is Yakuza," Fatima said.

"Check to see if he has Yakuza marking," Araki suggested.

Fatima nodded, and two men ripped off Nishin's bloody shirt. His skin was unblemished. Fatima shrugged. "There are those among the Yakuza who are unmarked in order to be able to do covert missions."

"He is not Yakuza," Araki said.

"Telling me what he is not is not very useful," Fatima said. "Tell me what he is."

"He is a member of an Organization the CPI has spent decades trying to infiltrate or at least find out what its real name is. The best we have come is to learn that it is referred to at times as the Far East Table. I told you this earlier."

Fatima frowned. "You mean the group people call the Organization, with a capital letter?"

Araki nodded.

"We have heard of this Far East Table," Fatima said. "I recently killed one of their members, but she could tell me nothing. If this man, Nishin, is an agent, I am willing to bet he knows little and would say nothing."

Araki shrugged. "It was the best lead we had. And we wanted to know why he came here to the Philippines and what his mission was."

Fatima frowned as she tried to piece together this puzzle of bodies around her. She had been after Shibimi because the Yakuza had sent her that way. Araki had been after Nishin, and he had been after Shibimi. Fatima felt a sudden rush of pressure as she realized the information she had received had not come from nowhere and there was a very good chance someone knew she had this information.

There was no time to fool around. She drew her pistol and walked over to Nishin. He was glaring up at her. She fired once, the round making a small black hole in the center of his forehead. She turned. Both Shibimi and Araki were staring at her wide-eyed.

Araki was the first to speak. "What did you do that for? He was my—"

"You will be very lucky to leave here alive," Fatima said. "He was a ronin, a soldier, who knew nothing other than he was here to kill this man." Fatima went over to Shibimi and placed the muzzle of her gun between his eyes. His face was impassive as he regarded her.

"Where is his guard?" Fatima called out, and Shibimi's eyes flickered ever so slightly.

Two of her men dragged up the wounded guard, his stomach heavily bandaged. They slammed him against the side of the building and he cried out in pain. Fatima jammed the muzzle of her gun right into his wound, and he screamed.

"Who are you?" she asked, keeping one eye on the old man. He was much too concerned about the old man to be a simple bodyguard. "How are you related to Shibimi?"

She jammed the gun once more, and he screamed, then she stepped back and waited. When he caught his breath, the man managed to speak. "I'm his grandson."

Fatima spun back to Shibimi and walked up to him. "I will make you a deal. You tell me what you know of the submarine I-104 and I will have my people take your grandson into Manila and drop him at the hospital. You do not tell me, he dies."

Shibimi closed his eyes for several moments, then opened them and nodded ever so slightly. Fatima gestured, and the two men holding the guard dragged the wounded man toward a waiting car.

"I am upholding my end," Fatima said. "Talk."

Shibimi watched his grandson tossed in the backseat of the car and as it drove away up the dirt trail. When it was out of sight he returned his eyes to Fatima. "There were three 400 series Sensuikan Toku–class submarines built near the end of the war: I-400, I-401, and I-402. They were the pride of the fleet. The largest submarines ever built up until the 1960s, when the first ballistic missile submarines were built. They were underwater aircraft carriers."

"I've never heard of such a thing," Fatima said, noting that Araki had gotten over her shock about Nishin's death rather quickly and was listening intently.

"I was assigned to the I-401," Shibimi said. "It was indeed huge. We were all stunned the first time we saw it. Over four hundred feet long and forty feet high. There were 144 men in the crew. It had a water-proof hangar built onto the deck in front of the conning tower. Inside were three bombers. Fully loaded with fuel, we had the potential to sail back and forth across the Pacific without refueling."

"Where *did* you sail?" Fatima demanded.

Shibimi closed his eyes and sighed. "The I-401 was built with a specific mission in mind. We were to sail to the Panama Canal and use our three planes to bomb it, shutting it to traffic. But the war ended before we could do that mission. We were at sea when the surrender was signed. We'd been at sea for two months. Doing trial runs. First heading toward the Panama Canal. Then sent north toward the American West Coast, where we were to rendezvous with a freighter and take on biological weapons to attack San Diego and Los Angeles."

"Biological weapons developed by Unit 731," Fatima said.

Shibimi looked startled, then nodded. "Yes. But that mission was canceled when we were within fifty miles of San Diego. No explanation was given. We were directed to rendezvous with a ship in the South Pacific, east of Australia. It was a long journey back across the ocean.

"When we arrived at the location, we were shocked to see an American submarine tender. They were as shocked as we were, but they had the same orders. They refueled us. And we received new orders. To head here, to the Philippines."

"Where you were met again by Americans," Fatima said.

Shibimi nodded. "Yes. We surfaced at night, not far from here, off Corregidor. Then an American cargo ship came alongside. Our three airplanes were dumped overboard. In the hangar were placed numerous, unmarked crates."

"Golden Lily," Fatima said. "Part of it."

"Yes," Shibimi said. "Although neither I, nor any member of the crew, knew it then. We also took on a large amount of food store. And received sailing orders once more."

"To go to Antarctica," Fatima said.

"If you know all this, then why are you asking me?" Shibimi said.

"I don't know everything," Fatima said. "Where in Antarctica?"

"Due south. We sailed to the edge of the ice pack of the Ross Sea. Then we waited until it was summer and the pack had receded as far as it could. The captain was the only one who knew what we were doing. The rest of us just followed orders. We picked up random radio transmissions at times. We found out about the dropping of the atomic bombs. Details of the surrender."

Shibimi's eyes grew distant. "That's when the suicides began. A man whose family had been in Nagasaki was first. Then others. In the first month while we sat off the coast, eight men killed themselves. They saw no hope, no reason to live. The captain would not explain what our mission was. Then something strange happened."

Shibimi fell silent for a few moments, and Fatima gestured for one of her men to give him some water. His wound had stopped bleeding.

"What happened?" Fatima finally asked.

"Two more submarines arrived," Shibimi said.

"American?" Fatima asked.

"No, German," Shibimi said. "Because I was Kempetai, I talked to the member of one of the crews who was Gestapo. He told me an interesting story. He said the Germans called Antarctica Neuschwabenland and considered it part of the Third Reich. Or had. The Third Reich no longer existed by the time we met. He told me that before the war, the Germans had sent planes down to Antarctica and dropped pennons with Nazi flags over as much of the land as they could, a naïve way of trying to claim the land as theirs.

"In 1943, Admiral Donitz, who commanded the German submarine forces, claimed that the Germans had created a fortress in Antarctica, a boast of a rather feeble attempt to establish a base there. But the agent told me this was not the first time his submarine, U-530, had been to Antarctica. In fact, it was its sixth trip. And every time they brought supplies and, like us, un-marked crates. This was their last trip along with their sister ship the U-977."

"What happened then?" Fatima asked. She found it strange to be talking about such a cold and faraway land here in the middle of the sweltering Filipino jungle. And to have a man who was in the Japanese Kempetai talking about meeting a Gestapo agent off the shores of Antarctica.

"A landing party was organized under the command of one of the German officers who had obviously been there before and was experienced in traversing the land. It consisted mostly of Germans, but a few members of our crew were part of it. They struck out over the ice cap covering the Ross Sea.

"We waited. And finally we received a radio call from the party that they were in place. All three subma-rines submerged. One of the German ships was in the lead. You have to remember, we were sailing almost blind under the ice. We homed in on the sonar signal the land party was broadcasting.

"When we arrived, we found that the land party had blasted holes through the ice so that each submarine was able to extend a snorkel and radio transmitter up to the surface. But that was it." Shibimi fell silent for a moment. "It made no sense to the rest of the crew. We couldn't surface. We couldn't bring the land party aboard. The captain didn't give the rest of the crew time to. He ordered almost everyone with the exception of myself and his executive officer into the rear crew compartment and the engine room. Then he had us seal the hatch from our side.

"I think it was merciful what we did. We were cold anyway. Our country had been devastated in the war. Surrender was not an option. Most of us had nothing to go home to, and if we did, we would have been in disgrace. We pumped the air out of the rear compartments. It was over relatively quickly. Relative, when you hear the echoed screams of men dying and their banging on the hatches and pipes and hull. One hundred and twenty-nine men were killed."

Fatima glanced over at Araki. She had gotten more than she had bargained for on this mission.

Shibimi continued. "The captain then said we must commit hari-kari. He said it would be his place as captain to be last. However, those were not my orders. I had to act quickly. I drew my pistol and shot the executive officer and captain. I powered the ship down except for the radio, which I put on a certain frequency at low power to continuously transmit. Then I put on a dry suit and a rebreather. I went into the escape hatch in the conning tower. I sealed myself in then opened the outer hatch.

"The water was cold even with the dry suit, on the verge of becoming ice. It was pitch-black under the ice. I made my way by feel to the snorkel and radio transmitter. I grabbed on and made my way up in the darkness, fearful that I would find them enclosed in ice when I reached the ice pack. But the hole that had been blasted had not completely iced in yet. I was able to wiggle into it, pulling my way up, still afraid that as I got closer to the surface it would be sealed in.

"I barely made it. I did hit ice. I had a pick with me. In that tight space I chipped away, my air diminishing, and then I broke through. About six inches of ice had already formed, and I was able to crawl through, onto the surface. It was night. I saw a single lantern, like a beacon, in one of the tents the ground party had taken. I staggered over to it, the water on the outside of my dry suit freezing as I did so. I made it inside. A stove was still going, but they were all dead.

"The Germans had drank poisoned wine. The Japanese had used the knives and guns to kill themselves. I stripped off my dry suit and scavenged for cold weather clothing. Then I slept among the dead for a long time. When I awoke, I gathered supplies.

"Then I made my way back to the coast. A six-day journey for me on foot. When I got to the coast a trawler was waiting for me. The crew knew nothing of me or why they were picking me up. They brought me back to Japan, where I could report the mission accomplished."

Shibimi stopped speaking.

"Where were these submarines left?" Fatima asked.

"After all these years," Shibimi said, "I still remember the coordinates." He spoke them, and Fatima copied them down.

"What else have you done for the Far East Table?" Fatima asked.

Shibimi gave a bitter laugh. "That was it. Why do you think I am here in the Philippines driving a stupid tugboat and peddling in arms? They tried to kill me, and I escaped. I came here and here I have been all my life. They wait for me." His voice had dropped. "The souls of those men, they wait for me."

"Then join them," Fatima said as she fired her pistol.

Then she turned to Araki. The Japanese woman stared back at her. "What are you going to do to me?"

"Do you want to know the truth?" Fatima asked.

Araki nodded.

"Then you must come with me."

"Where?"

"To Antarctica, of course." Fatima turned to one of the Abu Sayif. "Dispose of the bodies," she ordered. "I want the freighter to be prepared. Take her to Manila and link her up with the crew. I will need everyone at the ship."

Oahu

"We're going to rack up quite a few frequent flier miles on this trip." Tai was looking at the flight itinerary Royce had just given them. " Depart Honolulu for New Zealand. Cross the international date line en route. Arrive Wellington, New Zealand, on Saturday evening at 2100 hours local."

"The passports I've given you," Royce said, "are real and should raise no problems. From New Zealand you count on Logan to take you to Antarctica."

"What about communications?" Tai asked.

Royce slid a small case across the table. "Satellite radio. You might not get the best reception in Antarctica but you should be able to punch through a text message."

"Gear?" Vaughn asked.

"Will be waiting for you in New Zealand," Royce said.

"Including weapons?" Vaughn pressed.

"Including weapons," Royce reassured him.

Vaughn stood and looked at Tai. "All right. Let's get cold."

Manila

Fatima checked the coordinates Shibimi had given her. Then she made her way to the front of the map store and paid the proprietor. She slid the map inside her jacket and opened the door with a feeling of excitement that she was on the trail of something that might unlock the secret of the Organization.

She left the store and hopped on the motorcycle she had taken from the village. She roared through the streets to the rendezvous she had set up on her way in. She was headed to another ethnic-oriented part of Manila—not Japanese this time, but Korean. She raced through the narrow streets, avoiding cars, trucks, bikes, and pedestrians.

She turned down an alley and came to a halt. She took her helmet off, left it on the seat and entered the back door of a small store. An old Korean man was seated on a stool just inside, a blanket over his lap. Fatima saw the large double-O shape of the end of a sawed-off shotgun trained on her.

"I am unarmed," she said.

"What do you want?" the man demanded. "Your call said you had important information."

"I believe I know where some American nuclear weapons are stored," Fatima said.

The old man snorted. "I can tell you where many American nuclear weapons are stored in South Korea and in Japan."

"But these are not in South Korea or in Japan. Or in the United States or anyplace where there are currently America forces."

The old man stared at her. "How can this be?"

"The Americans built a secret military base right after World War II," Fatima said. "They went back there at least one time and put four nuclear weapons in it. And now it is abandoned, and I believe the weapons might still be there."

"Impossible," the old man said. "Even the Americans are not that stupid. Where is this base?"

"Antarctica."

The old man blinked. "That is—" He fell silent as he thought about it. "Are you certain?"

"I am certain there is an American base that was abandoned there," Fatima said. "I am not certain about the weapons, but it is likely they are still there. Even if they no longer work, they will still have their cores, which can be used. And even without that, the discovery of such a thing would be of great embarrassment to the Americans."

"Antarctica is a large place," the old man said. "Where exactly is this place?"

"I am heading down there to find out," Fatima said. "Would your superiors be interested in knowing the location?"

The old man simply nodded.

"Then I will contact you in the same manner over satellite when I know more," Fatima said, not wanting to give up any more information right now.

"All right," the old man agreed. "I will wait for more information."

Which Fatima knew to be a lie. He would be on the satellite phone as soon as she left, contacting his superiors. But that is what she wanted. She nodded back at him and walked back out the door.

As she grabbed her helmet off the motorcycle seat, she noted a van blocking her in. Fatima put the helmet on, cranked the engine, and waited for the driver of the van to take the hint and move. After thirty seconds of nothing she beeped her horn. She couldn't make out the truck's occupants through the tinted windshield.

"Damn it," she muttered as she got off her bike, walked up to the passenger side and rapped on the door. The cargo door slid open and a man leaped out, wrapped her in a bear hug and rolled with her back into the rear, the door sliding shut.

Fatima kicked backward, feeling her boot strike home, but the man holding her didn't make a noise. She desperately struggled, but her arms were locked to her side with a grip of steel. She felt a prick in her wrist and looked down to see a needle sliding into her flesh. She watched as the plunger descended.

The last thing her conscious mind processed was the van pulling out into traffic.

CHAPTER 5

Oahu

"This could all be a setup," Tai said as the plane lifted off the runway.

Vaughn had his eyes closed. "At least if it is, we're going first-class."

"Why should we believe anything Royce tells us?" Tai asked.

"Why shouldn't we?" Vaughn asked in turn. He opened his eyes. "I don't know what the truth is about anything. But even when I was in the real Army, I wasn't too sure about the truth either. Were you?"

Tai sighed. "I believed in what I was doing."

"I believed in my team," Vaughn said. "But it got shot up doing a mission on orders that I wonder about now. My brother-in-law was killed. Men who trusted me, trusted my orders, died. And now I can say 'I was just following orders.'"

"Oh, bullshit," Tai said. "Now you're getting into where the ultimate truth is. What it is. A bunch of crap."

"Then what are we doing on this plane?" Vaughn asked. "Why are you here?"

Now it was Tai's turn to close her eyes. "I want to find out who is behind all this. I want to find out who got your brother-in-law killed, and my sister too. And I want to make them pay."

Surprisingly, Vaughn laughed. "That, I can understand. Revenge. But you think we're going to make the slightest bit of difference?"

"We did in Hawaii."

"All right." Vaughn nodded. "We did. And we will here. Or freeze to death trying."

Tokyo, Japan

The head of the Far East Table stared out the window and pondered recent developments. Bad news comes in three, and he had just received the third part.

Kaito being killed in Hong Kong.

Being summoned to Geneva to discuss the I-401 and someplace called the Citadel.

And now Nishin disappearing in the Philippines on a simple assassination mission to avenge Kaito's death.

He looked down at his desk and the flimsy report on I-401. It had indeed been commandeered by the Far East Table near the end of World War II to be sent on a covert mission for the Organization.

And that was all the report said.

He picked up the secure phone and punched in number two on the speed dial. The call was bounced through satellites to the United States, specifically the Nevada desert.

The call was answered on the third ring. "Yes?"

"Have you received a summons to Geneva?"

"Yes. I will be departing shortly."

"Regarding the Citadel?"

"Yes."

The head of the Far East Table reined in his irritation. "And what do you know of it?"

"It's in Antarctica. It was initially established in 1947, the same year the place I am right now was established. But somehow information about it was compartmentalized even from the Table to a large extent. One of our agents, who you know—David Lansale—was the one who did this. And he raised the issue by sending information about it to the Abu Sayif."

"I tried to have Fatima killed, but my agent has disappeared."

The voice on the other end took on a gloating edge. "I have a man in the Philippines who has just captured her. He will terminate her after interrogation."

"We must do more than that," the head of the Far East Table said. "When we go to Geneva, we must present them with a plan to completely wipe this issue out."

"What do you propose?"

"We alert resources to be prepared to intercede in Antarctica as needed. I will do what I can on my end, but you have more available to operate in that part of the world."

There was a short silence. "All right. I will do that. I will see you in Geneva."

Manila

Fatima had been coming awake for brief interludes over the past hour, but every time she approached lucidity a large wave of blackness again engulfed her. This time, though, as she opened her eyes, she could actually think. There were vague memories flitting about her brain, trying to tell her something had happened over the past hour that she needed to recall, but try as she might, no concrete memory could form. There were disturbing visions of what seemed like very bad dreams, but as she took in her surroundings, the present nightmare banished thoughts of worrying about the immediate past.

With slow sweeps of her eyes, she checked out the situation. She was lying on the floor in a filth-strewn room—the walls an eclectic splatter of spray paint and punctured Sheetrock. A single lightbulb burned in the ceiling, casting long shadows through the room. A wooden door beckoned to the world outside. Her wrists were handcuffed behind her, the steel cutting into her skin uncomfortably.

She was considering sliding her hands down her back and pushing her feet through, to at least get her hands in front of her body, when the door opened and the man from the van walked in.

Fatima was truly worried now because the man made no attempt to disguise his identity. That meant he was not concerned about her identifying him in the future, which meant she did not have a future. He had hair cut tight against his skull, his bright blue eyes emanating both intelligence and malice. The fact he was not Filipino was of concern also.

After staring at her for a few minutes, he finally

broke the silence and spoke in an Australian accent: "Good day, Miss Fatima. You don't have to worry. I've already gotten what I needed from you." At Fatima's confused look, he smiled. "It's part of the miracle of modern medicine. The first shot I gave you caused unconsciousness. The second one made you talk." He squatted down and gazed into her eyes. "You don't remember talking and giving me the coordinates, do you?"

Fatima didn't answer. She curled up in a tight ball, her knees to her chest. The man poked her in the shoulder. "There's no need for you to play stupid with me. It was foolish of you to go to the North Koreans. Don't you think that shop is watched all the time? I know quite a bit about you. Part of the perks of the job. You told me everything I asked. You told me some quite interesting personal information about yourself."

Fatima closed her eyes and starting rocking back and forth. He slapped her on the face. "Don't tune out on me." He smiled, but it was only a moving of muscles in his face that didn't touch the coldness of his eyes. "It's kind of like looking into someone's soul when they're under. Imagine being able to ask someone any question you want and get an honest answer?"

His eyes were flashes of blue, catching the light from the flickering bulb above him. He pulled a pistol with a suppressor on the muzzle out of a shoulder holster. He put the muzzle against her temple and stared deep into her eyes. They remained like that for almost a minute, a lifetime for Fatima, who had stopped breathing, every nerve in her body screaming.

Suddenly he pulled the pistol back. "Most people consider you a terrorist. If it didn't violate my orders, I could turn you over to the Americans, dead or alive, and get a nice bounty. But then I would be dead also. Still, it is tempting."

Fatima muttered something under her breath.

"What was that?" the man demanded.

She whispered to herself again. The man knelt next to her and grabbed her shoulders, pulling her to her knees. "Talk louder."

Fatima leaned forward, pressing her chest against his.

"That's not going to work," the man said, but he didn't pull back.

Fatima moved her body up and down slightly. She could feel him beginning to grow hard. "Not in the head," she said in a low voice.

"What?"

"Please don't shoot me in the head."

The man laughed. "Why not?"

"Please. I'll make it worth your while not to."

The man pushed her back roughly and stood up. He moved a few feet away and stared at her, his eyes flashing. Fatima forced herself awkwardly back to her knees and shuffled toward him. He backed up until he was against the wall. She felt the skin on her knees tear as she moved, but tried to keep a lustful look on her face.

She pressed her head into the man's crotch.

"I asked you about this," he said. "I know what you like."

Fatima gave what she hoped was a good approximation of a sexual moan. With her teeth, she unzipped his pants, not an easy maneuver. He reached down and grabbed her head as he entered her mouth.

Fatima bit down with every ounce of energy she had. The man screamed and doubled over. She whipped her head out of his grasp and rolled away from him. As she did so, she brought her knees to her chest and slipped her hands over her feet to put them in front of her body. She jumped to her feet and ran at him then, swinging her hands like a club as she did. The blow knocked him sideways, still doubled over. She leapt on his back, looped her manacled hands over his head and pulled back tight on his neck.

He gasped for breath and tried to shake her off. He twisted the hand with the gun and pulled the trigger, the round ripping through Fatima's shirt but not hitting her. He fired again as she kept the pressure up. Then he straightened and threw himself backward against the wall, slamming her into it, but she didn't let go.

He dropped to his knees, finally letting go of the gun. Fatima kept the pressure tight. He fell forward, taking her with him, but still she didn't let go. It was too quick. Sure enough, after a couple seconds of playing dead, he suddenly rolled, pinning her beneath him. But she sensed his strength weakening.

Then he was still.

Fatima counted sixty to herself as she kept the chokehold with the cuffs. Slowly she let go. Awkwardly, with her bound hands, she searched his pockets until she found the key for the cuffs and maneuvered it out. Then, holding it in her teeth, she unlocked herself. Hands free now, she searched his pockets and found a United States diplomatic passport, which she kept. His name meant nothing to her. The fact that it was a diplomatic passport confirmed what she had suspected: once more the long hand of the United States was after her. It was a good thing she was leaving the Philippines for a while.

Without a backward glance she left the room and headed out of the abandoned warehouse.

Washington, D.C.

The Intelligence Support Agency was a branch of the Pentagon that tried to coordinate the massive flow of data that poured in from all the various intelligence subdivisions of the military. Hundreds of analysts sat in cubicles scrolling through data on their computers, trying to separate intelligence from information. The former was usable data, the latter not. They also handled intelligence requests from the various parts of the military trying to coordinate with the rest of the military-industrial complex so that the right hand could at least have a clue what the left hand was doing.

Bob Festoon was a third of the way through his inbox when he came upon an encrypted request from Majestic-12 Area 51. It caught his interest because rarely did anything from Majestic come through here. So rare were its communiqués and so little was known about the organization that there were some who said it didn't really exist—that it was just a cover-up for something else.

Festoon had even tried accessing data on both Majestic and Area 51 and discovered little even in the ISA's highly classified database. Area 51 was a place whose real purpose was unknown and whose existence was officially denied, yet there had been shows on A&E about it. Majestic-12 was shrouded in even more secrecy.

There were many theories, and Festoon was familiar with most of them. There were those who claimed the government had contact with aliens at the site and they were trading for information and technology. The more radical theorists stated that the items of barter from the human side were allowing the aliens to conduct mutilations on cattle and other livestock and also to abduct

humans for various experiments. There were some who
even claimed that the aliens were interbreeding with
the humans.

Another theory was that Area 51 was the place the
government was testing its own latest supersecret aircraft. Festoon knew for a fact that the F-117 Stealth
Fighter had been test-flown out there for years before
being revealed to the public. The latest "secret" plane
that was being tested was called Aurora, and estimates
had the plane flying anywhere from Mach 4 to Mach
20 and capable of going high enough to place satellites
into orbit. Festoon had seen three references to Aurora
in official top secret message traffic, so he was confident that it existed. However, the official government
line still was that Majestic-12 and the Area 51 complex
didn't exist.

Festoon finished decoding the message and then
stared at it for a few seconds before turning to his computer:

Request all information on Antarctic Base,
code-named Citadel.
Established 1949 by military during Operation High Jump.
ASAP

He accessed military records and quickly searched
the database. After twenty minutes of fruitless effort he
was convinced of one thing: there was no record in the
ISA's classified database of the Citadel.

Which made it likely, Festoon thought, that this
Citadel didn't exist. The Intelligence Support Agency
was lavishly funded by the Pentagon's multi-billion-
dollar black budget and accountable to no one but the

National Security Council, its tentacles reaching into every domestic and foreign source of information. The ISA was more than a gathering agency, though. It also acted on the information it received, implementing numerous covert actions in the name of national security both in the United States and overseas.

The ISA had numerous contacts throughout the business world, men and women in critical places that the ISA worked with, also forwarding the interests of the military and, concurrently, the massive industrial complex that supported the military. It was the covert arm of the military-industrial complex that President Eisenhower had so feared, and its power was far greater than even those briefed on its existence dared believe.

Festoon encoded the information given by the computer and its conclusion that the Citadel didn't exist and electronically dispatched it to Majestic-12. He also filed a routine report on the request and put it in the massive pipeline of such reports that circulated throughout the ISA. He picked up the next piece of paper in his in-box and went to work on that.

Oahu, Hawaii

Royce listened to the satellite phone ring and ring and knew that things had gone wrong in the Philippines. The initial call from his agent after capturing Fatima had been succinct, and the news about her going to the North Koreans was startling and troubling. The fact that she also knew about the bombs was just as bad.

He hit the End button and dialed another number of a contact in the Philippines. He ordered the man who answered to check the warehouse where the first agent had been interrogating Fatima.

Then he sat back in the chair and considered the situation. He was in the observation post of a rather unique bunker complex built on Fort Shafter on the outskirts of Honolulu. Built during World War II, when the fear of Japanese invasion of the island was very real, it had housed an air defense coordination center, tunneled deep in a lava ridge line. Now it housed the WestCom Sim-Center, which stood for Western Command, Simulation Center. It was the place where the major commands of the United States military in the Pacific theater played their war games using sophisticated computer simulations. It was currently empty, as no war games were being conducted, the military being more occupied with the real wars going on in Afghanistan and Iraq.

Royce typed on his laptop keyboard, which he had linked by Firewire into the Sim-Center's mainframe. On the large video display in the war room below him, a map of Antarctica was displayed. For the first time, Royce felt irritation with his friend David Lansale. What the hell had David done down there? And why was Lansale, even after death, playing him off against Fatima and the Abu Sayif about the Citadel?

He typed in another command and the map shifted, showing the Korean peninsula. One of the most critical military spots in the world that had the potential to go hot very quickly.

Royce sighed. He knew that Vaughn and Tai would be landing in New Zealand soon, but this was growing much faster and much more dangerous than he had anticipated. His desire for knowledge about the Organization had to be balanced against external threats, and now those threats were growing larger.

Royce cleared the front screen. Then he began typing in a message to his contact in North America.

Auckland, New Zealand

Vaughn threw their bags into the back of the pickup truck, while Tai handed them to him. It was hard to believe their seemingly never-ending flight from Hawaii was finally over.

Vaughn didn't know what to make of Logan. About six-foot-two, tanned, with blond hair that Vaughn was sure the man spent quite a few dollars getting worked on, he had those rugged good looks that would have made him perfect for one of those beer commercials kayaking down white-water rapids while several beautiful women awaited him at the other end. Vaughn didn't like him in the slightest. There was a curious intensity about him that was offset by a very congenial, perfect smile that he shined on Tai as often as he could.

He did have to give Royce credit for one thing: he got them around customs and their gear into the back of the pickup without being checked. And he noted the hard cases already under a tarp in the back that held the weapons and other illegal equipment he had requested.

Tai slid in to sit in the middle, and Vaughn sat on the passenger side as Logan took the wheel. He drove them around the perimeter of the airfield until they came to an old, weather-beaten hangar.

"This is it," Logan said as he pulled up to the hangar. He glanced across Tai at Vaughn. "Mind opening it up?"

Vaughn got out of the truck and slid the large doors open, wide enough for Logan to drive through, then he stepped inside and slid them shut again. As Logan parked the truck, Vaughn looked around. Two planes were parked inside, and a man dressed in greasy overalls was working on one of them. Logan and Tai got out of the pickup.

"This is our aircraft," Logan announced, standing in front of the sleek two-engine plane the man was working on. Vaughn noted the skis bolted on over the wheels of the plane and extra fuel tanks hung under each wing. The man stopped working on the engine and looked at them.

"This is our pilot, Mike Brothers," Logan said.

Brothers acknowledged them with a grimy wave and went back to work, intent on whatever he was doing. Vaughn had no desire to interrupt a man working on an engine he was going to be counting on. Brothers looked like he had done more than his fair share of hard living, with his weather-beaten skin and pure white, thinning hair. Vaughn hoped he knew what he was doing.

"Brothers spent a couple of decades flying the bush in Australia," Logan said. "He's spent the last three years doing runs to Antarctica. The pay is better."

A man with simple motivations, Vaughn thought, reflecting back on the conversation he'd had with Tai on the plane.

"Over here," Logan said, leading them to a plywood board screwed to the hangar wall, which had maps tacked up on it.

Vaughn and Tai sat in the metal folding chairs in front of the maps while Logan stood next to the board.

"We're taking off first thing in the morning tomorrow," Logan announced.

"How long a flight?" Tai asked.

"Eight hours," Logan answered. "Earth First's base, which is where I've always gone before, is located here on Ross Island, about fifteen miles from McMurdo, so we use the runway there and then tractor over. There are eleven people down there right now, but seven are out on the ice shelf doing core tappings, so we'll be able to squeeze in with no problem."

Logan picked up a manila envelope and slid out several photos. "I got the copies of the pictures you sent me. I've tried to figure out where this Citadel can be using them. The Citadel appears to be set in a sort of basin, surrounded on three sides by mountains. Based on the flying time from High Jump Station—now Mc-Murdo—and aircraft type, the JRM Mars, I've estimated it to be between five and six hundred miles from McMurdo straight-line distance. I'm assuming they flew straight because you do not want to dick around in the air down there. The weather can change on you in a heartbeat."

Logan turned to the map. "Combing that with the mountains in the background, that places it in one of three spots: to the south, here at the edge of the Ross Ice Shelf in the Transarctic Mountains; to the east, at the edge of Marie Byrd Land, where King Edward the VII Land juts out into the Ross Sea; or to the northwest, here along the Adelie Coast.

"The order I just gave you is also the order in which I think we should look. Let me explain. Six hundred miles from McMurdo along the Adelie Coast puts you almost right smack on top of the French station, Dumont d'Urville. I doubt very much that the Citadel is in this area for several reasons. First, I think the French would have come across something if it was there. The

Russians also established a base there in '71 farther east along that coastline, here— Leningradskaya. And they haven't come across anything.

"Additionally, I, and many of my colleagues from Earth First, have been in this area several times conducting protests over the airstrip the French have been trying to build there the last four years. We have made numerous overflights of the area and spotted nothing. I know that the Russians have done extensive electromagnetic sensing missions around that area, trying to determine if there are any mineral deposits. I assume a lot of metal was used in the construction of the Citadel, so I think they would have uncovered it."

Logan tapped the map. "It's possible the base is here along the coast to the east, but I like the location in the Transarctic Mountains. I prefer it because if the purpose was to hide this base, putting it there would locate it much farther south than all bases established afterward, except for Amundsen-Scott Base, which sits right on top of the geographic South Pole itself. Also, this area is along the original route explorers used to reach the South Pole. Both Amundsen and Scott traversed the Ross Ice Shelf and traveled up glaciers into that mountain range. Nowadays, though, expeditions bypass the mountains, going around, either to the east or west. The area has not been extensively explored. Therefore it is my recommendation that we look first in this region."

He paused and looked at Tai, then Vaughn. When neither of them said anything, he continued. "What I've done is make a montage of the silhouettes of the mountains around the Citadel, along with the azimuths the pictures were taken at—I was fortunate that I was able to use the sun and shadows to judge that by. Then as we fly along the mountains, we try to match the outlines."

Vaughn was beginning to change his initial negative opinion of Logan. The man was obviously not stupid.

Logan held up a piece of paper with an outline of three jagged peaks poking above a sea of ice. "This is the view we should see along a due north azimuth. Mountains, whose peaks manage to make it above the ice, are called nunatuks down there. As you can see in this picture, we have these three very distinctive nunatuks, two large pointed ones on the flanks of this rounded one. This three mountain setup is what we should be looking for."

"How common are nunatuks?" Tai asked.

"Not as common as this map would make you believe with all these mountain ranges drawn on it," Logan replied. "The Antarctic ice sheet on the average is over twenty-five hundred meters thick. That's over eight-thousand feet. So a mountain has to be very high to clear the ice sheet.

"If we can find these three—and they are rather unique—and line them up exactly on azimuth, then we will be along the line that the Citadel lies on."

"This may be a stupid question," Vaughn said, "but wouldn't this place be totally covered up by now? After all these years, it would seem like there'd be quite a bit of snow on top."

"Good question." Logan rubbed his chin. "I think even the entrance and any air vents for the Citadel are most likely totally covered over by now, but not from snowfall. There isn't much accumulation down there, but the wind would pile ice and snow up against any exposed structure. However, I do have a plan for that.

"As I explained, we can get pretty close to its loca-

tion if we find these mountains. Once we do that, we
land and use sonar through the ice to try and find the
base. It's similar to the way fishermen look for schools
of fish. Earth First has two backpack sonar sets at the
base that they use for research on the ice cap. The core
tapping team didn't take them, so we can use those as
we ski along the azimuth to shoot down into the ice.
The metal and lack of density of the base ought to show
up clearly. According to the information you sent, the
Citadel covers a large area underground, so that should
help quite a bit."

Vaughn wondered what contingency the builders
had designed to find the place if it was covered up. He
doubted very much that they had overlooked that major
problem when they'd built it.

"What's the weather like?" Tai asked.

Logan walked over to a table and switched on a radio set. "Let's find out. We have high frequency contact
with our base, and just last month we finally got the
people over at McMurdo to give our station the most
current weather reports. Before that we were on our
own."

Vaughn thought it was interesting that McMurdo
hadn't been giving the weather to the Earth First people.
Typical government mentality. Earth First represented
a potential threat, so the party line was probably to ignore them at least, or more likely, to make their life
as miserable as possible. It was stupid, but who said
governments were smart? On the other hand, he imagined that the Earth First people weren't exactly trying
to ingratiate themselves with the various government
personnel down there, and the resulting attitude was
probably, "Why feed the dog that bites your hand?"

Logan fiddled with the dials and then picked up

the microphone. "Earth First South, this is Auckland. Over." He clicked off and looked at them.

There was no answer, and he repeated the message. Finally the radio crackled with a woman's voice. "Auckland, this is Earth First Base. Over."

"What's the weather look like? Over."

"The latest from McMurdo at 1900 Greenwich mean, present readings: temperature minus twenty-nine degrees Fahrenheit. Winds north-northwest at twenty-three knots. Barometric pressure 29.4 rising. Ceiling 1,200 feet, overcast. Visibility four miles with some blowing snow.

"Forecast is for the temperature to rise to minus twenty-one degrees Fahrenheit and the winds to continue at the same. Ceiling is expected to go up to around 1,500 feet with continued broken clouds. Visibility to extend to almost five miles. Over."

Logan replied. "Great. We'll give you a call once we're in the air and tell you when to expect us. Over."

"Roger. See you then. Out."

Tai frowned. "That sounds like pretty bad weather to me."

Logan smiled. "Actually that's good weather for Antarctica. The forecast is for eight hours, plus two on the far side for a safety margin. That report is a combination of inputs from d'Urville, the Soviets at Minsk Station, the Aussies at Wilkes, and several others. McMurdo collates them and then broadcasts every thirty minutes. Four hours out from McMurdo is our point of no return. That's when we get the latest weather relayed from Aurora Glacier and the pilot makes our decision whether to continue on or turn around and head back based on weather and fuel."

Vaughn turned as someone came up behind them.

Brothers stood there with two other men. One was an overweight man with a balding head, and the other an obvious weightlifter with muscles bulging under his overalls. His head was shaved, his black skin reflecting the overhead lights.

"Who is this?" Vaughn asked.

"Burke and Smithers," Logan said. "They're going with us as support."

"We don't need support," Vaughn said in a tone that brooked no argument.

Logan wasn't one, apparently, to accept that. "We aren't going onto the ice with only four people. We can't carry enough gear to survive. We have a standing policy—hell, everyone in Antarctica has a standing policy—of a minimum of five people in any surface party. And I assume sooner or later we're going to put boots down on the ice, right? And I vouch for them. They've done work for me when I've been contracted by Royce before."

Vaughn glanced at Tai, and she shook her head ever so slightly. He knew Logan was right—it helped to have extra bodies on hand—but for this mission he didn't trust anybody.

Brothers took the silence as a chance to step forward. He spoke with a strong Australian accent as he wiped off his hands with a grimy towel. "We're topped off, and I've got all your gear loaded. We'll be ready to roll at first light as long as the weather holds." He walked to the front of the room. "I've got extra fuel tanks on the wings and two bladders in the back all hooked up. We should have enough petrol to make it there."

"'Should have?'" Tai echoed.

Brothers smiled. "Just a phrase. It's a good airplane—a Cessna 411, if that means anything to you—

but Antarctica is a bit out of its normal range so we have to pack on all that extra fuel. I assume Logan has told you about the point of no return. It's not only there because of weather, but also because of the fuel situation. Once we go past it, we've got to make it to Earth First South Station because we won't have enough fuel to turn around and come back." The burly man shrugged and dismissed the fuel situation.

"All right. Here's your safety briefing. If we run into trouble, you do what I say without asking any questions. We go down in the ocean, the raft is under the copilot's seat. That's the one up front that I'm not sitting in. You'd better hope we stay afloat long enough to get the raft inflated and out the window because if you get dunked, the cold water will kill you in less than a minute.

"We go down on land and I don't make it to give you advice, then my advice now is stay with the plane. It's got an emergency transponder on board, and even if that gets busted, the plane is going to be the biggest thing rescuers could find. You go wandering around on the ice, you'll last a little longer than if you had hit the water, but not by much. The end result will be the same.

"There are first aid and emergency kits on board the plane. They're marked in red, and you can't miss 'em." Brothers smiled. "Any questions?" The other five people just stared at him. "All right then. See you in the morning."

Logan pointed at some boxes lined up against the wall. "I've got some cold weather gear here. Let's get your equipment squared away before I show you where you'll spend the night."

Area 51

Dyson, the head of the North American Table, was pressed back in his seat as the Gulfstream Jet roared down the runway that cut across the dry bed of Groom Lake. The plane needed only a fraction of the seven-mile-long concrete to get airborne.

He looked once more at the negative reply from the ISA concerning information about the Citadel, then put it down on the table in front of him. The potential embarrassment if the place did exist, and held four MK-17 thermonuclear weapons, was great. The fact that it was causing him problems with Geneva was also very bad.

The secure computer link buzzed, and words began scrolling across the screen. The message was brief and to the point: his agent in the Philippines had been found. Dead. And there was no sign of Fatima. Which meant she was free with the information Lansale had sent her. And he had no doubt where her destination would be: the Citadel.

If the Abu Sayif got its hands on the four Mark-17s— well, he didn't want to dwell on that.

But the information was even worse than that as the message continued: Fatima had met with a North Korean agent prior to being picked up by Royce's agent. Which meant the scant information he had about The Citadel and the bombs was probably en route to Pyong-yang.

Dyson checked his contacts and began making calls to begin maneuvering resources south toward Antarctica in preparation for possible intervention.

CHAPTER 6

South Pacific

The small freighter cut through the ocean heading southeast. Fatima stood on the bridge, Araki to her right, and looked ahead at endless ocean. The captain was in his chair to her left, the helmsman in front of him. The ship appeared old and rusted, but the engines were perfectly maintained, and the ship was cruising at a much faster speed than its appearance suggested it would.

"You have no idea who this man you killed worked for?" Araki asked.

"He was American," Fatima said.

"But that does not necessarily mean he was working for the American government," Araki said.

"Then who?" Fatima asked.

"Now you are playing me for the fool," Araki replied.

"Nishin was from the Organization," Fatima said. "Why would they have a second person there? It was too soon for someone from Japan to fly in if they discovered that Nishin was missing. So the American was on the ground already, waiting for me. If they were from the same Organization, why didn't they work together?"

"One was Japanese and one American," Araki said. "Perhaps the Organization has many arms to it?"

"Likely," Fatima allowed. "But he questioned me about the Citadel, of that I am certain. Why would he do that if the Organization built the Citadel and he was from it?"

To that, Araki had no answer. They stood there in silence for a while, feeling the ship roll as it punched through the waves.

Finally, Fatima spoke. "The only way we figure out what is going on is to find the base and subsequently figure out why the Organization built it, why it is so important that someone is willing to kill to hide its existence, and why Lansale sent me that information."

"Since you escaped, we're a step ahead of them," Araki said.

"Maybe," Fatima said. She turned to Araki. "Tell me what information you've withheld."

Araki sighed, then spoke. "David Lansale. I've heard of him. Before I came to the Philippines. His name was in the intelligence packet I was given."

Fatima nodded. "He parachuted into Japan during the Second World War. During the Doolittle raid. Met with representatives of the government to negotiate the Golden Lily."

Araki stared at her. "So you know more than I do."

"It appears so."

"Then perhaps you might tell me where we are going now?" Araki asked.

"Antarctica."

"We still have the problem of actually locating this place," Araki pointed out.

"We will try to go to where the I-401 and the two German submarines were abandoned," Fatima said.

Araki frowned. "Those submarines were left under the ice cap. They could have sunk to the bottom. Even if they are still locked in the ice, the ice moves, doesn't it?"

"It is all we have," Fatima simply said.

"And what will we do when we get there?"

"It is not a question of what *we* will do," Fatima said.

Araki stared at her. "What do you mean?"

"Do not worry yourself," Fatima said with a smile. "Just remember that the enemy of my enemy is my friend."

Airspace, South Pacific

"Roger, Earth First South Station. Passing point of no return and coming in. Out." Brothers turned in his seat toward the five passengers cramped in the back and yelled over the whine of the engines. "Weather is satisfactory all the way, so we're continuing on."

Burke, Smithers, Vaughn, Tai, and Logan sat amidst a jumble of equipment, with scarcely room to move an elbow. Vaughn had his eyes closed, trying to catch some sleep, but it was eluding him so far. He could hear Tai and Logan talking. Tai was trying to learn about operating in Antarctica, and Logan was trying to learn about Tai. Burke and Smithers appeared to be sleeping.

Vaughn opened his eyes. "How long have you worked for Royce?"

Logan was startled. "I don't rightly work for him. I do jobs for him when he calls."

"Why?" Vaughn asked.

Even under his tan, Logan's face flushed visibly red. "He pays well."

"And?" Vaughn pressed.

"And what?" Logan said angrily.

"What's he holding over you?" Vaughn pressed.

"Nothing," Logan snapped. He pulled his heavy Gore-Tex jacket tighter around himself and put his hood up. "I suggest we all get some sleep. We're going to need it." He shut his eyes.

Vaughn glanced at Tai. She shrugged and then closed her eyes also.

Two hours later Brothers's voice intruded over the numbing roar of the plane. "There's Antarctica."

Vaughn, along with the others, peered out the right side. "That's Cape Adare," Logan announced. "It's where the Ross Sea begins to the west. It's well over one thousand kilometers across the opening of the Ross Sea to the other side. The international dateline actually cuts right through the middle of the sea."

Dark peaks, streaked with snow and ice, poked through the low-lying clouds, overlooking the ocean. To the left, the sea ice stretched unbroken as far as the eye could see through a few gaps in the clouds.

As they continued south, more peaks appeared along the coast they were now paralleling as the ocean turned into the Ross Sea. Logan called the ranges out as they went by: the Admiralty Range; the Prince Albert Mountains; and finally, the Royal Society Range.

Brothers began to drop altitude as a single massive

mountain appeared straight ahead above the clouds, set apart from the others to the right. "That's Mount Erebus. Earth First South Station and McMurdo are both set on the base of Erebus on the far side. It, along with Mount Terror, make up most of Ross Island. Captain Ross, whom the island, the sea, and ice shelf are all named after, christened both mountains after the two ships that he used to explore the Antarctic," Logan explained.

"He had a ship named *Terror*?" Tai asked.

Logan laughed. "Yes. Interesting history to that ship. First, as Americans, you'll be thrilled to know it was originally outfitted as what the British called a bomb vessel, carrying heavy mortars. It was one of the ships that shelled Fort McHenry in the War of 1812 and inspired that fellow to write your 'Star-Spangled Banner.'

"But more importantly, the ship's later history is a lesson on how brutal conditions are here and in the Arctic. In the 1830s the *Terror* was on an exploration mission in Hudson Bay when it got caught in the ice. The ship was pressed over fifty feet up the side of a cliff by the pressure of the ice on its hull. It was repaired and was Captain Ross's second ship—he was in command of the *Erebus*—on his expedition down here from 1840 to 1843.

"They successfully did that mission but weren't so lucky on their next one to Baffin Bay. The ships were last seen entering the bay and then not heard from again for over a decade, until someone found both ships, completely abandoned by their crews and icebound. Not a single one of either ship's crew was ever found. One hundred percent casualties. Their bodies are still buried somewhere in the ice, as are a lot of other bodies."

"We're going down," Brothers yelled over his shoulder.

Tai was startled. "What?"

"We're going in for our landing," Brothers qualified with a smile.

"Smart-ass," Tai muttered.

"We don't have much of a runway," Brothers told them as they descended. "We land on the ice on the Ross Ice Shelf itself, as it's the flattest thing around. The reception party should have marked out a reasonably good stretch for us. We don't need much," he added in way of encouragement.

Vaughn watched the slopes of Erebus come closer, and then the plane punched into a thick cloud layer and all view was blanketed. Suddenly, the clouds parted and they were in the clear again. The plane was very low now, and Brothers banked hard left, over land.

"That's McMurdo Station!" Logan yelled. Vaughn pushed his face up against the glass and looked below. The sprawl of buildings and numerous large storage tanks surprised him— McMurdo was much larger than he had imagined. Somehow he had pictured something out of the old science fiction movie *The Thing*: a few Quonset huts huddled in the snow. At a rough guess he would say there were at least forty buildings down there.

"All right. Everyone buckle up." Brothers swung out over the ice now, very low. They roared over a snow tractor with a large red flag tied off to the top. Brothers pulled up and did another flyby. A man on top of the tractor was holding a green flag pointing in a northeasterly direction.

On the third pass, Brothers finally dipped his wings down. With a hiss and then a steady rumble, the skis touched the ice, a thin mist of snow pluming up on either side. Gradually, they slithered to a halt. Brothers turned the plane around and taxied it back to the tractor. Vaughn could now see that the tractor had a flatbed trailer hitched to it with several drums piled on top.

The silence as Brothers turned off the engines was as shocking as any loud sound. They'd lived with that noise for many hours. As their senses adjusted, the steady whine of wind bouncing off the skin of the plane became noticeable. With the airplane's heater off, the temperature immediately started dropping inside.

"Everyone bundle up." Logan was cinching down his hood.

Vaughn pulled his own cold weather equipment out of his duffel bag. He was wearing a Gore-Tex camouflage parka over Patagonia Pile jacket and bib pants that zipped on the sides and the crotch. Tai wore the same thing. Logan and his two men's outer layer was bright orange. They all had polypropylene underwear next to their bodies to wick away any moisture from their skin. Large rubber cold-weather boots—Logan had referred to them as Mickey Mouse boots— covered their feet. The boots had a layer of air trapped in them that insulated the feet remarkably well, but Vaughn knew from experience they also brought about a lot of foot sweating, which had to be carefully monitored.

Brothers swung open his door, and the blast of cold air slammed into Vaughn's lungs with one quick gulp. Brothers scrambled out and Vaughn followed suit, his feet crunching into the snow. Despite his cold weather training in Special Forces, he'd never felt such cold. The air stung his face, the only exposed part of his body. His skin rebelled, trying to shrink from the pain of the cold, and he felt his muscles tighten, as if he could make himself smaller and that would in some way make him warmer. He forced his muscles to relax.

The other members of the party piled out and stood looking around. To the north, Mount Erebus was a solid wall reaching up into the cloud covering. To the south, an endless line of ice disappeared where the clouds seemed to touch down. To the west, the Royal Society Range blotted out the space between cloud and ice. They looked amazingly close, as if they could be walked to in an hour or two, yet Vaughn knew from the map that they were almost a hundred miles away.

The tractor kicked into life, drawing his attention away from the scenery. It roared up, treads clattering, placing the trailer alongside the plane. The driver, looking like a bear in his bright orange garments, waved down at them, pumping his fist. He seemed to be in a bit of a rush.

"Let's offload," Logan called out.

As they busied themselves transferring the gear from plane to trailer, Smithers used a sledgehammer to drive ice pitons into the ground. One for each wing, one for the tail, and one for the nose; Brothers attached a rope to each piton to secure the plane to the ice.

Once all the equipment was off the aircraft, Vaughn watched as Logan gave Tai a boost up onto the wooden platform that made up the floor of the trailer. She tried to get as comfortable as possible among the bags and cases. Vaughn and the three other members of the party climbed on board, and all grabbed on for dear life as the driver threw the tractor into gear and roared off toward the looming form of Mount Erebus.

Logan leaned over to put his face between Vaughn and Tai. "Welcome to Antarctica."

Democratic People's Republic of Korea Embassy, Manila

The ambassador's aide frowned as the secretary entered the meeting room and hurried over to his chair. "Mr. Choegu, there is an urgent message for you," she whispered in his ear.

Making his excuses to the delegation of trade bureaucrats from Singapore, Choegu walked swiftly to his office. The encoded message sat on the center of his desk, only the word URGENT readable in Han Gul, the rest in unintelligible seven letter groups. He turned and unlocked the safe behind his desk and pulled out the onetime pad.

He wrote the letters out in longhand as he deciphered the message on a single sheet of paper with a hard plastic board underneath in order not to leave an impression copy. As the words coalesced into meaning, Choegu felt both excited and confused.

   —ABU SAYIF SAY THERE IS AN ABANDONED AMERICAN MILITARY BASE IN ANTARCTICA.
   —BASE IS SUPPOSED TO CONTAIN NUCLEAR WEAPONS.
   —WILL CONTINUE TO MONITOR AND RELAY INFORMATION AS SOON AS POSSIBLE.
   —ABU SAYIF WILL BE IN CONTACT WITH MORE INFORMATION SOON.
   —RAWSS.

Choegu knew who Rawss was—one of their deep cover agents in Manila. He didn't even try to sort out the various pieces of the puzzle. He immediately pulled out another onetime pad and transcribed the letters of the message verbatim as quickly as his hand could write.

Done, he rapidly walked up the stairs to the fourth floor of the embassy building. A guard with an automatic rifle stood in front of a steel door. Despite his rank and stature, Choegu had to show his identification card to the guard, who knew perfectly well who he was.

Satisfied, the guard opened the steel door and Choegu stepped inside. Another steel door awaited him. An eye appeared at the small peephole, and he once again showed his identification. The door opened and he entered.

"Sir?" the man who had let him in asked.

Choegu held out the piece of paper. "Send this immediately."

Earth First South Station, Antarctica

Tai's first glimpse of Earth First South Station confirmed what she had expected. A large, squat box building looking more like several trailer homes sealed together than a research station sat on the ice. Established several hundred meters from the base of Mount Erebus, it was painted bright red, and just to the right a cluster of antennas was tied off to a tower. A colorful banner reading EARTH FIRST was strung along the front.

It had taken the tractor almost forty-five minutes to get them off the ice shelf and up here to the station. As they pulled in front with a clatter, a couple of people stepped out of the building to greet them. As Logan did the introductions, Tai could see Vaughn hanging back.

She knew their camouflage cold weather suits didn't fit with the bright outfits and colorful banner hung on the outside of the station, and the lackluster handshakes from the station personnel confirmed that.

"Let's get our equipment inside," Logan ordered.

Vaughn helped Tai haul their gear bag inside, not wanting the Earth First people to handle it, especially the weapons cases. They were directed down a short corridor and into a small room barely containing three sets of bunk beds. Tai dumped her gear onto one bed while Vaughn put his across from her. Then they rejoined Logan in the mess hall/meeting room as Logan briefed a skinny bearded man on their mission to find the Citadel. Logan had introduced him as Peter McCabe, Earth First's foremost Antarctic expert. When Logan showed him the faxed photocopy of the picture, McCabe sat down at the table and looked at it for a long time.

"This looks familiar. It's rare that you have three nunatuks that close to each other." He pulled out a large chart. "Show me again where you think this place might be, based on the air time."

"The range of the resupply aircraft comes out to roughly five hundred miles." Logan traced a half arc around McMurdo Station.

"It's not to the west," McCabe firmly announced. "That would put it very close to the French station there. I've been in that area quite a bit lately, and I'd certainly recognize these peaks if they were in that area."

He stared at the map a long time, his eyes boring in as if he could see the actual ground from just looking at the two dimensional paper. Tai took the opportunity to look over at Vaughn. He appeared to be out of sorts around the civilians, and she shared some of his feelings.

McCabe turned the map around and placed the photo down on it. He tapped a spot on the far side of the Ross Sea. "It's here. I'd be willing to bet that middle peak is Mount Grace. The one on the right is McKinley Peak. The lower one on the left must be this one that has no name."

Logan shook his head. "Are you sure? I'd have thought they'd put the base farther south." He pointed at the map. "Down here along the Shackleton coast perhaps."

McCabe looked up. "No. That's Mount Grace. I knew I'd seen that silhouette before. To the south of it is the glacier where they launched the Byrd Land South Pole traverse in '60. When you fly out in that direction you put the glacier on the right and McKinley on your left. Then it's open ice until you hit the Executive Committee Mountain Range."

Vaughn spoke for the first time. "How soon can we take off again?" he asked Brothers.

The pilot was chewing on the end of his bushy mustache. "Ah, well, mate, the plane, it can take off right now. The problem is the pilot. I just put in eight nonstop hours and I could use a couple of hours to rest. How about in four hours?"

Tai could tell Vaughn wasn't happy about the delay. She half expected him to try and order the pilot to take off immediately. Vaughn sighed and looked around the table. Smithers and Burke had not said a word, but simply listened to the discussion.

"All right," Vaughn said. "It's presently 3:15 P.M. local time here. We take off at seven-fifteen. The—"

"What about darkness?" Tai interrupted. "We won't be able to find the place in the dark."

Logan laughed. "There is no night in the summer

down here. The sun gets a little lower on the horizon, but it never sets."

"As I said," Vaughn continued, "I want everyone gathered in this room ready to go at six. That will give us plenty of time to make it down to the plane and be in the air at seven-fifteen. Are there any questions?"

Tai saw McCabe looking at Logan, his eyes full of questions about the two people in military camouflage, but the man had the common sense not to say anything in front of Vaughn.

Vaughn looked over at her. "I'm going to get some sleep. I'll see you all at six."

He left the conference room then, but reappeared almost immediately, his duffel bag over his shoulder.

"Where are you going?" Tai asked as he placed his hand on the door leading outside.

"I'm going to sleep outside. I'll be on the lee side of the building when you want me." With that he stepped out, and the door slammed shut behind him.

"You brought a weird man with you, Tai," was Logan's only comment before he turned to his crew and to give some more instructions.

Tai tugged on her parka, grabbed her backpack, and went outside after Vaughn. She found him on the far side of the building, digging in the snow. He briefly glanced up at her, but she said nothing, watching him.

After completing the slit in the snow, he removed the bungi cord from around a Therm-a-Rest pad and laid it down on the bottom of the trench. Unscrewing the valve on the top corner, the pad quickly expanded to full size, about an inch and a half thick, by a foot and a half wide, by six long.

Then he pulled out his sleeping bag. It was compressed inside a stuff sack, and he released the cinches and unrolled the bag. Vaughn then stretched a poncho across the top of the trench, fixing down the ends with snow, leaving an opening just large enough to crawl in. All done, he put the shovel down in the hole along with his bag in a place he had dug out near the head.

"Why are you sleeping out here?" Tai finally asked, unable to restrain her curiosity.

Vaughn looked up at her. "It takes about four days to acclimatize to a radically new environment. Or at least it takes me four days. Besides, I hate sleeping that close to a bunch of people. I'm a very light sleeper, and the slightest noise wakes me up." He smiled. "Hell, tell the nature lovers in there that I'm just loving nature."

"What's that?" Tai asked as he started to slip into a thin bag.

"It's a vapor barrier, or VB liner, that goes inside the sleeping bag," he explained. "The liner keeps my perspiration inside it. Makes for a damp sleep, but it's better for me to be damp than the bag. I can dry out. I might not be in circumstances where I can dry the bag out, and a wet sleeping bag will kill you here."

He proceeded to slide all the way in until the only thing visible from the trench was his face. Tai leaned over. "I guess I'll build my own snow trench."

"Good idea," Vaughn said.

"I need to send a sitrep to Royce first."

Vaughn looked at her. "Sure that's a good idea?"

"Let's not get into that," Tai replied.

"Whatever," Vaughn said, and shut his eyes.

Tai walked a dozen yards away and pulled out the small satcom radio from her backpack. She knelt in the snow, opened the small satellite dish and oriented it, then hooked the radio to it. She checked to make sure she had a clear bounce back from the Milstar satellite, which was just on the northern horizon.

Using a pen on the small keyboard on the radio, she summarized their situation and their intent to search for the Citadel shortly. Then she broke the gear down and put it back in the pack.

Tai went inside the base to the bunk room where their gear was stored. No one else was around. She opened one of the weapons cases, pulled out a 9mm pistol, loaded a magazine in it, and slid it in one of the pockets of her parka. She took a second one out and did the same, putting it in the opposite pocket. Then she pulled out her air mattress and sleeping bag from her duffel bag. As she turned for the door, it was thrown open. Vaughn stood there.

"The mess hall now!" he barked, and was gone as quickly as he'd come.

Tai rushed to the mess hall to find Vaughn leaning over an unconscious Brothers. The pilot was slumped in a chair, his clothes covered with melting ice and snow.

"What happened?" she asked.

"I found him outside, lying in the snow, just like this." Vaughn was checking the pilot's bare hands for frostbite as he spoke. "Another five minutes and he'd have frozen to death."

"How'd you find him?" Tai inquired.

"I heard a noise. Sounded like the main door slamming shut. I don't know." He shrugged. "Something just didn't seem right, so I got up and checked."

As Vaughn explained, the other members of the team filed in until all were assembled.

"So what happened to him?" Logan wanted to know. "Did he fall and knock himself out?"

Vaughn shook his head. "I don't think so." He broke open a medical kit and pulled out some smelling salts, waving them under Brothers's nose. The pilot gagged briefly, and then his eyes flickered open. He reached up for his head and moaned. Tai stepped forward and looked. A large purplish bruise was visible through the thinning hair on the back of the pilot's head.

Vaughn moved around to face Brothers. "What happened?" he asked.

Brothers tried shaking his head, but the pain got the better of him and he held still. "Shit. I don't know. I was going to take a piss and was in the corridor when someone whacked me on the back of the head. That's all I remember."

Six sets of eyes met, flickered to one another and then back to Brothers. The silence lasted almost a full minute, and then Vaughn asked, "Was anybody awake when he left?"

The three other men shook their heads.

Vaughn turned to Tai. "When I came in, all three were in their beds and appeared to be sleeping. You were in your room. The three people from Earth First were all accounted for also."

"That leaves you, then, doesn't it?" Logan observed.

Vaughn shrugged. "Then it would have been pretty stupid of me to have rescued him, wouldn't it?"

Tai decided to take charge before things went totally to shit. "Are you able to fly?" she asked Brothers.

He nodded carefully. "Aye. I don't think I have any permanent damage."

"Then we leave now." Vaughn turned to Smithers and Burke. "Get your gear ready to go. We leave for the plane in fifteen minutes."

Logan gestured at Brothers. "What about whoever

knocked him out? I don't think it was chance that it was the pilot who was attacked. Somebody is trying to stop us from getting to this Citadel."

"And that's why we're leaving right away," Vaughn replied. "You have as much of an idea who did it as I do. But if we wait around here any longer, whoever it is will have a chance to do something else. I don't want to give them the opportunity. Let's load out."

When the others left the room to get their gear, Tai looked at Vaughn. "We've been infiltrated."

"No shit," he said.

Tai took one of the pistols out and offered it to Vaughn. He took it, checking the magazine. "Make sure you keep it close to your body," he said. "The gun is sweating in here and will freeze up if you don't keep it warm."

Tai nodded, took her pistol out, opened her parka and pile shirt and stuck it inside. "Going to be hard to get to in a hurry if I need it."

Vaughn was doing the same. He shrugged. "Everything is going to take longer down here. Let's hope if we need the guns, whoever we need them against is just as slow."

CHAPTER 7

Geneva, Switzerland

Dyson was not used to being made to wait. Before becoming the head of the North American Table, he had been CEO of one of the top three corporations in America. He'd advised Presidents. Been on the boards of dozens of organizations. He was worth untold billions.

And now he waited after having been summoned like an errant schoolboy to the principal's office.

After forty minutes the door to the Intelligence Center opened. There was no secretary to usher him in. Just the open door. Dyson got up and walked through, eyes blinking as he tried to adjust to the dimmer light inside. He saw the four Assessors in their chairs. He headed for the fifth chair, glancing at the large video displays lining the walls, trying to get a quick glimpse to see if any of the data referred to the current situation he had been summoned for. He could see that one of the large screens displayed a map of Antarctica, but his quick look couldn't reveal anything else.

He sat down, picked up the headset and put it on. He had never met the High Counsel in person. As far as he knew, none of the heads of the various Tables ever had.

"We have received your report," the High Counsel said, his voice coming through the headset. "It was woefully lacking in information. I want to assume that during your flight here you had time to reflect and come up with possible explanations."

Dyson cleared his throat. "I believe David Lansale planned all of this a long time ago, and he set it up that if he died, this information would be released to cause us problems."

"Explain."

"Understand that this is speculation on my part, not hard data," Dyson said.

"We understand."

Dyson could see that two of the four Assessors were watching him, the other two intent on the screens.

"I've tried to line up what we do know and added in the unknown of Lansale's motivations. Lansale was a very good agent, one of our best, and he participated in many top level assignments. But our psych profiles—which we did not have when he was first recruited out of the Office of Strategic Services in World War II—indicate he had maverick tendencies. He questioned things. I believe he questioned who he worked for.

"This all started when he parachuted into Japan as part of Doolittle's raid in World War II. He rendezvoused with Emperor Hirohito's nephew, Prince Chichibu, to negotiate for us. Part of those negotiations were the Golden Lily, the fledgling Japanese atomic weapon program, clemency for the Imperial family—all this is in your database. He did as he was ordered to do, and the mission was a success.

"However, I believe he did more than he was ordered to do. I think he began planning this Citadel operation. After all, the Japanese submarine, I-401, was tasked during the waning days of the war to conduct a mission to Antarctica *prior* to the establishment of the Citadel."

"Do we know what was on the I-401 or the two German submarines?" the High Counsel asked.

"I believe the I-401 carried part of the Golden Lily. We always knew parts of it were missing. Abayon and the Abu Sayif, of course, have recently revealed they held a significant portion of the treasure on Jolo Island, but there are still many missing pieces."

"And the German submarines?"

The American head shifted in his seat. "It might be part of the Nazi Black Eagle treasure. Most likely some of it that has never been accounted for in public or by us. But I fear that they also might have carried weapons of mass destruction." Dyson noted that all four Assessors were now looking at him.

"Explain," the High Counsel said.

"We know the Germans sent uranium to Japan via U-boat after they surrendered and before the Japanese did. Lansale helped keep that from developing into anything via his Japanese contacts in the Far East Table. But—we also know from Operation Paper Clip that a large amount of experimental nerve gas that the Germans developed went missing at the end of the war. I believe some of that gas was on those two U-boats that linked up with the I-401."

"And your agent did not get the location of the I-401 and the two German submarines, correct?"

"He only called in the information. He was supposed to fully debrief Royce later. He never made it to later. His body was found, and there was no sign of Fatima. We have to assume she's on the trail of the I-401."

There was a long silence. Then finally the High Counsel spoke. "You will remain here at the castle until the head of the Far East Table arrives. We will then coordinate our actions."

Ross Ice Shelf, Antarctica

Brothers pulled in the yoke, and the heavily laden Cessna bounced a few times and then was in the air. Reaching sufficient altitude, the plane banked and headed for the search area. Vaughn was crowded in the back with Tai, Logan, Smithers, and Burke. The plane was almost as crowded with people and equipment as it had been on the flight from New Zealand. If they found the area the base was in, Vaughn wanted to be prepared to land and try to find it. He was keeping a close eye on Brothers, not sure the knock on the head hadn't affected the pilot.

Their course followed the edge of the Ross Ice Shelf to the east. Ross Island faded behind them, and after an hour and a half Roosevelt Island appeared below and then slid to the rear. They slowly decreased the distance to the Ford Mountain Range, looming up in front of them. As they approached the first mountains, Brothers increased power, and the wings groped in the thin air for even more altitude until he had sufficient height to clear them.

While the magnificence of the peaks that jutted out

of the white impressed Vaughn, what struck him more was the depth of the sea of ice that swept the flanks of those mountains. It was hard to imagine an ice sheet almost two miles thick.

Brothers piloted them over a glacier and through a pass, putting them on the opposite side of the mountain range. Now they turned north, flew along the eastern side of the mountains, looking to their left, searching for the three mountains. Vaughn had taped the photocopy of the picture against the bulkhead above the left side window, and he and Logan were scanning in that direction.

Brothers flew straight up the middle of the mountain chain. The weather was remarkably clear, and the peaks seemed startlingly close to Vaughn. It seemed possible to reach a hand out the window and caress the rock. He glanced right at the map board on Logan's lap. He had their route marked on the plastic cover with grease pencil.

"Everyone look carefully," Logan yelled out over the whine of the engine. "McKinley should be coming up soon." His words disappeared into the rumble of the engine without any reply from the others.

"That's McKinley," Brothers yelled out from the front a short while later. He immediately banked to the left, and the nose of the aircraft settled on a northeasterly route.

Vaughn tapped Logan on the shoulder, gesturing for the map board. Logan passed it back, and Vaughn oriented it, checking the map against what he could see below.

"Can we move to the right a little bit?" he called out to Brothers.

Visibility was unrestricted, and far out to the front

through a gap in the range they could even see the ice
pack on the coast. To the left and right, isolated moun-
taintops poked out of the white carpet of ice.

"There. That's it," Vaughn calmly announced.

Three peaks, backdropped against further nunatuks.
Tai leaned across Vaughn, her body tight against his as
she looked up at the Xerox taped on the fuselage and
then out again. She leaned forward and tapped Brothers
on the shoulder. "There. We're pretty close on line."

Vaughn looked at their guide and asked, "What do
you think, Logan?"

Logan nodded. "Close. You have to consider the fact
that the photo was taken from the ground. We're up
much higher than that.

"Brothers," he called out, "drop down and let's see
how they look."

Brothers did that, and they circled down until they
were barely a hundred feet above the ice. Then the pilot
pointed the nose straight at the peaks, and all six of the
plane's occupants stared ahead.

Tai was the first to break the silence. "That's it. Let's
land."

"All right," Brothers said, looking over his shoulder.
"Let me find a flat stretch. We don't want to be buckling our landing gear. It's a long walk back to Base."

Brothers flew along and then did a long loop to circle around again. And again. And again, all the time
searching the ice-covered ground. Vaughn was almost
certain they were in the right area. The three peaks
matched, and the basin was surrounded on three sides
by mountains. The bowl was about twelve miles long
by thirty wide, open to the south. If they could land and
get an azimuth on the peaks to exactly match the photo,
he believed they could get very close to the Citadel.

The passes revealed no sign of any structure, but that didn't surprise him. The ice and blown snow would have covered the above-surface portions of the Citadel long ago.

"All right," Brothers announced. "I've got a stretch that looks like it might work."

"'Might'?" Tai repeated.

Brothers ignored her. "Everyone make sure you're buckled up tight."

Brothers slowly pushed forward on the yoke and reduced throttle. The ice crept closer and closer to the plane as they descended.

"Let's hope there are no crevasses," the pilot said in a cheerful tone.

Then the skis touched and they were down—for the moment.

"Shit," Burke yelled as they became airborne again, bouncing over a small ridge and then slamming back down on the ice once more.

The plane was shuddering, and the right wing tipped down as that ski hit a divot in the ice. They turned right slightly, and then Brothers straightened them out. The plane gradually came to a halt.

"Well, that was fun," he said.

Vaughn looked over his shoulder. "Can you taxi closer to those three nunatuks until we get on the exact right azimuth from the photo?"

"I can do it," Brothers said, but he glanced back at Logan. "The question is: how stable is the ice here?"

Logan licked his lips. "Actually, the ice should be all right here. We're on a pretty solid base. You have to worry about crevasses when you're on a glacier, but we're above solid ground now. Should be all right."

"Let's do it," Vaughn ordered.

"To the right," Tai said. Brothers looked at her questioningly. "If you want to line them up, go to the right."

The pilot increased throttle and worked his pedals. The Cessna slithered along.

"Hold it," Tai called out after three minutes of moving very slowly. "What do you all think?"

Six sets of eyes peered to the north.

"Yes." Vaughn was the first to answer.

"Yes." Logan echoed him. The other three said nothing.

"Let's get skiing." Vaughn unbuckled. He slapped Logan on the shoulder. "Which do you want? North or south?"

Kaesong, North Korea

The headquarters for the North Korean Special Forces is located just twenty-five miles north of the famous border city, Panmunjom. This location puts it in close proximity to the demilitarized zone, where many of its unit's covert activities are conducted. Tonight, however, General Guk Yol, the army Chief of Staff and former commander of the Special Forces Branch, had his eyes focused on a map that had never been unfurled in his operations room before. The fact that his staff had even been able to find the map was quite an accomplishment on such short notice. It was only forty-five minutes since General Yol had been awakened by the duty officer and given Choegu's message from Manila.

Yol pointed a gnarled finger, broken many times in hand-to-hand combat training, at the map. "It is there, sir."

There were only two people in the world that General Yol had ever shown such deference to. One had been Kim Il Sung, the leader of North Korea for forty years. The other was the man who presently stood opposite him looking at the map—Kim's son, Kim Jong Il. "It is very far away."

"Yes, sir, but it is a golden opportunity. It gives us a lever that is the perfect solution to the problem that has kept us from implementing the Orange III plan."

Kim Jong, long the designated heir to Kim Il Sung, and now the ruler, rubbed the side of his face. The recent reduction of American forces in South Korea had left that threat a paper tiger. With the Americans embroiled in Iraq and Afghanistan, they were stretched perilously thin. Kim had no doubt his massive army—sixth largest in the world—could now overcome their enemies to the south. The problem was the real threat the Americans still held: their tactical nuclear weapons.

Korea is a land of mountains and narrow plains. It is along those narrow plains that any offensive movement has to advance. And tactical nuclear weapons were the ideal countermeasure to such movement. If that one factor could be removed, the entire balance of power in the peninsula would shift to the North's favor.

In late 1991 the United States had removed all tactical nuclear weapons from the peninsula itself in a gesture to force the North Koreans to abandon their nuclear weapon program. The gesture had been ignored for the simple reason that it was seen as an empty one. The Americans maintained more than enough tactical nuclear weapons on the planes, submarines, and cruise missiles of the Seventh Fleet to more than make up for the lack of land-based ones.

Orange III was the classified operations plans,

known as OPLAN, for a northern invasion of South Korea. Unfortunately, Kim Jong Il rued, his father had never approved the implementation of the plan because of the high risk and cost potential if it failed—and fail it most likely would if the Americans used their nuclear weapons.

The fact that the North Koreans had their own small arsenal of nukes did not change that balance for two simple reasons. First, they only had limited abilities to project those weapons a few hundred kilometers into the south—they could never touch the United States itself to keep it from using the weapons. Second, tactical nuclear weapons favored the defender—not the attacker.

But now there was a window of opportunity. This new information could make Orange III a reality if it was used properly.

Kim looked up at his old friend. "I cannot believe that the American government has abandoned nuclear weapons in this place."

Yol smiled, showing stained teeth, the result of constantly smoking cigarettes. "Imperialists are like that, sir. Not only does one hand not know what the other is doing in the U.S. government, but fingers on the same hand are often in the dark as to the action of the other fingers."

"But the bombs—how could they have just been left there?"

"I don't know, sir. But it appears they are. Unguarded for the time being. We must seize the opportunity."

Kim was more cautious than his military commander. "Could it be a trap set by the Americans?"

Yol considered that very briefly. "I see no reason for the Americans to do that."

"But can we use these weapons even if we find them?"

"That, I do not know until we get our hands on them."

"And how can we do that?" Kim asked.

Yol turned to the map. "It is a long way," he admitted. "But we need not have to cover the entire distance."

Kim frowned. "Why not?"

Yol pulled down a larger scaled map that showed the entire Pacific region all the way down to Antarctica. "Because we have a team that could do the job right here." He tapped the map, indicating Indonesia. "If you will give me the permission, sir."

"You have a plan, then?"

Yol smiled. "Yes, sir."

Kim settled back in his seat. "Let me hear it."

Yol tapped a button, and three Special Forces officers carrying charts and paper hustled into the room. A lieutenant colonel took over the briefing, his pointer going to the same spot in Indonesia. As he progressed, the pointer slid down to Antarctica and then north again, but didn't come back to the Korean peninsula.

At the end of fifteen minutes, Kim had caught Yol's enthusiasm. The briefing officers wrapped up and left the room, leaving the two of them alone. Kim Jong II had known General Yol for his entire adult life. He had only one question for his old friend: "It is a very daring plan. You think you can do it?"

"Yes."

"Send the message and begin all the preparations."

Antarctica

Vaughn slid to a halt and looked back over his shoulder. The plane didn't look very far away, but he estimated he'd come at least four miles. He reached for the sonar emitter slung over his shoulder and pointed it down. As he pressed the trigger, he watched the small screen on the back. Negative. After five seconds he turned it off and reshouldered it.

Every thirty push-offs with his right ski, he halted and repeated the process, with the same negative result. At least the cross-country skiing felt good and kept him warm. He was moving north, so he had the mountains to his front. His course was centered on the middle peak. He estimated it was about four to five miles ahead of him, and sensed he was moving slightly uphill as he continued. The surface was definitely not as flat as it had appeared from the air, and he appreciated Brothers's talents even more. Occasionally Vaughn crossed low ridges of compressed ice and had to traverse to get over them.

Twenty-seven. Twenty-eight. Twenty-nine. Thirty. The echo just below the surface shocked Vaughn for a moment. He blinked and stared at the screen for ten seconds. It was still there. He looked around the immediate area. The surface ice was relatively even except for a six-foot ridge running in an angle across his front. There was no sign of anything man-made.

He pulled his backpack off, slid out one of the thin plastic poles with a flag attached and stuck it in the ice. Then he began to ski, ten paces only now, past the flag, trying to search out the dimensions of whatever it was under the ice. He continued to receive a positive response as he approached the ridge.

Vaughn traversed up the small incline of ice and stood on top of the buckled ice. His flag was over eighty meters away. This had to be the base. He noted an outcropping from the ice ridge about ten meters away and skied along the top to it. Snow had piled up, forming a large block, perhaps fifteen feet to a side and eight feet high. Vaughn aimed the sonar into the snow pile. Positive response. There was something in there too.

He looked to the south. His view of the plane was blocked by a large ridge he had crossed about a mile back. He secured the sonar over his shoulder and skied down off the ridge and back to his ruck. He was getting tired but threw it over his shoulder and set out to the south with long distance-eating glides on the skis.

Tai shivered and considered asking Brothers to crank the engine to get the heat going, but she held off. They only had so much fuel, and they'd been on the ice for almost three hours. The windows had fogged over from the breathing of the remaining occupants, and she used her mitten to scrape a small hole in her porthole so she could peer out.

A figure appeared on the horizon, skiing toward the plane with smooth, powerful strides. She kept the glass clear and watched the bundled man come closer.

"One of them is back," she said.

Smithers swung open the side door, and the wind removed what little body heat had built up inside the plane. The skier stepped out of his bindings and passed the skis in, where Smithers slid them along the floor. The man stepped in and shut the door behind him.

"Anything?" Tai asked as Logan slid his parka hood down.

"Nothing." He slumped down in his seat and leaned back. "I went about eight kilometers out and took a slightly different route back and picked up nothing."

There was a roar as Brothers started the engines. In

a minute welcome heat poured out of the vents, and the windows started slowly clearing.

"Let's taxi north and pick up Vaughn on his way back," Tai suggested.

Brothers shook his head. "Uh-uh. I know where the safe runway is to take off on." He pointed out the front window. "Right back the way we came. Plus there's too many small ridges that way. We wouldn't get far."

"Besides," Logan added, "we don't know if Vaughn is taking a straight-back route. Even though it isn't likely, we might just miss him."

Tai sighed and resumed her watch out the window. Brothers shut off the engines after five minutes, and the heat slowly dissipated out the skin of the plane.

The pilot turned in his seat and tapped his headset. "I just got the weather report from McMurdo," he said. "It doesn't sound good. They only give us another three to four hours max of good weather and then we're going to get hit with high winds, which means very low visibility."

Tai knew they weren't going anywhere without Vaughn. She wondered what was taking him so long. He should have been back a half hour ago according to the plan.

Twenty minutes later Smithers called out. "I see him."

Tai leaned over and looked out the opposite side porthole. Vaughn was rapidly moving toward the plane. They opened the door as he arrived, and he threw his backpack in, followed by the skis and himself.

"Anything?" Tai asked.

"Yes."

She waited, but Vaughn was busy cleaning the snow off his boots and then shutting the door. "Well?"

Vaughn removed his snow goggles and smiled. His voice, though, was weak with exertion. "There's something under the ice about four miles from here. I checked it as much as I could and left a flag there. It's pretty big, whatever it is. At least eighty meters long, maybe more. It's either your base or a big-ass flying saucer that got buried under the ice."

Everyone in the plane looked at Tai expectantly, waiting for her instructions. Vaughn accepted a cup of coffee from Smithers's thermos and cradled it in his hands.

"Can we land up there?" she asked him.

Vaughn nodded. "I think there's a good level area to the north of the spot. I couldn't really tell because I didn't ski over it, but I think it's worth a look." He looked forward at Brothers. "It runs northwest-southeast."

Brothers shook his head. "We've got bad weather coming. If we don't head for home now we may get stuck out here."

"What happens if we're stuck out here?" Tai asked.

He shrugged. "We have our emergency gear, but it depends how long the weather stays bad. It could stay bad for a week, in which case it could be an awfully long time to be cooped up in this plane on top of the ice."

"I don't think staying here's a good idea," Vaughn threw in.

"What if we get into the base?" Tai said.

"What?" Vaughn was confused.

"What if we get into the Citadel? It would be out of the wind. They probably left quite a bit of supplies in there."

Vaughn was shaking his head. "Even if what I found

is the Citadel, it was all covered up. How are we going to get in?"

Tai was considering the idea. "They had to have an access shaft."

"I think I found it when I was checking out the dimensions," Vaughn said. "There is something that's covered with blown snow next to an ice ridge."

"We've got shovels and pickaxes in the plane's gear. We can give it a shot," Tai suggested.

"I don't like it." Logan shook his head. "If you want my opinion, we go back to Earth First South and wait until we get good weather. We know where the place is now and can come back."

Brothers agreed. "I don't like the idea, missy," he said to Tai. "I think we ought to go back."

She leaned forward in her seat. "We're going to have to weather out this storm somewhere—either at Earth First South or here. If we stay here, at least we won't get caught in the bad weather flying back. Plus, you have to remember we still have that forty-five-minute tractor ride back to the station from the ice shelf once we land. I think landing up near the base site and trying to dig in is the better option." She knew that time was the most precious commodity they had now. She made a command decision. "Let's try to land near the site."

CHAPTER 8

Antarctica

This second landing had been smoother than the first, and the plane was now staked down, three hundred meters to the north of the ice ridge. Next to the ridge itself, Tai, Vaughn, and Smithers were hacking at the ice and snow on the protuberance, while Burke and Logan swept the loose debris away with shovels.

It was obvious to Vaughn there was a man-made object underneath this snow. The shape was too linear to have occurred naturally. He swung the pick, and a section of ice splintered off. His next swing almost broke his hand as the point bounced off something solid. With his gloves, he began wiping ice and snow away, exposing metal.

"I've got something!" he yelled. The others gathered around and stared at his discovery. The metal was painted white, and the pick had gouged the smooth surface.

"Let's clear it out," Logan said, dropping his pick and grabbing a shovel. Shoulder-to-shoulder, Vaughn and Logan used the edge of their shovels to enlarge the clear space on the metal. Soon they exposed a flat sheet of metal, almost three meters wide by two high.

Logan stepped back and looked at it. "This has to be some sort of surface shaft."

"Where's the door, then?" Tai asked.

"There's four sides," Vaughn replied as he began excavating around the corner to the right. Smithers joined him. Without a word, Logan and Burke started on the corner to the left.

As they cut into the ice, they leveled off the area around the shaft, making it flush with the surface of the ice on the nonridge side. The wind had picked up and snow was beginning to lift and blow across the basin.

Vaughn worked smoothly, trying not to break into a sweat. As his body heat rose, he removed his parka in order to equalize the temperature, stuffing it into his rucksack. He warned the others to make sure they did the same.

A meter from the edge he discovered a seam in the metal. He scraped ice away up and down and then to the right. Gradually a door appeared. On the far right side there was a spoked metal wheel. Once the door was completely uncovered he stepped back.

"Do you think it will work?" he asked Logan. The rest of the party had gathered around as Vaughn finished clearing the door.

Logan was running his hands along the seam. "I don't know," he replied. "It ought to. It shouldn't have frozen up, as the temperature here never gets above freezing to produce the moisture needed for that. Let's give it a try."

Vaughn stepped back as Logan gripped the wheel and leaned into it. The metal didn't budge.

"Here, let me try." Smithers placed the handle of the pick through one of the spokes of the wheel and squatted down. Slowly he started to exert pressure up.

"Watch out!" Vaughn yelled as the wood handle broke. The free piece ricocheted off the door and hit Smithers in the head. Dazed, he fell back onto the ice.

"Damn." Smithers sat there rubbing his head through the parka hood. "That hurts."

Vaughn thought it would be darkly amusing if they had found the Citadel but couldn't get in. The only thing that truly worried him was the weather. He had silently gone along with Tai's decision, but now he was beginning to have second thoughts. The sky was dark with clouds now, and the wind was howling, knifing through his clothes. They needed to get out of the wind, and there were only two choices: go into the base or back to the plane.

He looked at Smithers again. Something dark was seeping through his hood. "Shit," Vaughn muttered. "Stay down," he ordered as Smithers tried standing up. He carefully pushed the big man's hood down. The inside was caked with blood that had already frozen. The gash from the wood wasn't hard to find on the man's bald head. It was about three inches long and didn't appear to be deep.

"What's wrong?" Tai asked.

Without answering, Vaughn opened the first aid kit attached to the outside of his rucksack and pulled out a sterile gauze pack. He quickly tore it open and then put his mittens back on before pressing the cloth up against the cut. It immediately turned bright red as the blood soaked through.

"He got cut," Logan said. "It's not deep, but scalp wounds bleed a lot because the blood vessels are right on the surface."

"We need to go back to the plane now and settle in," Vaughn said. "Hopefully, this thing will blow over quickly."

Brothers shook his head. "I don't think so, mate. McMurdo says this is a big front. We may be stuck for days."

Vaughn looked at Tai. She took a deep, icy breath, then took charge. "All right." She pointed at Burke. "You hold the bandage in place. Make sure you keep the pressure on." She gestured to Vaughn, Brothers, and Logan. "Let's all get on this thing."

They grabbed hold.

"On my count of three," Tai said, "we turn counter-clockwise. Ready? One. Two. Three."

They leaned into the wheel and strained. To no avail.

"Again. Ready? One. Two. Three."

The second attempt was also a failure.

"All right," Tai said, taking deep breaths. "Let's take a break for a second."

Vaughn looked at the wheel. "How about we try it the other way? Clockwise?"

Tai nodded, and they all reassumed their positions. "Ready?" Tai asked. "One. Two. Three."

They all leaned into it, and with a loud screech the wheel moved ever so slightly.

"Again," Tai gasped. "One. Two. Three."

The wheel turned almost a full inch.

"Again."

As they continued to labor, the wheel turned inch by inch. It was slow and hard, but it moved. Vaughn estimated they made a full revolution of the wheel after five minutes of effort. Yet there was no indication they'd unclocked the door. They went at it again, the wheel moving somewhat easier now, and managed another two complete revolutions. And then it stopped. No amount of effort could get it to move any more.

"I think we've gone as far as we can go," Vaughn said.

Logan tapped the metal door. "I'd say it opens inward. It makes sense down here. You want doors to open in because the outside could be blocked by snow or ice."

Vaughn sat down on the ice, his back to the center of the door. He jammed his feet into the ice and snow as best he could then pushed. The others stared at him for a moment, then Logan sat on one side and Tai on the other. Together they put pressure on the door. With a low creak, a small gap appeared on the right side, and they all adjusted, keeping up the pressure. The door swung open wider, the three scrambling to keep the momentum going until it was wide enough for a person to slip through.

"Hold it!" Vaughn finally called out, and they stopped. He got to his feet and peered around the edge. In the darkness beyond he could just make out a metal landing and staircase. The Citadel beckoned. Tai pressed into his side, shining a flashlight in.

"Ladies first," Vaughn said.

Tai slipped in, followed by Vaughn.

The stairs did a ninety-degree turn and seemed to descend directly down into the depths. An open area next to the top of the stairs had a pulley system rigged on top, suggesting that was the way heavy gear could be transported up and down.

Tai shined the light down, and it showed wood planking about twenty feet down and something else at the bottom of the stairs, but from their position they could only make out a vague outline.

Tai leaned over the railing and shone the light directly down. "Oh, shit," she muttered.

Vaughn leaned over also. What had been a vague form was now clearly the body of a man lying at the base of the stairs, facedown, his hands stretched out in front of him, almost an act of supplication.

"Great," Vaughn muttered. "Come on."

Tai cautiously followed Vaughn down the metal steps. The man hadn't moved. When they reached the bottom, Vaughn shone his own light on the body, revealing a figure clothed in Army-issue clothes, circa the 1950s. Three black holes were stenciled in the back of the man's jacket, surrounded by a red frame of blood. Vaughn knelt down and turned the body over. Sightless eyes peered out from a young face, forever frozen in the surprised grimace that must have come as the bullets slammed into his back.

Vaughn looked closely at the face of the corpse, marveling at the frozen preservation. He wondered how long the man had been dead. He looked up at Tai. "Let's get everyone in here before the storm gets worse."

Indonesia

Among the tens of thousands of islands that made up the Republic of Indonesia, this was one of the smaller and less significant. At least to most outsiders. It was an island whose lone small village had been completely wiped out by the tsunami that struck on December 26, 2004.

The village was now reoccupied. But not by fishermen and their families, as the old village had been. It was occupied by a strange international conglomeration. One drawn together from secret meetings around the world. Surprisingly, it was a group that owed its formation to one man: the President of the United States. Because gathered on this small island, working together and training each other, were small elements from the various countries that had been dubbed the Axis of Evil and from the terrorist organizations the United States was at war with.

There were Al Qaeda operatives, Iranian commandoes, a small group of representatives from the Abu Sayif, remnants of Saddam Hussein's elite inner circle, and an elite Special Forces team from North Korea.

This latter group kept itself apart from the others as much as possible. Mainly because their commander considered his men to be real soldiers and the others to be terrorists at best, although they considered themselves freedom fighters.

The commander, Major Min, once more read through the message his radio operator had decoded twenty minutes ago. It was the longest message he had ever seen transmitted over high frequency radio in all his years of special operations. He was holding a complete operations plan (OPLAN) for a new mission that was to commence immediately.

Min's face twisted in a sneer as he read the concept of operations. Those desk-bound fools in Kaesong! He looked up at the thatched roof of the hut that comprised his team's headquarters. Hyun was a small man, less than five and a half feet tall and weighing no more than

120 pounds dripping wet. He was the spitting image of Bruce Lee, the major difference being that Min had actually killed many more men than Bruce Lee had ever simulated killing in his movies.

"Get me Hyun," he snapped at Kim Chong Man. As his executive officer scurried out to the airstrip, Min leafed through the pages of the OPLAN, his mind trying to rationalize the words. This was going to be difficult, very difficult.

Min had been on this island for four months, supposedly advising the other groups on various Special Forces techniques, particularly bomb-making and covert operations. At least that's what they were supposed to be doing. Min had found that the other groups did not like getting advice. In his personal opinion, the real reason he and his men were here was to make a small political statement to these other groups that North Korea supported them in some manner.

Min had been in Special Forces for twenty-one years and had run more than his share of classified missions, so he was no stranger to being awakened in the middle of the night and handed an OPLAN. This one, however, was different in several important aspects. The first was the fact that it was outside of his immediate area of operations. The second was the strategic significance of the mission. It all looked very nice on paper, but implementation was going to require great sacrifices and effort. One of Min's favorite adages was that nothing was impossible to the man who didn't have to do it.

Typical bureaucratic thinking, Min thought with disdain as he read through. It was the same type of thinking that had left him in the DMZ infiltration tunnel north of Seoul two years ago when they should have pulled out at the first sign of compromise. Indecision in his chain of command had left him and his old team in there long enough for the South Koreans to flood it. Min shuddered as he remembered the torrent of water pouring into the tunnel and the muffled screams of the men who couldn't escape.

Hyun stepped in and snapped a salute, breaking Min out of his black reverie. "Captain Hyun reporting as ordered, sir."

Min looked at the short man in the flight suit with undisguised disgust. "What is your aircraft's range?"

Hyun blinked. "It is 6,500 kilometers with a one hour reserve, sir."

"We need to go 9,700 kilometers."

Hyun looked at Kim, who had accompanied the pilot in, and then back at the major. "We will have to refuel somewhere then, sir."

"If we had someplace to land and refuel I would have told you that." Min's voice was ice cold. "We need to travel 9,700 kilometers without refueling."

"That is impossible, sir."

"Make it possible. You have one hour to be ready to leave." Min turned his gaze to his XO. "Bring the team in and I will brief them."

Antarctica

"How long do you think he's been down here?" Vaughn asked as the rest of the party piled up their gear in the dimly lit space at the base of the stairs. The three flashlights combined with the dull reflected light from the still open door to produce a gloomy effect. The man wore unmarked Army fatigues under olive-drab cold-weather gear. There was no name tag on his shirt. He had the insignia of a captain pinned to his collar.

"He was probably the last one," Tai said, then corrected herself. "Well, the next to last one in here. Sometime in the fifties."

Vaughn pulled a poncho out of his rucksack and gently draped it over the body. "Whoever he worked for shot him in the back to keep him from talking about what he did and what he saw here. Judging by the size of the wounds, I'd say it was a small caliber gun. Probably a .22. You have to be damn good to kill someone with a gun that small."

Tai turned to the rest of the group. "We have got to find out everything we can about this place. I want to know who built it and why."

Vaughn began organizing the group. He stared down the corridor, his eyes trying to pick up details. His flashlight reflected off the metal sides and faded out after thirty feet. The ceiling, ten feet above, consisted of steel struts holding metal sheeting that blocked out the ice and snow. Conduits, pipes, and wires crisscrossed the ceiling, going in all directions. The corridor itself was about ten feet wide, and the floor was made up of wood planks, each separated by a few inches to allow snow and ice to fall through the cracks to the sloping steel floor below.

It was as cold down here as it was outside, but at least they were out of the wind. Vaughn went over to Smithers. "How's the head?"

Smithers pulled back the bandage. "I think the bleeding has stopped." He looked around. "We could use some heat, though."

Logan spoke up. "There ought to be some sort of generator or space heaters down here."

"You think they would still work after all this time?" Vaughn asked.

Logan nodded. "Oh, yes. Antarctica is the perfect place to preserve things. This body is proof of that—the man looks the same as the day he died. Think about it—the temperature never gets above freezing. There's no moisture. No bacteria.

"There are supplies in Shackleton's hut on Ross Island that were placed there in 1907 and are still edible today. I have no doubt that if we find the power source down here, or even a portable heater, we can get it going." He pointed his flashlight at a lightbulb set in a protective cage on the ceiling. "We might even get the lights on."

Tai shined her lights down the corridor. "Where do you think we'd find the power source?"

Logan shrugged. "I don't know. Let's go take a look."

Vaughn turned to the rest of the party. "Brothers, Burke, stay here with Smithers. Break out your sleeping bags and get in them. We're going to see if we can find the power source and get some heat going."

Vaughn, Tai, and Logan walked down the wood planking. After thirty feet the walls disappeared on either side and they entered a cross corridor. Straight ahead was a door. To the left, the corridor had a door, which was shut. To the right, the corridor was open for about ten feet, then a pile of ice and snow blocked the way.

Logan shined his light where pipes in the ceiling disappeared into the pile. "Looks like that's where some ice buckled the ceiling."

"Let's try the door on the left," Tai suggested.

They turned left and tried that door. It wasn't locked and opened easily. The flashlights revealed a room about thirty feet long and ten wide, full of electronic equipment.

"Looks like some sort of communications setup," Tai said. "Everything's way out of date, though."

Logan pointed his light at a pair of large boxes that hung down from the ceiling, one at either end. "This is one of the prefab units. Looks like they're each heated separately by those space heaters. That leaves the corridors under the ice at outside temperatures. The top of each unit is probably heavily insulated to keep the rising heat in."

"How would the power be provided?" Vaughn asked.

"Most likely oil burning generators," Logan said. "That's what runs the majority of the bases here, although they would have had to airlift in all that oil. At McMurdo they bring it in by ship, so it's not a major logistical problem. Here, I don't know."

Tai nodded. "The man I talked to who helped build this place said that they brought in a quite a few bladders of fuel."

Vaughn turned for the door. "We need to find whatever it is that burns that fuel, then."

Next, they went to the door that had been straight across. This unit seemed to be a nicely set-up living quarters. There were three sleeping areas, each separated by a thin wall. Traversing the entire length, they came to a door on the far side. They exited that and were faced with another side corridor extending off to the right and another door directly in front.

"Let's go straight through until we get to the end," Vaughn said. . If there's nothing in this row, we'll work up the next one over."

Logan swung open the door and they stepped in. Large stainless steel tanks lined both sides of a narrow walkway. The tanks were open on the top, and banks of dead lights hung low over them. There were pumps and various tubes arrayed throughout the room.

"What is this?"

Logan shined his flashlight inside one of the tanks. "I don't know. It reminds me of something I've seen before, but I can't place it right now."

They walked the length of that unit and went through the door. The last unit on the row beckoned. Logan pushed open the door and they walked in.

"Ah, this is more like it," Logan said as he turned the flashlight on the machinery inside. "This must be the power room. Look, there's a control panel." He walked over to a console full of dials and switches to the left of the door. "There's the 'on' for the master power, but I'm sure we have no battery power."

He pressed the button with his thumb. Nothing.

"There must be a small auxiliary generator around here to start the main off of." He flashed the light on the other side. "Here we go."

Vaughn watched as he knelt down next to a medium-sized portable generator and unscrewed a cap, shining his flashlight inside. "It's even got fuel. Hold the light while I prime it."

Vaughn hovered over his shoulder as Logan worked. After about five minutes Logan stood. "All right. Let's give it a shot." He held a knob attached to a cord in his hand and pulled.

"Shit," he muttered as the cord didn't move. He pulled more carefully, and the cord slowly unwound. Then he squatted and thrust upward. The engine turned over once with a burp. "Damn. This thing is stubborn."

Vaughn didn't say a word. He found it remarkable that they were trying to start a generator that had sat down there for almost half a century. The concept of a place where nothing deteriorated or rusted was a hard one to grasp.

After five more tries the engine coughed, sputtered, and turned over for almost ten seconds before dying.

"I've got it now." Logan adjusted the choke and pulled once more. The generator sputtered and then roared into life. He let it run on high for a few minutes and then turned the choke down.

"All right. Let's see how we get the main started while that warms up." He took the flashlight from Vaughn's hands, played it over the control panel and laughed. "They've got all the instructions right here, almost as if they expected someone who didn't know how to run this thing to try and start it. Hell, it's even numbered.

"Okay, we've already accomplished step one by getting the auxiliary started. The next step is to open up the main fuel line." He moved to the left of the console and looked up. "Here's the valve."

Vaughn heard a few seconds of metal screeching.

"Okay. We've got fuel. Now we prime this baby." Logan worked for a few minutes, following the instructions step by step. "Last—but not least—we open the power line from the aux to the main generator and give it some juice."

Vaughn watched as lights flickered and glowed on the console. Gradually they steadied. Logan looked over the gauges. "Ready?" he asked.

"Yes."

He pressed the starter button. The lights on the board dimmed, and they heard a sputtering noise behind the console. The sputtering shifted to a whine and then a rhythmic rumble after thirty seconds.

Logan was examining another row of controls to the right. "Here's a bunch of switches labeled north, middle and south, east and west tunnels." Vaughn looked over his shoulder at the schematic of the corridors of the base. At least he could get oriented now. The surface shaft where they had come down opened onto the north end of the east corridor.

Logan threw all the switches, and light suddenly streamed in through the open doorway. "All right!" he yelled.

Vaughn looked at the doorway and flicked on the light switch just inside of it. The room was flooded with the glow from the overheads. He looked down at the other end of the room. "What's that for?"

Logan turned. The entire far end of the unit was filled with massive control panels with uncountable gauges. It made the main generator board look puny. A three-by-three-foot panel with a triangular warning sign was recessed into the left side. Logan walked the twenty feet to it and looked the setup over.

"Oh my God. I don't believe it. I don't fucking believe it."

Tai and Vaughn hurried up to him. "What's the matter?" Tai asked.

Logan looked at Vaughn, his face ashen. "This is the control panel for a nuclear reactor."

CHAPTER 9

Geneva, Switzerland

The head of the North American Table stood up when his counterpart from the Far East entered the anteroom to the Intelligence Center. They barely had time to greet each other as the door opened and one of the Assessors gestured for them to come into the I.C.

An extra chair had been set up, and the two took their places in the center of the room. The video screens around the room flickered with various images and data, none of which the two got to take in, because as soon as they put on their headsets, the High Counsel spoke.

"There have been reports from various sources that a small team left New Zealand and traveled to the Earth First South Station in Antarctica. This small team subsequently departed by aircraft from the station on a mission of unknown intent. We find this intelligence to be highly disturbing, given the timing, Senior Assessor."

The Senior Assessor took over. "The computer estimates that there is a seventy-eight percent chance this team—three members of which are known to have worked for Agent Royce before—is searching for the Citadel. However, we have received no report from Royce that he has dispatched such a team."

Dyson glanced at his counterpart and waited.

"Explanation, Dyson?" the High Counsel demanded.

"Sir, I don't have any further information on that. If Royce dispatched a team, it might be to track down Fatima if she is heading down there."

"Not likely," the Senior Assessor said. "Fatima's whereabouts are unknown, but if she is in Antarctica right now, she would have had to fly, and we would know about it. So she is not there."

"He could be setting up an ambush," Dyson suggested.

The High Assessor didn't accept this explanation. "Royce worked for Lansale, who was behind the building of the Citadel and the compartmentalization of information about it. Lansale sent the packet to Fatima. It is possible that he gave information to Royce about the Citadel, and Royce is trying to determine the accuracy of that information. But he still should have filed a report on this to Area 51. No such report has been filed. Unless ... "

The last word hung in the air, and Dyson protested immediately. "We received no report."

"And then there is the issue of the I-401," the High Counsel continued. "No report was ever filed on it."

"Because we knew nothing of it," the head of the Far East Table said. "Much was lost at the end of World War II. If our Table was involved in the I-401 mission, the information was destroyed in the ruin of Japan near the end of the war."

"Easy excuse," the High Counsel snapped. "Did you practice that on your flight here?" There was no chance for a reply as the High Counsel continued. "However, we believe you because the data supports you. The computer has done a Course of Action Projection on this entire mess. You are dismissed for the moment. Wait in the anteroom."

The head of the Far East Table quickly left the Intelligence Center.

"We want to know about Majestic-12," the High Counsel said to Dyson when he was left alone in the center of the room.

"It's a cover story we use—" he began, but was quickly cut off.

"That has been North America's line for over half a century," the High Counsel said. "But Majestic-12 is real, isn't it? And you're the head of it. The one thing that has kept the Organization intact for centuries has been absolute loyalty. Any time that loyalty has been breached, the penalty has been swift and severe.

"Majestic-12," the High Counsel continued, "was formed in the heady days after World War II when the United States thought it was all-powerful. It was formed by members of the North American Table who instituted a coup against those who would not go along. That should have been a warning sign picked up here, but there was so much going on in the world at the time that it was missed. A serious oversight. So ever since then, the North American Table has worn two faces.

One it presents here. The other it keeps hidden from us as Majestic-12.

"The computer projects this as the reason there have been recent problems with various agents in the North American division. They have received conflicting taskings. Although we never have to explain tasking to our agents, they are not stupid people. So while it would appear Lansale and perhaps Royce are rogue, we think the problem lies elsewhere. With Majestic-12. And we will act accordingly."

Dyson started to get up, but that action was abruptly terminated as metal clamps snapped out of the armrests and legs of the chair, locking him in place.

"You *will* tell us all you know," the High Counsel said.

A door on the opposite side of the Intelligence Center opened, and a man walked in carrying an old-fashioned doctor's black bag.

"Meet the new Curator," the High Counsel said as the man pulled a stainless steel table over next to the chair and opened his bag. He began laying out various implements on the table, the nature and implications of which caused Dyson to break out in a cold sweat.

"You can make it easy, or you can make it hard on yourself," the High Counsel said. "We don't really care."

Antarctica

"How could they have put a nuclear reactor down here?" Brothers asked. "I thought reactors were huge and had lots of safety devices and all that."

They were back in the first hallway, linking up with the rest of the team. Vaughn had given a brief summary to the other three members, who were still huddled in their sleeping bags.

"I say we go to the first set of living quarters you found and set up," he said. Then Vaughn threw his gear over his shoulder and headed off. The others quickly got up, gathered their gear and followed. They left the body outside in the corridor, covered with a blanket, letting the cold continue its task of preservation.

Entering the room, Vaughn switched on the ceiling heaters as the rest of the team settled in. Logan was still agitated by their most recent discovery—almost more than he had been over the discovery of the body. He now answered the question Brothers had raised in the corridor. "McMurdo had a nuclear reactor. The U.S. Navy set it up in '61 and got it on line in '62. They thought it would alleviate bringing in all the fuel oil every summer and be a cheap and effective way to keep McMurdo supplied with power."

"What happened?" Smithers was feeling better and seated on a chair, leaning back against the wall.

"The plant was closed in '72. They had a leakage of coolant water into the steam generator tank. The Navy shut the thing down, and it took them three years to remove it. When we get back to Earth First South Station, I can show you where the reactor was. They'd put it on Observatory Hill right near Erebus, which in and of itself wasn't too bright, as Erebus is still an active volcano.

"They shipped the reactor and 101 drums of radioactive earth back to the U.S. and buried it somewhere there. But even that didn't make the site clean enough. The Navy had to come back and dig out quite a bit more earth and ship it back. The site was only finally opened up for what the military termed 'unrestricted use' in 1979."

"There's no way they could have left a reactor down here unattended since the fifties," Vaughn said. "I don't know much about them, but I do know they require constant attention."

Logan nodded. "You're right. This one must be off line, and the rods aren't here. The plan must have been that whenever they were going to reoccupy this place, they'd bring the rods with them and use the oil generators until they could bring the reactor on line. But even so, the fact that the U.S. government put a nuclear reactor—even one without the nuclear fuel—down here and abandoned it is unbelievable."

Burke was more concerned with immediate matters. "What now? We have to wait the storm out, but what do you want to do in the meantime?"

Vaughn stood in front of the group. "We need to explore this place. Now that the lights are on, we should be able to figure out what this place was built for and maybe who built it." He looked at Smithers. "Can you help?"

Smithers nodded. "The bleeding has stopped. As long as I don't hit my head again I should be all right."

Logan grabbed his flashlight and headed for the door. "I'm going down to the power plant to see if I can't find out where the actual reactor is and take a look. They had to have offset it from this base a ways, and maybe I can find the location."

Logan, Burke, and Smithers left the room rapidly, leaving Tai, Vaughn, and Brothers. The pilot walked over to one of the beds and flopped down on it. "I'm going to catch me some shut-eye so I'll be ready to fly when this storm does break." With that, he pulled the pillow over his head.

"Let's take a walk," Vaughn suggested to Tai.

They left the rapidly warming room and returned to the first building they'd entered, the communications center. Vaughn turned on the heaters, then checked the gear lining the wall. "They've got a lot of redundant commo equipment here." He pointed. "That's an HF—high frequency—radio. A pair of them. Several FM, shorter range stuff." He fiddled with the knobs. A dull hiss was all that came out of the speakers.

Tai pointed to one corner of the room, where a bunch of wires disappeared into the ceiling. "There are the leads that go to the antennas."

"Which probably blew away on the surface a long time ago," Vaughn said as he turned the radio off.

A transmitter on the other side of the room caught Vaughn's attention. Several large boxes containing long-lasting batteries surrounded it. A placard on the front read: CITADEL TRANSPONDER. FREQUENCY 45.83.

"What's that?" Tai asked.

"That's how the builders of the base planned to find it once it was covered over. The transponder—if the batteries were still working—is initiated by an incoming plane's radio. The pilot dials up the proper frequency—45.83—on the radio and presses his transmit button. That turns on the transponder. The pilot then homes in on the radio beacon.

"It's the same system set up at small airfields. It allows pilots to turn on the runway lights when they approach at night and there's no one in the tower. The antenna for this transponder is probably built into the roof of the access shaft."

Vaughn checked the transponder, but as he suspected, the batteries were long dead. However, one gauge indicated they were slowly recharging now that the power to the base was on.

"Let's move on," he said. They exited, and Vaughn paused. "Let's get oriented. Let's call the row of units closest to the entry shaft Row A. The next will be Row B, and so on. The long column to the left is One, the middle Two, and the one on the right Three. Thus we have just left Unit A2, which appeared to be a communications setup.

"This tunnel, designated the north tunnel on the power supply board, is blocked heading to Unit A1. We might be able to get to that unit by going up the west tunnel, but we will hold off on that until we work our way over there.

"Unit B3 is living quarters, where we have temporarily left our equipment and our pilot is catching some sleep." He opened the door directly across. "We are now entering Unit B2."

The first thing that caught his eye as he went through the door was Burke at the electric stove. Burke waved a ladle at them and then went back to stirring a large pot on top of the electric stove. "Dinner will be ready in about thirty minutes."

Vaughn led the way through the kitchen and dining area. "This appears to be the central area for meals, and probably was designed to double as the meeting area for the community that was to live here."

Tai followed him as they went to the next unit in line. This one was another set of living quarters except more lavish than the one they had set up in. There were two bedrooms and a small living room. Tai moved into the smaller bedroom and immediately noticed a large blue binder conspicuously placed on top of the bed. An envelope was taped to the binder.

She picked up the binder and stuck it in her backpack, then rejoined Vaughn in the other room. They went through the door and into C2, which turned out to be another set of living quarters. Then they crossed over to C3, which contained the strange metal tanks and light fixtures they had discovered earlier with Logan. Then on to D3, checking out the control panel for the nuclear reactor. Vaughn noticed just to the left of the panel that the grating was off and a dark tunnel beckoned. A small sign above it was labeled: POWER ACCESS TUNNEL.

"That must be where Logan has gone," Vaughn said. He led the way to the next unit, D2, which turned out to be an extremely well-stocked library. Not only were there numerous books on the shelves, but several file cabinets full of microfiche and three microfiche readers were set up on tables.

"Precomputer days," Tai noted.

Unit D1 was a dispensary with enough equipment to outfit a minor surgery. The shelves were stocked with numerous drugs.

C1 was an indoor greenhouse. Large banks of lights lined the ceiling, and trays filled with frozen soil were held in racks. There were lights on the bottom of the racks on down to the floor. Someone had spent quite a bit of time making every inch of space functional in the small room.

The west tunnel was blocked halfway up between B1 and B2 by the buckling of the ice ridge. Unit B1 itself was crushed halfway through. It appeared to be another bunk room.

Vaughn went back out into the main center tunnel. They'd been in all the units except A1, which was blocked. He now turned his attention to the set of large double doors on both ends of the main tunnel. He and Tai pulled open the set to the west. A large dark tunnel appeared. Groping inside the doors, Vaughn found a lever, which he pulled down. Sparks sputtered out of the ceiling, and then nothing. Using their flashlights, they probed the darkness, only to be met by the same wall of buckled ice that blocked off Unit A1. It had cut across the base diagonally and continued on through here.

"Let's try the other side," Vaughn said, led the way down the main cross tunnel and opened the doors there. He threw the lever, and large arc lights went on, revealing a massive tunnel burrowed out of the ice, extending almost two hundred meters straight ahead. There was a clear central passageway, but the rest of the twenty-meter-wide tunnel was crammed with mountains of supplies.

"Geez," Tai muttered as she took it in. "They were ready for a long stay."

Vaughn moved down the aisle, checking the labels on the boxes. Most of it was food. The last fifty meters of the storage tunnel housed a dozen snowmobiles, a bulldozer, a backhoe, several snow tractors of various sizes, and two large cabins on skis that looked like they could be hooked up to the back of the larger tractors.

The tunnel ended at a metal grating that ramped up and ended in the ceiling. "What do you make of that?" Tai asked.

"I think that's how they planned on getting these vehicles out of here," Vaughn replied. He pointed at sections of the metal grating stacked to the side. "They probably planned on running the bulldozer up the ramp and putting down the grating as they went until they reached the surface."

Tai looked at her watch. "Let's go to the mess hall and get some of that food."

They retraced their steps back to the east tunnel and

turned right until they got to the shaft. When they entered the mess hall, Burke was ladling something into Logan's bowl.

"What did you find?" Vaughn asked Logan.

He looked up from his bowl. "I went down the access shaft to the reactor, but it was blocked by ice about fifty meters in. I assume the reactor is out that way another hundred meters or so."

Tai had the binder out and was paging through it. "The reactor is five hundred meters straight-line distance from the power room. Southwest," she said. "As you guessed, the rods aren't in. They were supposed to be brought in and put in place when the base was activated."

Everyone turned and looked at her. "You found the instruction book for this Tinkertoy set?" Vaughn said.

Logan got up and looked at the binder, flipping some pages. "Hydroponics!" he exclaimed, studying the diagram of the base and the label for Unit C3. "I knew I'd seen that somewhere before. They have a setup like that at UCLA."

"What's hydroponics?" Burke asked.

"It's the cultivation of plants in water rather than soil. They set aside Unit C3 to grow food just like the greenhouse in C1, except this one uses water instead of dirt." Logan shook his head. "But I don't understand why they needed to dedicate two units of their base to growing food when they have all the supplies in the ice storage tunnels." He pointed down at the diagram. "The one blocked ice tunnel to the west looks as if it's as large as the one to the east. That's a hell of a lot of food and supplies."

"It doesn't look like they thought they could count on a resupply," Vaughn remarked as looked at the pages. The binder listed the location of equipment and supplies along with instructions for the use of various equipment, but it didn't say anything about the purpose of the base or who was supposed to use it.

"Look at how far off they offset the reactor," Logan commented. "Over a quarter of a mile away. With all that ice in between, that made a very effective shield from the main base."

Vaughn's eyes focused on the one unit they hadn't been able to look at it. "Check out what Unit A1 is labeled: 'Special supply and armory.'" He looked up at Tai. "We have to get into that. It will be where the bombs are."

Tai nodded, reached into her pocket and pulled out a letter. "I also found this."

Vaughn handed her a pocket-nife with the blade open. She slit the top of the letter and pulled out a one-page handwritten note.

"Read it aloud." Logan said.

Vaughn cleared her throat and began reading.

"21 December 1956
To Whom It May Concern,

I have no clue who will read this letter or if it will ever be read.
You might be here trying to find out the truth.
You might be here in a desperate last stand against unknown enemies or threats.
Since I don't know who is reading or what the circumstances are, the less said, the better. Make of this place what you will.

David Lansale"

"The bastards set up a survivalist base down here," Logan said.

Vaughn shook his head. "No. It appears that way, but if you think about what Lansale wrote, he had no idea who would be the next people to come in here. And why they would be coming. This place was his ace in the hole for several different possibilities."

"Well," Logan said, "this place sure is set up to be a refuge in case of all-out nuclear war. Considering the time frame in which it was built and restocked into the mid-fifties, that was a pretty big concern. There are no worthwhile targets in Antarctica for a nuke, the winds off the coast would keep fallout to a minimum, and we've seen how the cold and lack of humidity would keep things preserved."

"Great place to live," Smithers muttered.

"It's also about as remote as you can get in Antarctica," Logan added. "Due north of here is the South Pacific Ocean—a spot on the middle of it is the world's farthest point from dry land. Without having an intermediary base like McMurdo, a direct flight here, especially back when this was built, is almost impossible."

Everyone turned as Brothers stomped back in, shaking snow off his coat. "I just poked my head out the door, and the weather's finally gone to crap. We won't be flying anywhere for a while."

South Pacific

"Why have you kept me alive?" Araki demanded of Fatima.

They were alone in the freighter's small galley, trying to get some food down as the ship lurched through the waves, pounding its way south. Fatima had a cup of coffee cradled in her thin hands, as much to keep them warm as to drink.

"So you can tell your superiors the truth," Fatima said. "You were tracking Nishin for a reason. To learn more, correct?"

"Yes."

"Are you learning?"

"Yes."

"Then that is why you are still alive." Fatima took a sip of her coffee. "The world is at war, yet no one really seems to know what the sides are or who is fighting who. The more information everyone has, the clearer things will become."

Indonesia

"I have prepared the plane to fly 9,700 kilometers, sir." Captain Hyun stood underneath the massive nose of his plane.

"How?" No congratulations. Min didn't believe in them.

"Normal range is 6,500 kilometers. If we also use the one-hour reserve fuel supply, our possible range is extended to 7,125 kilometers. We will make the additional 2,575 kilometers using three of the fuel bladders here at the airfield. I have loaded them on board, and we will hand pump the fuel from the bladders to the main tanks as we progress."

Min nodded. His narrow eyes watched his team members loading their gear on board the aircraft. They'd been instructed only to gather their equipment. Min wanted to wait until they were in the air before fully briefing the team.

"May I inquire where we are going, sir?" Hyun held up his flight charts. "I need to plan a route."

"South," Min answered.

Hyun frowned. "South, sir? To Australia? New Zealand?"

"No. Straight south. Over the ocean."

"But, with all due respect, sir, there's nothing to the south."

Min turned his coal black eyes on the pilot, cutting him off. "You fly the plane, Captain. Let me worry about everything else. We take off in ten minutes."

Hyun stiffly saluted and retreated into the belly of his plane. Min stepped back and ran his eyes along the silhouette of the Soviet-made IL-18. It was an old plane, built in the late fifties. Four large propeller engines mounted on its wings reminded him of an old style airliner. With the plane many years obsolete, the Russians had dumped it on their so-called North Korean allies in exchange for desperately needed hard currency. The plane was the way Min and his fellow commandos had traveled to the small dirt runway on this island, and it was their only way out and back to North Korea.

Kim snapped to attention before him. "All loaded, sir!"

Min nodded. "Let us board then and take off."

Antarctica

Tai worked the small tractor's plow, carefully scraping away slivers of ice from the blockage. She wished the corridors were large enough to bring the bulldozer out from storage. She was sure that would have punched through in no time. As it was, the small tractor was very difficult to maneuver in the narrow confines of the west tunnel. She enjoyed doing work that didn't require thinking. As long as she concentrated on the task at hand she could keep the dark thoughts at bay. Despite her protestations to Vaughn, she felt like she was flying blind here, not sure who or what to believe.

The other members of the party—minus Brothers, who was seated in the mess hall reading a book—were standing in back of her, shovels in hand and waiting. Easing down on the accelerator, Tai pushed the corner of the plow blade into the ice. She'd been at it now for fifteen minutes and had worked through almost five feet of ice and snow. Of course, she reminded herself, they might not find anything on the other side. The ice also might have crushed everything behind the cave-in.

After scraping off another six inches, she dropped the blade, drew back the debris and piled it against the wall of Unit B1. She rolled forward again and dug in the blade. The tractor suddenly lurched, and Tai had to slam on the brakes as the blade broke through. She backed off and shut down the engine.

Vaughn came forward with a flashlight and shined the light through the hole. They could see wood planking on the other side—the continuation of the west corridor.

"Shovel time," Vaughn said. The others came forward, and they carefully began enlarging the hole Tai had punched.

When it was large enough for a person to go through, Vaughn gestured for Tai to lead the way. She slid through, followed by Vaughn, Logan, Smithers, and Burke. They moved up to where the west corridor met a north one. Vaughn went to the door of Unit A1 and swung it open. The five stepped inside. The glow of their flashlights lit up a well-equipped arms room.

Vaughn tried the light switch on the off chance a power cable from the rest of the base might still be functioning, but got nothing. He walked along the racks, noting the weapons. Two dozen M-1 rifles in mint condition. Some old .30 caliber machine guns and .45 caliber pistols. The walls of the unit were stacked with ammunition for the weapons. It was a gun collector's dream. Vaughn noted several cases of explosives.

"Why did they need all this down here?" Logan asked as he picked up a pistol.

"To prepare for anything," Vaughn said, picking up an M-1 rifle.

Vaughn put the rifle down as he spotted a door on the side of the unit facing to the west. None of the other units had had such a door. He went to it and tried the handle. It was locked.

Tai came up. "What do you think?" she asked, nodding toward the door.

"We haven't found them yet," Vaughn said. He grabbed one of the .45 pistols and loaded it. Then he went to the door and fired three rounds through the lock, startling the others.

"Damn, what's wrong with you?" Logan demanded.

Vaughn ignored them as he shoved the door open. He shined his flashlight through, revealing a large ice chamber, about one hundred feet wide by two hundred long. He immediately saw six crates, four of them very large, two of them somewhat smaller. Stenciled on the outside were the words: MACHINED GOODS. Beyond those six crates were numerous smaller crates, stacked on top of each other, filling the entire space.

Pure bullshit, Vaughn thought as he walked up to one of the large crates. He turned and grabbed a bayonet off one of the shelves. He pulled the blade free and went up to the nearest large crate, placed the point under it and, putting his body weight on it, levered up. With a loud screech the top moved a half an inch.

"What did you find?" Logan asked as he and Tai came in and watched.

"I don't know," Vaughn grunted as he pushed again. He slid the blade around and carefully applied pressure every foot or so. Slowly the top lifted. Vaughn put his fingers under the lid and pulled up. The top popped off, and he pushed it to the side. A large, gray, cylindrical object, rounded at one end and with fins at the other, was inside, resting on a wood cradle.

"They put a fucking bomb in here?" Logan exclaimed.

Vaughn bent over to examine it with a growing feeling of coldness in his stomach. Lansale's papers had indicated this would be what they found, but he hadn't truly believed it. A serial number was stamped on a small metal plate, halfway down the casing. Vaughn read the ID and then slowly straightened.

"It's an MK-17 thermonuclear weapon," he said. He pointed with the bayonet at the other three large cases. "Four altogether."

"Fuck," Logan said.

"What's in the smaller two cases marked 'Heavy Equipment'?" Tai asked. "And the rest?"

"Probably not party supplies," Vaughn said as he went over to one. He pried it open. Another, smaller, bomb. He checked the serial number. "Each nuclear weapon has a special serial number—this one also has the proper designator for a nuclear weapon. If I remember rightly, this looks like an MK/B 61, which is a pretty standard nuclear payload for planes back in the fifties." He looked back at Logan in the dim light cast by their flashlights. "You may know something about nuclear reactors, but I know about nuclear weapons, and that's a goddamn nuclear weapon."

"How do you know so much about nuclear weapons?" Logan asked as he came over and looked into the crate.

Vaughn pointed his flashlight at the bomb. "I was on a nuke team for a little while when I first arrived in the 10th Special Forces Group. A nuke team had the mission to emplace a tactical ADM—that's atomic demolitions munitions. We were supposed to infiltrate behind enemy lines, put the bomb in the right spot, arm it and then get the hell out before it blew."

"What about the rest of the crates?" Tai asked.

Vaughn walked to the stacks of crates past the bombs. There were at least a thousand of these of varying sizes and shapes. He opened one and saw three paintings, carefully wrapped inside. He glanced at Tai. "The Golden Lily. Or at least part of it."

Logan whistled as he broke open a small crate and pulled out a bar of gold. "There must be millions of dollars worth of stuff here."

"Yo!" Burke called out. He was farther in the cavern and pointing at a stack of crates. They had swastikas stenciled on the sides. "How the hell did these get here?"

"Who knows?" Vaughn said as he pried open the top to one. He froze when he saw what was inside.

"What the hell is that?"

Vaughn carefully pulled out one of the gray metal canisters. "Sarin nerve agent. The Nazis developed it during the war." He looked around. There were at least twenty similar crates. "God knows what other deadly stuff is in here, mixed with the treasure." He put the canister back in the crate.

"There's enough WMD stuff in here—" Tai began, then shook her head. "This is a cluster-fuck. Why would someone put all this here? And how did it get here? I think MacIntosh would have said something to us if he'd seen any of this coming in."

"These two newer nukes had to be put in here in the sixties or seventies," Vaughn said. "Lansale must have kept moving stuff down here over the years."

"But why?" Tai asked.

"Got me," Vaughn responded.

Logan seemed mesmerized by the cold gray steel of the nuclear weapon. "You said you knew quite a bit about nuclear weapons. Can that thing be detonated?"

Vaughn closed his eyes briefly, trying to remember. "There are a lot of safeties on a nuclear weapon. We used to have to pass a test every three months that required us to flawlessly complete forty-three separate steps to emplace and arm our nuke.

"On your standard nuclear weapon you've got an enable plug, ready/safe switch, separation timer, pulse thermal batteries, pulse battery actuator, time delay switch, and a whole bunch of other things that all have to be done correctly. Despite all that, though, if someone knows what they're doing, and they have enough time to tinker with it, I have no doubt that they could initiate it, except for one thing. You can't even begin without—" He stopped and blinked.

"What one thing?" Tai asked, finally looking up from the bomb.

Vaughn turned and headed out of the unit.

"Where are you going?" Logan yelled. When he didn't answer, they followed.

Vaughn made his way directly to the mess hall. Brothers looked up as he stormed in and grabbed the blue binder off the counter. He thumbed through, turning to the index. He had started reading it from the beginning when he'd found it earlier and only gotten halfway through. Now he ran his finger down the index as the others crowded around. It stopped at a section labeled: EMERGENCY PROCEDURES.

Vaughn rapidly flipped through until he found the section. There was a page that referred them to the operating manual for the reactor in the power room if there were any problems with it. The second page talked about getting the tractors out of the east ice storage room using the ramps. The third page was a handwritten note. Vaughn recognized the handwriting from the note that had been taped to the outside of the binder:

THE PALs AND ARMING INSTRUC-
TIONS ARE IN THE SAFE.
LANSALE.

Vaughn closed his eyes. "Oh fuck!"

"What does that mean?" Tai asked as she looked over his shoulder.

Vaughn opened his eyes and looked at her. "Let's go out in the hallway." He led Tai and Logan out, taking the binder with him. "As I was telling you—if someone knows what they're doing, they can get by all the safeties on those bombs but one. The first and most critical safety is the permissive access link, or PAL. That's the code that allows you to even begin to arm the bomb. The code and bomb are never kept together, for security reasons. The MK/B has a multiple code six-digit, coded switch with limited try followed by lockout. That means you get two shots at the right codes, and if you get it wrong both times, you don't get a third shot—the bomb shuts down."

Vaughn stabbed his finger down at the paper. "Except it appears that the PALs for those two newer bombs are here in the base." He turned back to the index and scanned. "Here." He turned to the correct page, where a diagram of a unit was displayed. "The safe with the PAL codes and arming instructions is located in Unit A2."

CHAPTER 10

Antarctica

"Latest weather from McMurdo calls for at least another twenty-four to forty-eight hours of this storm," Brothers informed the group gathered around the mess table. "I took a look outside about ten minutes ago and couldn't see more than five feet from the door. The wind is howling out there."

The warm air from the overhead heaters blew gently across Tai as she looked about the room. They had discovered the base. They had discovered the four MK-17s and two, newer weapons. They'd found nerve agents and stolen treasure. Yet they still weren't any closer to knowing what or who exactly the Organization was. They'd tried the safe, but it was locked tight, and they didn't have the combination, which seemed to make Vaughn a bit calmer about the whole thing.

Tai had her doubts about the viability of the nuclear weapons, but she had to trust that Vaughn had more experience in that area.

Everyone was exhausted, that was obvious. "I suggest we all get some sleep," Tai said. "When we get up, I'd like to dig out the west tunnel and completely open it up to Unit A1." Most of the group headed off to the quarters, but Vaughn remained behind, as Tai had expected.

"What do you think?" she asked.

"I think we got a problem," Vaughn said. "We didn't find out anything more about the Organization, and I'm getting the feeling this whole place was a setup by Lansale, an ace in the hole, almost literally. I'm worried about the bombs. They worry me a lot. Because we're the ones who are sitting on them now."

Tai sighed. "What should we do about them?"

"I don't know," Vaughn said. "It's weird, but the people who built this place and put those weapons down here are probably all retired or dead now. Why do you think no one has been down here in so long? Why do you think the batteries on the transponder were dead?"

"Do you really think those weapons could still work?"

"The MK-17s? Probably not. The MK/B, fifty-fifty. And even if they don't work, they still have their cores. A lot of people would love to get their hands on those."

"What kind of damage could those MK/Bs do?"

Vaughn shook his head. "That depends."

"On what?"

"On what they're set at. I think the MK/B has four settings for yield, ranging from ten to five hundred kilotons. So it depends on what it's set at."

"You mean you can change the power of the bomb by flipping a switch?"

Vaughn gave her a weak smile. "Pretty neat, huh? The theory is, the bomb is set for required yield prior to a mission depending on the target profile. I'm sure there's an access panel on the casing that opens to that control. I for one don't plan on messing with it."

"Well, say, what will a ten kiloton blast do?" Tai felt somewhat embarrassed to be asking since she felt she ought to know more about the subject, but the military branch she'd been in was more focused on the war on terror than on nuclear weapons.

"A kiloton is equal to a thousand tons of TNT. So 10K is ten thousand tons of TNT. If it blew here, ten kilotons would take this base out, but not much more than that as far as blast goes."

Vaughn leaned back in the chair as he went on. "There are five effects of a nuclear explosion. Most people only think of two—the blast and the radiation. The blast, which is the kinetic energy, uses about half the energy of the bomb. That's what blows things up. It's the shock wave of compressed air that radiates out from the bomb at supersonic speed. If the bomb goes off underground, that wave is muffled, but it takes out whatever it blows near, creating a crater. If it's an air burst or above the surface, then the blast does more damage. You not only have to worry about the original wave but also the high winds that are then generated by the overpressure. We're talking winds of over two hundred miles an hour, so it can be pretty destructive.

"There are two types of radiation: prompt and delayed. Prompt is that which is immediately generated by the explosion, and it uses about five percent of the energy of the bomb. It's in the form of gamma rays, neutrons, and beta particles. We measure those in rads. Six hundred rads and you have a ninety percent chance of dying in three to four weeks."

"How many rads would these bombs put out?" Tai asked.

Vaughn shrugged. "I can't answer that. It depends on the strength of the blast, whether it goes off in the air or underground, and your relative location to ground zero. Plus how well shielded you are. Usually, you'll die of blast or thermal before you have to worry about prompt radiation

"If you survive the initial effects, the real one you usually have to worry about is delayed—also known as fallout. However, with the strong winds down here, the fallout will get dispersed over quite a large area. The other good side of that is that there isn't anybody down here to be affected by it. In a more populated and less windy area, fallout can be devastating.

"The other two effects are thermal and electromagnetic pulse. Thermal causes quite a bit of damage in built-up areas because it starts fires. The flash will blind and burn you even before the blast wave reaches, if you're exposed to it. Thermal uses up about one-third of the energy of the bomb.

"Electro-magnetic pulse, known as EMP, is the one effect that few people know about. When the bomb goes off, it sends out electromagnetic waves, just like radio, except thousands of times stronger. That wave will destroy most electronics in its path for quite a long distance."

Vaughn continued, even though it was obvious he was depressed dredging all this information up. "The bottom line is that no one really knows exactly what effect nuclear weapons will have on people. There are too many variables. The only times they've ever been used against people—at Hiroshima and Nagasaki—were so long ago, and those bombs were so different from the MK/B and even the MK-17 thermonuclear ones, that the data is not very valid.

"I think Nikita Khrushchev, surprisingly enough, summed up the effect of nuclear war quite well. He said the survivors would envy the dead."

Tai and Vaughn were silent for a few moments. Then Vaughn tried to smile. "We used to have debates in the team room about our nuclear mission. Most guys were worried about simple and more personal things like whether the firing delay we had been told was in our ADMs was actually there. Most of the team believed that once we emplaced and initiated our bombs, they'd go off immediately. The figuring was that if the team managed to successfully emplace the bomb and arm it, the powers-that-be wouldn't take the chance on an hour delay to let the team get to safety."

"What about if there's a fire down here?" Tai asked. "Would those bombs go off?"

"The MK/B has thermal safety devices that would prevent accidental detonation due to fire," Vaughn replied.

"Do you think we should open the safe?" Tai asked.

Vaughn shook his head. "I looked at it. It's set in the ground and requires a combination. We don't have that. I recommend we don't mess with it. We've got the bombs. You don't need the codes."

Cape Cod, Massachusetts

The old man was jogging along the deserted beach, his shuffling pace leaving a trail of footprints just above the surf line. His head was slightly bowed, the sparse white hair reflecting the setting sun. His head cocked slightly as the sound of helicopter blades crept over the sand, but his feet kept their steady rhythm.

A shadow flashed by and a UH-60 Blackhawk helicopter flitted by, less than thirty feet above the ground. The man's feet finally came to a halt, as the helicopter flared, kicking up sand. The old man covered his eyes as the wheels touched and two men in unmarked khaki hopped off.

They ran over to him. There was no badge flashed or words spoken. They were all players and knew the rules. The old man allowed them to escort him onto the aircraft. It lifted and immediately sped off at maximum speed to the west, toward nearby Otis Air Force Base.

The incoming tide washed over the footsteps, and within twenty minutes all traces of the lone jogger were gone.

Airspace, South Pacific Ocean

Major Min looked up from the plans he and his XO were poring over as Captain Hyun approached. Min was impressed that Hyun had waited almost four hours before coming out of the cockpit and approaching him. The interior of the IL-18 was stripped bare except for Min's team, their equipment, and the fuel bladders. The team was spread out along the vibrating steel floor, either sleeping or preparing their equipment for the infiltration.

"Sir, may I speak to you?" Hyun inquired.

Min nodded.

"Sir, as captain of this airplane it is my duty to inform you that we do not have enough fuel, even with all this," Hyun waved a hand at the bladders, "to make landfall in this direction. In two hours we will be too low on fuel to be able to turn around and make it back to Indonesia."

"There's land ahead," Min quietly remarked.

Hyun blinked. "We are heading for the South Pole, sir. There are no all-weather airstrips suitable for this aircraft down there."

Min shrugged. "I know that. My team will parachute out, and then you will attempt to land on the ice and snow farther away to ensure operational security. I will leave one of the members of my team on board to help you travel to our exfiltration point."

Hyun blanched. "But, sir—" He halted, at a loss for words.

Min stood. "But what, Captain?"

Hyun shook his head. "Nothing, sir." He turned and retreated to his cockpit.

Senior Lieutenant Kim looked at his team leader. "Our captain is a weak man."

Min turned his attention back to the papers. "Are you satisfied that your men know the parts of the plan that they need to?"

Kim nodded. "Yes, sir."

"Have you picked who will stay with the plane?"

"Yes, sir. Sergeant Chong has volunteered."

"Good."

Kim scratched his chin. "The only thing I don't understand, sir, is why we are doing this."

No one else would have dared to say that to Min, but the two of them had spent four years working together. They'd infiltrated the South Koran coastline three times and conducted extremely successful reconnaissance missions there. They owed their lives to each other.

"There are U.S. nuclear weapons at our objectives."

Kim didn't show any surprise. "But you briefed us that there was no one there. No military."

"Correct."

Now Kim was surprised. "You mean these bombs are unguarded?"

Min nodded. "Yes. Our objective is to seize those weapons along with their arming codes and instructions. And to leave no trace of our presence there."

"How will we do that and what will we do with the weapons? I thought our government already had nuclear weapons?"

"We are not going back home with the weapons." Min shook his head. "The rest is not for you to know yet, my friend. You will be told when it is time. Suffice it to say that if we are successful, Orange III will be implemented, and it will succeed."

Min leaned back in his seat as his executive officer moved away. Although this whole plan was jury-rigged on short notice, there was quite a bit of precedent for the entire operation. The primary wartime mission of the North Korean Special Forces was to seize or destroy U.S. nuclear weapons. Min had helped draw up plans for direct action missions against overseas targets, including U.S. 7th Fleet bases in Japan and the Philippines, and even Pearl Harbor in Hawaii.

North Korea had never been particularly shy about striking at their enemies outside their own borders, and the Special Forces had been involved in every action. In 1968 thirty-one Special Forces soldiers had infiltrated across the DMZ and made their way down to Seoul to raid the Blue House, home of the South Korean president. The mission failed, with twenty-eight men killed, two missing, and only one captured.

Shortly after that attack, on January 23, 1968, KPA Special Forces men in high speed attack craft seized the USS *Pueblo*. Later that year a large SF force of almost a hundred men conducted landings on the coast of South Korea in an attempt to raise the populace against the government. It failed, but such failures didn't daunt the North Korean government.

In 1969 a U.S. electronic warfare aircraft was shot down by North Korea, killing all thirty-one U.S. service members on board.

As security stiffened in South Korea over the decade of the 1970s, North Korea moved its attentions overseas, ignoring international reactions. In 1983 three PKA Special Forces officers planted a bomb in Rangoon in an attempt to kill the visiting South Korean president. That mission also failed.

Later in 1983 four North Korean merchant ships infiltrated the Gulf of California to conduct monitoring operations against the United States mainland. One of the ships was seized by the Mexican authorities, but that didn't prevent the North Koreans from continuing such operations.

Min knew that history, and he also knew more than the average North Korean about the changes that had been sweeping the world in the past decade. Spending time overseas, even in remote Indonesia, he had been exposed to more information than those in the tightly controlled society in his homeland ever received. The breakup of the Soviet Union had never been acknowledged by Pyongyang, except in cryptically worded exhortations to the people telling them they were the last true bastion of communism in the world. In fact, Min truly believed he was part of the last line in the war against western imperialism. He believed that if this mission succeeded, he would strike a blow greater than any of his Special Forces predecessors. That was enough for him.

Antarctica

Tai knew there was no way she would be able to sleep. "There is one thing I think we have to do," she said.

"What?" Vaughn asked. They paused as the door to the mess hall opened and Logan walked in. He grabbed a cup of coffee. "Mind if I join you?"

Tai glanced at Vaughn, then shrugged. "All right."

"Didn't plan on sitting on top of a couple of nukes," Logan said. "This is a messuck. You two figured out what's next?"

"We're working on it," Vaughn said.

Tai put down her coffee mug. "We need to make sure these bombs can't be used. We need to destroy the PAL codes."

"How do you propose we do that?" Vaughn asked.

"We blow up the safe that holds them."

Vaughn shook his head. "Destroying the codes doesn't do enough. Besides, the codes in the safe might not be the only ones. Someone else, somewhere, probably has a copy. Probably buried deep in some classified file cabinet. But there is a way to neutralize the bombs. Or at least keep them from being activated."

"How?" Tai asked.

"I told you that those two newer bombs have a six-digit PAL code that allows limited tries followed by lockout. I can enter two wrong codes and cause both bombs to go into lockout. That will mean that they can't be exploded."

"Bullshit!" They both looked at Logan in surprise. "How do we know you don't already have the codes and will arm the bombs with the correct six digits instead of the wrong ones?"

"Why would I do that?" Vaughn asked.

"I don't fucking know!" Logan turned to Tai. "Listen to me. What's to stop Vaughn from arming the bomb with a time delay? Then he kills us or just holds us at gun point and leaves, taking Brothers with him. If one of those goes off, all evidence of this base will be gone."

"I know Vaughn better than I know you," Tai said to Logan. "I trust him."

Safe House, Pine Barrens, New Jersey

The old man looked up as the door opened and two men walked in. The short one carried a briefcase, the taller one carried nothing. Knowing he would never get their real names, the old man immediately labeled them the Short Man and the Tall Man. The Short Man placed the briefcase on the desk, and they both stared at the old man.

Finally, he could take it no longer. "What do you want?"

Not a word had been said to him since he'd been picked up on the beach, flown to Otis Air Force Base, cross-loaded onto a military jet to Fort Dix, then driven to this house in the middle of nowhere.

The taller one, whom the man had correctly guessed was in charge, spoke. "We need information, Colonel Whitaker."

"I'm retired."

Silence reigned.

"What information?" Whitaker finally asked.

"We need information on an operation you were involved with. An operation we have no record of."

The Short Man flicked open the locks on the briefcase.

Whitaker frowned as he searched his memory. "That was a long time ago."

"The Citadel?" the Tall Man asked.

Whitaker felt his stomach flip.

The Short Man lifted the lid on the briefcase. Then he turned it so Whitaker could see the contents. Various hypodermic needles were arrayed in the padding on the top, and serum vials were secured in the bottom. The Tall Man gestured at the contents with a wave of his hand.

"The art of interrogation has progressed to much more sophisticated levels than what you dealt with when you were on active duty. We're less crude and much more effective.

"You know, of course, that everyone talks eventually." The Tall Man reached in and pulled out a needle, holding it up to the light. "With these sophisticated drugs, that eventually comes much faster. Unfortunately, the side effects, particularly for a man of your advanced years, cannot always be controlled." He put the needle down. "Why is it that there are no records of the Citadel?"

Whitaker considered his options. "What do I get out of this?"

The Tall Man shrugged. "It depends on what you tell us."

Whitaker sighed. He knew what the Tall Man had said was true—he would talk sooner or later. He'd been on the other side of this table too many times not to know that. Jesus, to have it all come to this because of that stupid base! He talked.

"I was the ops supervisor for the construction of the Citadel in 1947 in Antarctica. It was a group of buildings—twelve, to be exact—that were buried under the ice. The sections—"

The Tall Man interrupted. "What we want to know is who was behind the op and why."

"I worked directly for Sidney Souers."

"Who?" the Tall Man asked.

"The first director of Central Intelligence," Whitaker explained.

The Short Man had pulled out a PDA, punching information into it. He held it out now in front of the Tall Man, who read it and nodded. "Souers was a founding member of Majestic-12, wasn't he?"

"Yes."

The two men exchanged glances. "How did Souers give you this assignment?"

"Personal briefing." Whitaker sighed. "It was an unofficially sanctioned mission—no paper trail and denial if uncovered. Souers brought me back to Washington from Japan, where I was doing work trying to track down some of their scientists. When I got to D.C., Souers told me he had a mission that could be very profitable to both of us and had the President's blessing."

"Who was Souers working for?"

Whitaker shrugged. "I don't know."

"Souers never told you who the place was for or even what it was designed for?"

"It was easy to see what it was designed for," Whitaker said. "It was a survival shelter. As far as the who goes, it had to be somebody that had quite a bit of money and resources, along with leverage with the White House."

"Tell us about Lansale," the Tall Man said.

"Who?"

The Tall Man looked at him dispassionately. He turned to his partner. "I'll be back in an hour. Prep him."

"Wait a second!" Whitaker shouted as the Short Man pulled out a vial of clear liquid and picked up the nearby needle. "I'm telling you everything. You said if I cooperated that wouldn't be necessary."

"I said it depended. You just told us you did free-lance work while at the ISA. You broke the rules, and now we're going to find out what other rules you might have broken in your career."

The Short Man approached with the needle.

Antarctica

They'd managed to clear not only the west tunnel of ice, but also the entryway into the west ice storage area. That room was as large as the eastern one, but there was no ramp at the end. It was also stocked with supplies and food. Then, using the diagram in the instructor binder, they turned their attention to trying to find the site of the inert nuclear reactor.

Now, Tai was lying behind Logan and Vaughn in the power access tunnel. The tunnel was made of corrugated steel tubing approximately three feet in diameter. They'd been digging here by hand for two hours already. It was slow work because as they removed ice, they had to drag it back out on a blanket the length of the tunnel, where Tai would take it and dispose of it along the south ice wall.

She thought it might have been easier to go up to the surface, try to use the sonar to find the reactor, and then try to dig out its access shaft. But then the weather would have been a problem. She'd gone up to the main surface shaft not long ago with Vaughn and Logan and taken a look outside. As Brothers had said, visibility was close to zero as the wind lashed the countryside with a wall of white. Ten feet from the doorway a person would be lost, and only find their way back with a large degree of luck. It was hard to believe the latest radio message from McMurdo that the intensity of the storm was actually lessening.

Looking into the blowing snow, feeling the icy talons of cold ripping at her clothes through the open door and thinking about the frozen body lying at the foot of the stairs, Tai recalled something she'd read during her two-hour guard shift: the fate of Captain Lawrence Oates, a member of Scott's ill-fated 1911-1912 South Pole expedition. Scott's party had arrived at the South Pole after man-hauling their sleds most of the way, only to discover a tent and note that Norwegian Roald Amundsen had left behind, proving that Amundsen had beaten him there by a month.

On their return trip, running out of food and in the middle of a blizzard, Oates, suffering from severe frostbite, walked out of the party's campsite into the blowing snow and disappeared, sacrificing himself so the party could continue on more quickly. His noble gesture was all for naught, though, as the rest of Scott's party died only eleven miles from a supply depot. Their bodies were discovered eight months later, along with Scott's journal, which told the sad tale.

"I've got an opening," Vaughn said, snapping Tai out of her ice-bound reverie. He was poking his shovel ahead, through the ice. Then he and Logan scratched away, widening the opening. The tunnel continued for another ten feet before angling off to the right.

"Let's see what we have," Vaughn said as he led the way.

The environmentalist followed, and Tai crawled along behind them on her hands and knees, her Gore-Tex pants sliding on the steel. Fifty more feet and they reached a thick hatch. Vaughn turned the wheel and the door slowly opened. Another two hundred feet. Then another hatch. They squeezed out of the second one and could finally stand. A small, shielded room opened out onto the reactor's core. Radiation warning signs were plastered all over the walls. Tai looked through the thick glass at the slots where the rods were to be inserted in the reactor core itself. In front of the glass was a small control panel with a few seats.

Logan shook his head. "Unbelievable. They really thought something as poorly constructed as this could work. No wonder the one at McMurdo had to be taken apart."

"You have to remember this was put in a long time ago," Vaughn reminded him.

"Hell, even twenty or thirty years ago someone should have had more common sense." Logan ran his hands over the thick glass separating them from the core. "Why are people so stupid?"

"So we have nukes and a nuclear power plant," Tai said. "But we're still not any closer to the Organization."

Vaughn peered once more through the thick glass at the inert core of the reactor. "You know, we might not be any closer, but it might be closer to us."

"What do you mean?" Tai asked.

Vaughn looked at Logan. "You once accused me of trying to take out Brothers. But I *know* I didn't do that. And I think whoever did only did it to try and slow us down a little bit, not stop us. Because sabotaging the plane would have worked much better. And the only reason to slow us down is if someone is behind us."

"We know Fatima and the Abu Sayif—" Tai began, then paused as she considered what he was saying. "You think the Organization will come here?"

Vaughn shrugged. "Sooner or later. I don't think our trip down here escaped scrutiny."

"What do we do, then?" Tai asked.

"Depends on who shows up," Vaughn said.

Airspace, Antarctica

Min watched as Sergeant Chong finished securing the steel cable that would hold their static lines to the roof of the aircraft, just in front of the aft passenger door. Min had never parachuted out of an IL-18 before, but he knew it had been done. This type of aircraft was not specifically designed for paratrooper operations, but the team was doing what it was best at: improvising.

Min looked out a small porthole at the ocean dotted with icebergs far below. They were flying at the plane's maximum altitude. Looking forward as best he could, he made out a dark line indicating the storm blanketing the continent ahead. The report they'd intercepted from McMurdo Station indicated the severity of the weather, but also that the storm should be gradually lessening in intensity. Jumping into high winds was never a good idea, a factor those who had come up with this brilliant idea had obviously not taken into account.

Min checked his watch. They were less than an hour

and a half from the target. "Time to rig!" he yelled to
his team.

Splitting into buddy teams, the nine men who would
be jumping began to put on their parachutes, Sergeant
Chong helping the odd man. Min threw his main parachute on his back and buckled the leg and chest straps,
securing it to his body and making sure it was cinched
down tight. The reserve was hooked onto the front.
Rucksacks were clipped on below the reserve, and automatic weapons tied down on top of the reserves.

After Sergeant Chong, acting as jumpmaster, in-
spected all the men, they took their seats, each man
lost in his own thoughts, contemplating the jump and
the mission ahead. Min pulled the OPLAN out of his
carry-on bag and checked the numbers in the communication section. With those in mind, he waddled his
way up the center of the cargo bay to the cockpit.

Antarctica

The wind had actually diminished, although it was
still kicking along with gusts up to thirty-five miles an
hour. Visibility was increasing to almost fifty feet at
times. The slight break in the storm could last for minutes or hours.

Below the surface, in the base, Tai, Vaughn, and Logan were crawling back from the reactor access tunnel. Burke, Smithers, and Brothers were sleeping, so
there was no one in the communications room to notice
when the small red light on the transponder flickered,
then turned green.

CHAPTER 11

Airspace, Antarctica

Sergeant Chong was wearing a headset that allowed him to communicate with Captain Hyun in the cockpit. Chong stood next to the rear passenger door, his hands on the opening handle. A rope was wrapped about his waist, securing him to the inside of the plane. The plane itself, buffeted by winds, was bobbing and weaving. Up front the pilots were flying blind, eyes glued to the transponder needle and praying a mountainside didn't suddenly appear out of the swirling clouds.

"One minute out, sir!" he yelled to Major Min.

Min turned and looked over his shoulder at the men. "Remove the coverings on your canopy releases," he ordered. The jumpers popped the metal covering on each shoulder. These metal pieces protected the small steel cable loops that controlled the connection of the harness to the parachute risers; pulling the loops would release the risers, separating the jumper from his parachute. Doing this in the air would result in death, but Min had a reason for taking this dangerous step prior to exiting the aircraft.

He shuffled a little closer to the door, his parachute and rucksack doubling his weight. "Open the door," he ordered Chong. "Activate trackers," he called back to the rest of the team. Then Min reached down and activated the small transponder/receiver strapped to his right forearm.

Chong twisted the handle on the door. It swung in with a freezing swoosh. They'd depressurized a half hour ago and were now flying in the middle of the storm and still descending. They were at an estimated altitude of 1,500 feet above the ground.

Snow swirled in the open door, along with bone-chilling cold. Min didn't even bother taking a look—he knew he wouldn't be able to see a few feet, never mind the ground. The plan was to jump as soon as Hyun relayed that the needle focusing on the transponder swung from forward to rear, indicating they'd flown over the beacon.

"One minute," Chong relayed. The one-minute warning was Hyun's best guess, meaning that the needle had started to shiver in its case in the cockpit.

Min grabbed either side of the door with his gloved hands, his eyes on Chong, waiting for the go. The seconds went by slowly, and Min realized he was losing the feeling in his hands, but there was nothing he could do about it.

Chong suddenly stiffened. "Go!" he screamed.

Min pulled forward and threw himself into the turbulent white fog. Behind him, the other eight men followed as fast as they could get out of the aircraft.

Min fell to the end of the eighteen-foot static line, which popped the closing tie on his main parachute. The pack split open and the parachute slid out, struggling to deploy against the wind. He felt the opening jolt and looked up to make sure he had a good canopy.

He couldn't tell what the wind was doing to the chute, nor could he see the ground. With numbed hands, he reached down to find the release for his rucksack so it would drop below him on its lowering line and he wouldn't smash into the ground with it still attached.

Min was still trying to find the quick releases when he did exactly that: his feet hit ice, then his sideways speed, built up by the wind, slammed his head into the ice, the helmet absorbing some of the blow.

Min blinked as stars exploded inside his head. Now the lack of feeling in his hands truly started to work against him. He scrabbled at his right shoulder with both hands, trying to find the canopy release; he'd never have been able to grasp and pop the cover under these circumstances, proving his risky decision in the plane was been correct. The wind took hold of his parachute, skiing him across the icy surface, his parka and cold weather pants sliding across the ice and snow, his head rattling as he hit small bumps.

Finally his numbed fingers found the cable loop. Min pushed with his gloved right thumb underneath, grabbed his right wrist with his left hand and pulled with all the strength in both arms. The riser released and the canopy flipped over, letting the wind out. Then he lay on his back, trying to gather his wits. He knew he needed to be up and moving but his head was still spinning.

Min had no idea how long he'd been lying there

when a figure appeared out of the snow, right wrist held
before his face, the receiver there homing in on Min's
transmitter. The small face of the receiver blipped with
a red light, indicating the direction of the team leader's
device. By following the red dot, the team could as-
semble on Min.

The soldier immediately ran to the apex of Min's
parachute and began S-rolling it, gathering the canopy
in. Min finally turned over and got to one knee. He
popped the chest release for his harness and slipped it
off, then pulled his weapon off the top of the reserve
and made sure it was still functioning.

As Min was stuffing his chute into his rucksack,
other figures appeared out of the blowing snow. He
could see that two men were hurt: Sergeant Yong apparently had a broken arm that the medic, Corporal
Sun, was still working on, and Corporal Lee was limp-
ing. Min counted heads. Seven, besides himself. One
was missing.

"Where is Song?" he yelled to the others above the
roar of the wind.

When there was no immediate answer, Min quickly
ordered the team on line. "Turn off all receivers!" He
pushed a button on his transmitter, and it became a receiver, picking up the different frequency that Song's
wrist guidance device had been set to send on.

Min headed in the direction the red dot indicated, his
team flanking him on either side. His first priority was
accountability of all personnel. He broke into a trot,
his men keeping pace, Yong and Lee gritting their teeth
to ignore the pain of their injuries. Min was actually
satisfied so far that he had eight of his nine men—he'd
expected at least twenty-five percent casualties on the
jump.

They found Song, his body fortunately jammed up between two blocks of ice, otherwise it might have been blown all the way to the mountains. As two men ran around to collapse the parachute and gather it in, Min knelt down next to his soldier. Song's eyes were unfocused and glassy, and Min unsnapped the man's helmet. As he pulled it off he immediately spotted the caked blood and frozen, exposed brain matter that had oozed through the cracked skull.

Min looked up at Senior Lieutenant Kim. "Have two men pull him with us to the target."

Min pulled his mitten off and quickly reset his wrist transmitter/receiver to receive on the transponder frequency. He turned his face into the wind. The target was in that direction.

"I'm going to check the weather," Brothers announced.

"Don't stay too long," Burke called out from the stove as Brothers zipped his parka up. "The food will be ready in about five minutes."

"Who wants to go with me?" Brothers asked as he headed for the door to check on the weather and, if possible, his plane.

Smithers hopped up from his chair. "I'll join you. I'd like to take a look outside. Feeling a little cooped up in here."

Vaughn glanced around the mess hall at the remaining members of the party. Logan had recovered the instruction manual for the nuclear reactor from the control room and was poring through it. Tai was staring intently at whatever was displayed on the screen of her portable computer.

Vaughn was not happy with the current situation. There was little of the base left to explore. Other than the note from Lansale, they had found nothing of much value. If publicized, the nukes and stock of Nazi nerve agent would cause a scandal, but a scandal wasn't exactly a threat. When the weather cleared they would head back and report in to Royce. Maybe he could do more with the information.

Min froze and peered through the driving snow. There was something large looming directly in front of him. He moved forward ten feet on his hands and knees until he was sure it was the surface shaft, about forty feet ahead. Using hand and arm signals, he sent two men scurrying around each flank to encircle the entrance.

There was a black wedge open on Min's side, and he could make out some movement there. Staying low, he continued forward, slowly closing the distance. His team was poised behind him, awaiting his instructions. He silently worked the bolt on his weapon, making sure it wasn't frozen.

After five minutes two figures appeared in the doorway. One walked out a few feet. The other one just stood there peering out, almost directly at Min.

Brothers shivered under the lash of the cold, but the release from the claustrophobic darkness of the base more than made up for the pain. The shots sounded like muffled pops, and Brothers turned, astounded as Smithers pirouetted into the snow, the bullet tearing through his shoulder. Brothers stared at the blood seeping out from Smithers for a split second.

Min moved forward at the run, his team dashing behind him. In two seconds he'd closed half the distance to the door before he was spotted. He fired another sustained burst from his AK, and the man dove for the door. The man who had been shot was yelling after his comrade, crawling for the opening.

Min slipped on the ice and immediately rolled back to his feet, keeping his eyes on the door. He was twenty feet from the door when it started to swing shut. The wounded man was slithering through, barely missing get caught in it.

Min ran up and pointed at the door. "Lieutenant Kim! Open this!"

Vaughn met Brothers halfway down the stairs of the shaft. "What the hell happened?"

Brothers slumped down and sat on the metal steps, his breath coming in ragged gasps. "Smithers was shot!"

"What?" Vaughn said, grabbing him by the arm. He looked up the stairs. "Where is he now?"

"Up there."

A dull echo sounded from above as two shots rang out. Vaughn let go of Brothers and sprinted up the remaining stairs. Smithers lay on the top landing, blood flowing from a wound in his shoulder. The door was shut. Vaughn slid the blade of the broken pick they'd left there through the wheel and jammed it against the side wall. Then he pulled out a bandage from his vest and wrapped it around Smithers's wound.

"Who was shooting?" he asked.

"No fucking idea," Smithers responded. "Brothers damn near left me out there."

Vaughn turned as the rest of the party assembled on the stairs around Brothers, yelling confused questions at him. They'd heard the initial rifle fire as if from a

great distance in the mess hall and had immediately
come to see what was happening.

"Everyone shut up!" Vaughn yelled sharply. He
helped Smithers down the stairs. "All right. Tell us
what happened."

Smithers took a deep breath. "I caught a glimpse of
several people moving out there. Someone was shooting. That's it. I don't know any more."

Vaughn craned his head. There were no more sounds
from the door. That worried him.

"Who could have done that?" Tai asked just as the
same question flashed through Vaughn's mind.

"Someone either wants us dead, or they want the
goddamn bombs, or both." Even as he answered,
Vaughn knew what the immediate course of action had
to be. "All right. Listen up and do what I say. I don't
know who these people are. For all we know they could
be Americans, but one thing's for sure: they aren't
friendly. They didn't hesitate to shoot.

"Logan, you take Brothers, Burke, and Smithers to
the reactor. I want you to wait by the first door. If you
hear Tai or me, you open it. If it's anybody else, retreat
and shut the second one, securing that one too. You all
should be safe in there."

He turned to the Tai. "You come with me."

"What are you going to do?" she asked.

"What I should have done when we first found the
bombs."

"Maybe we can talk to these people," Logan weakly
suggested.

Vaughn grabbed him by the shoulders. "They aren't
here to ask questions. If they get in and catch us, we'll
all be dead. We don't have time to stand here discussing
things." He pushed him toward the corridor. "Move!"

The four headed off down the east tunnel. Vaughn sprinted for the armory, with Tai behind. He threw open the door and headed directly for the cases lining the wall as he called over his shoulder, "Grab two M-1s, two pistols and ammo!"

As she did that, he went through the door to the bombs. Vaughn looked in the case at the bombs. He wasn't even sure which access panel opened onto the PAL keypad. There were at least six metal plates secured with numerous Philips head screws that he could see on the top side of the bomb. He didn't have time for that. He needed a more expedient way to neutralize the bombs.

Meanwhile, Tai used a bayonet to open a crate of .30 caliber ammunition. She threw a couple of bandoliers over her shoulder. Then she secured two .45 caliber pistols along with ammunition and magazines.

Vaughn ran back in and grabbed a crate marked C-4 and tore the lid off. He took out several blocks of the plastique, then looked for caps and fuses. He found them on the other side of the room. For good measure, he grabbed a few other goodies.

Tai was struggling with a clip of ammunition and the M-1 she held. Vaughn grabbed the other rifle and a bandolier. "Like this," he said as he slammed a clip home through the top.

Tai nodded and did the same. "What are you going to do?"

"We destroy the PAL codes. It's the quickest thing we can do. Come on."

He led her to Unit A2. "Keep an eye on the corridor," he ordered as he lay out a couple blocks of C-4 and a fuse in front of him next to the safe. As he was unwinding the detonating cord the sharp crack of an explosion roared through the base. Vaughn slid the block of old C-4 against the safe, primed it, and ran out the det cord as quickly as he could.

He pulled the initiator.

Nothing.

"Fuck," he muttered.

"What's wrong?" Tai asked.

"Either the fuse or the cord or the C-4 or all of them are too old," Vaughn said. He forgot about the explosives and grabbed his M-1. They'd run out of time.

Min was the first to leap in through the blasted door. Weapon first, he sidled down the stairs, his men right behind, the muzzles of their weapons searching out every corner.

Stopping short of the first intersection, Min deployed his men in two-man teams. He'd gotten a sketch of the layout of the base in the OPLAN, so he had an idea of where he was and what lay ahead. He signaled for two teams to head down the east tunnel, clearing in that direction; he would take the rest directly to A2 to secure the codes, and then to A1 to get the bombs.

As the first two men stepped forward into the intersection, a burst of fire ripped into them, slamming them to the floor. Min slid the muzzle of his AK-47 around the corner and blindly fired a magazine in that direction as Kim pulled one of the men back undercover. The other lay motionless in the center of the intersection.

"Smoke," Min ordered.

Lee took a grenade off his combat vest, pulled the pin, and threw it in the north tunnel. Bright red smoke immediately billowed out and filled the corridor.

"Go," Min ordered, gesturing.

Two men stepped into the corridor and moved slowly forward, while two more sprinted across the side corridor to loop around and catch whoever had done the firing from the flank.

Vaughn was sure he had hit two of them as he slammed home another clip into the M-1. All he'd seen were two men bundled up in dark-colored clothes, not enough to make an ID. He and Tai were just to the south of the intersection of the north and west tunnels, using the corner of B2 to protect them.

Vaughn gave the smoke enough time to completely fill the corridor and then pulled the trigger on the M-1 as fast as he could, emptying the clip. As he slammed another clip in to reload, the enemy replied with several bursts of automatic fire that ricocheted off the walls.

"They're going to try and flank us," he told Tai. "Let's go."

Weapon at the ready, Vaughn moved into the smoke-filled corridor, heading for the door on the north end of B2. He opened it and slid in just as he spotted two figures out of the corner of his eyes. He quietly shut the door behind Tai as the two men passed by, moving toward their old location.

Vaughn made his way through the mess hall to the far door. Were the flankers already around, or were they right in front of the door? Fuck it, he thought, swung the door open and stepped out. No one.

He opened the door to C2 and hustled Tai through. Then across into the south tunnel. Vaughn moved out into that hallway—he could hear voices yelling in a foreign tongue back in the direction they had come from. He recognized the language with a quiet chill—Han

Gul, Korean, with a strange accent he had never heard. North Korean, he had to assume.

Vaughn had his finger on the trigger and almost fired as he spotted a figure coming toward them. But it was Smithers, an M-1 in his hand. "Thought you might need some help," he said.

"All right," Vaughn said. He leaned with his back against the outside wall of the library. Tai was looking at him calmly, the M-1 across her lap. Smithers knelt down close to them. Vaughn whispered his plan. "We have to cross and get in the generator room. If these guys have their shit together, they've left someone watching the east tunnel.

"We go together, Tai on the right, me in the center, Smithers on the left. If there's someone there, I'm going to fire. Both of you keep going no matter what. If I don't make it, go to the access tunnel to the left of the control panel. Crawl down it till you come to the first hatch. Logan should be on the other side. Call out and have him open it, then go in and make sure you seal both hatches. Do you understand?"

Tai and Smithers nodded.

"Ready? *Go!*"

Vaughn stepped out, weapon tight against his shoulder, aiming up the tunnel. He fired at the same time the two Koreans at the other end did. Whether it was by sound or feel, he couldn't quite say, he sensed the bullets passing by him.

In the second and a half it took to cross the corridor, Vaughn had emptied his magazine, as had the two men. Miraculously, he was untouched as he slid into the safety of the cover of Unit C3.

The scream that tore through the air informed him that Smithers hadn't been as fortunate. Vaughn spun around. The man was lying in the middle of the tunnel, hands grasped to his left leg, blood pouring over it. His M-1 lay on the floor, forgotten.

Even as Vaughn started to move to go out and pull him to safety, a burst of automatic fire walked up the floor, sending chips of wood flying, and then the rounds stitched a pattern across Smithers's midsection, the velocity of the rounds punching him three feet down the south tunnel, where he came to rest, dead.

"Leave him," Tai called out, looking over her shoulder.

Vaughn followed her, hoping the Koreans would move cautiously down the corridor. He slid into the power access tunnel. There was no way he could replace the grate from the inside, so there would be little doubt about which direction he had gone in. They'd have to trust to the strength of the double hatches.

He crawled on his hands and knees right behind Tai, the distance to the first hatch, and waited as she pounded on it. "It's me. Tai."

The wheel slowly turned, then the door opened, Logan's face framed by the hatch. Tai went first, and then Vaughn slid through. "Shut it," he ordered, and slumped against the corrugated steel tubing that made up the wall. "Secure it."

Logan flipped over the latch, locking the handle. "Where's Smithers?"

"Dead," Vaughn said. He looked around the tunnel and pulled off one of the OD green bags he had draped over his shoulders.

"What are you doing?" Logan asked.

"If they blew in the top door, they can probably blow this one in too. I want to leave them a surprise that will make them think twice about doing the second one."

* * *

Airspace, Antarctica

Captain Hyun craned his neck, looking out the window. They had just cleared the last mountains and broken into intermittent cloud cover, leaving the storm behind. The sea of ice that surrounded Antarctica was spread out below as far as he could see to the north. There was no way he could land on that.

"We must turn back and try to land," he pleaded with the impassive Sergeant Chong. "We are almost out of fuel. We could land at McMurdo and get refueled."

Chong fingered his slung AK-47, took a deep breath, held it, then pulled the trigger. The first round blew the copilot's brains against the right windshield.

"What are you doing?" Hyun screamed, twisting in his seat, his eyes growing wide as the gaping muzzle of the AK-47 turned in his direction. "If you kill me, there will be no one to fly the plane," he desperately reasoned.

Chong's finger increased pressure on the trigger.

"Please!" Hyun begged.

Chong shot him through the chest three times, disgusted with his pleading. The third round knocked the pilot out of his seat. Without hands on the controls, the plane continued to fly forward smoothly. Chong reached over and pushed down on the yoke. The nose of the plane turned downward.

When the angle became too steep, the plane plummeted out of control toward the ice-covered water. The nose hit first, and the rest of the plane crumpled and compressed as it punched through the ice into the freezing water below.

In five minutes a disappearing black smear was all that was left to mark the grave of the IL-8.

Antarctica

Min looked at the primed block of old C-4 lying on top of the untouched safe and frowned. Someone in the other party had been smart, but not quick enough.

"Open that safe, but make sure you don't destroy the contents," he instructed Lieutenant Kim.

Kim slid his backpack off and pulled out his more modern explosives, molding the plastique with his fingers, shaping the charge to blow the door off.

Sergeant Jae stuck his head in the door. "They are down a tunnel blocked by a steel door, sir."

Min nodded. "Blow the door and kill them."

Jae nodded and sprinted away.

Min checked his watch. Chong was most likely dead by now, along with Hyun and his copilot. Nam had been killed when they crossed the intersection. Ho had been wounded, although not severely. Song had also been killed moving forward. Yong and Lee had been injured in the jump. That left three wounded and four healthy men. Not good.

"Clear!" Kim yelled as he finished priming the charge. He unraveled detonating cord as they left the unit. "Firing!" Kim pulled the igniter, and the soft burp of a controlled explosion echoed out the door.

Min walked in and checked the results. The door of the safe was off its hinges, the contents untouched. He pulled out the paper and leafed through it until he found what he needed.

Kim gathered his gear. "I will assist Sergeant Jae."

Min nodded his concurrence, engrossed in translating the documents.

* * *

Vaughn stared at the pack full of explosives, wondering if it was worth his time to even try to rig them, given what had happened when he tried to blow the safe.

"What are you doing?" Logan demanded.

"I'm thinking of blowing the tunnel," Vaughn said.

"We'll be trapped then!" Logan exclaimed.

"If I don't do it," Vaughn said, "we'll be dead."

The argument was interrupted by the deep rumble of an explosion, reverberating down the tunnel.

"That's the first door," Vaughn said.

A second, sharper explosion followed by screams could be faintly heard through the thick steel door.

"That's the mine," Vaughn said. "At least *it* worked. That will make them think twice about taking out this door."

Min looked at the mangled remains of Sergeant Jae. The corrugated steel tunnel had intensified the effects of the antipersonnel mine. Jae's body had taken most of the impact, but some had gotten by him, and Yong's right arm and leg were saturated with a load of shrapnel. Sun had given Yong a shot of morphine, and his screaming had stopped.

Kim came crawling back through the blood. "I can still blow the second door, sir."

"I know." Min rubbed his chin. He had not expected such a fight. In fact, he had not expected any fight at all. He had been so concerned with simply getting here that he had not war-gamed possible events upon arrival sufficiently. Now was time to cut his losses.

"Leave the door." Min announced.

Kim looked up at his team leader in surprise. "But they are still alive in there. Our orders are to leave no trace."

Min nodded grimly. "I know."

CHAPTER 12

Antarctica

"What the hell is going on?" Logan asked of no one in particular.

Vaughn was seated on the floor with his rifle near the tunnel entrance to the reactor. He held a fuse initiator in his hand. Tai was seated next to him, a pistol in her lap. Logan was sitting in one of the chairs in the room next to Burke. Brothers had his back up against the thick glass separating them from the reactor core.

"I'm surprised they haven't blown the second door yet," Vaughn remarked.

"Maybe they just wanted the bombs and have taken them and left?" Logan offered hopefully.

"But how did they know the bombs were down here?" Tai wondered aloud.

"Most likely the same way we did," Vaughn said.

Tai shook her head. "Royce said that the Abu Sayif received a packet from Lansale. You said they spoke Korean. How could the Koreans have found out about this?"

"That all doesn't matter now," Logan cut in. "We need to decide what we're going to do."

Do?" Vaughn laughed bitterly. "There's nothing we can do."

"If they're stealing the bombs we need to stop them," Logan said.

Vaughn stood and walked over. He thrust the M-1 out. "Here. You take this and go stop them. Of course, they've probably rigged that door on the other side just like I rigged it on this side. But hey, I'm not going to stop you, if that's what you want to do."

Logan didn't take the weapon. "What do you suggest?"

"I suggest we sit tight for now." He pointed at the three bags piled in the corner. "There's food in those. Enough to last us a week or so. We also have sleeping bags. Even if they turn off the power and we lose the heat, we'll be able to survive until they get what they want and leave."

"Why did you put that food and those sleeping bags in here?" Tai asked. She'd noticed them when they'd first entered and had wondered about it.

"Contingency planning," Vaughn replied. "Once you found those bombs, I figured there was a chance we might get some visitors. I was trained to what-if and worst case things. Except I didn't think our visitors would come in shooting. I was thinking more in terms of some spooks from our own government coming down and wanting to take us away to little padded cells." Vaughn pointed up. "There's a hatch in the ceiling that probably opens onto an access tunnel to the surface, but there's nothing up there for us either right now."

"You said they spoke Korean," Tai repeated. "You mean they're from North Korea?"

Vaughn's answer surprised her. "I don't know. Both North and South speak Han Gul. I was stationed in the South for a little while, so I recognize it. But it's possible that those might be South Korean troops out there for all I know. There's a lot of people in the world who'd like to get their hands on a U.S. made nuclear weapon and the Golden Lily and not be too concerned about who they have to kill to do it."

"But they'll never get away with it!" Burke said. "I mean, how can they cover this up?"

Vaughn shrugged. "I don't know. I don't even know how they got here. They couldn't have landed a plane in that weather. Maybe they jumped, but if they did in those winds, they're better men than I. I also don't know how they plan on getting away. But I can tell you one thing. I'm sure whoever is in charge of them has thought of answers to those questions or they wouldn't be out there."

"Do you think they'll steal my plane?" Brothers asked.

Vaughn shook his head. "I doubt it. The weather is still crappy up there. We couldn't use it either if we got out. I think they might try to walk out. For all I know they came here on some sort of over-snow vehicle and are going to use that to leave.

"Whether it's North or South Koreans out there, one thing's for certain. They're hard soldiers, and they're used to operating in cold weather. They've already taken several casualties, mainly because I don't think they expected any opposition. From here on out they'll be ready for us if we make a move. So I say we sit tight."

Tai was at a loss for words. She felt like they ought to be doing something, but Vaughn's cold logic made sense.

"So you say we just let them walk away with nuclear weapons?" Logan demanded.

Vaughn shrugged. "You're free to go and stop them." He looked over and his eyes met Tai's. "We didn't put those bombs down here, so they're really not our problem, are they? Actually, if you get down to it, this is the Organization's problem. They put the bombs and this base here. So maybe this will turn out all for the best."

Vaughn's words were met with silence.

The MK/B 61 nuclear bomb weighs 772 pounds. Using the same small tractor that Tai had used to clear out the armory, Min's men pulled the first bomb along the hallway to the east ice storage tunnel. There, they placed it on a large sled and secured it with ropes.

Corporal Sun had started the large bulldozer and was up on the steel grating ramp, cutting away at the ice with the blade, aiming for the surface. As soon as he cut through they would take the large SUSV tractor and head out. The SUSV consisted of a large engine section on treads that could seat three men up front, and a second section on tracks that was pulled along and could fit ten men and all their supplies. Min watched Sun's efforts for a few minutes and then went back to the armory.

South Pacific

"Captain James Cook was the first to sail around Antarctica, from 1773 to 1775, yet he never once spotted land, the ice pack keeping him well out of landfall."

Fatima sipped a cup of coffee as she listened to the captain. She and Araki were on the bridge of the freighter, the heaters going full-blast, fighting against the Antarctic wind that blasted against the glass that separated them from the world outside.

"The first party ever to land on Antarctic land and spend the winter did not succeed until well over a century later, in 1895. And in the slightly more than a century since, men in ships have been able to accomplish little more in these vicious seas."

"Your point?" Fatima asked.

The captain glanced at her, and then returned his focus to the sea ahead. He had a copy of the OPLAN in his hands and had just finished reading it. "These idiots in Pyongyang want us to pick people up off the coast of Antarctica." He laughed. "As if by a simple command such a thing could happen. Let's see what you have to say when we hit the ice pack in the morning. Whoever it was that wanted to get picked up will have to come to us—not the other way around."

"All right," Fatima said. "Once we make contact with them, I will inform them of this."

The captain twisted his head and peered into the distance as the lookout phoned in another iceberg off the port bow. "It's going to get worse," he lamented.

"It always does," Fatima agreed.

Antarctica

The way to the surface was clear, and Sergeant Sun had managed to drive the SUSV up the uneven ramp to the surface, where it sat rumbling on the ice cap, the sled hitched behind it. Major Min walked back down the ramp and across the base to the armory, where Sergeant Yong was propped up, back against the wall, his weapon on his knees. His wounded arm and leg were swathed in bandages. The bodies of Jae, Song, and Nam were laid out in the hallway under ponchos.

Min was uncertain what words would be correct to say good-bye to his soldier, so he simply stood in front of his man and saluted. Yong looked up and returned the gesture with his nonwounded arm. Before he had second thoughts, Min turned and swiftly walked back to the east ice storage room. He climbed up the ramp and crunched across the ice to the cab of the SUSV. He got into the cab and nodded at Sun. The medic threw the vehicle in gear, and the treads slowly started turning. At a crawl of ten miles an hour they headed away from the base. Min directed the driver to their one last stop before heading for the mountains lining the coast. The sled bobbed along in their wake, its cargo securely tied down.

Geneva

Dyson's body was strapped to the chair in the middle of the Intelligence Center. His dead eyes stared straight ahead. The man who had been "working" on him packed up his equipment and left the center.

Then the High Counsel spoke to the Assessors. "I want a Course of Action Projection based on what we just learned about Majestic-12."

"With what parameters?" the Senior Assessor asked.

"I want to know what the possible outcomes will be if we exterminate Majestic-12."

Pine Barrens, New Jersey

The two men walked down the corridor, the squeak of their shoes echoing off the cinder-block walls. They went into a small room with a secure satellite link to Geneva. "I got everything out of Whitaker," the Tall Man said into the mike. "He put the bomb on the airplane carrying the engineers."

"Why?" the Senior Assessor asked.

"To keep the location secret and for $500,000. He also helped wiped out the convoy that accompanied the four MK-17 bombs down there."

"That was years later, so Lansale kept him on retainer. What about the submarines?"

"He didn't know about those."

"Terminate him."

Pentagon

As questions bombarded him, the head of the Intelligence Service Agency didn't like the role reversal. The hastily assembled officers and senior administration officials wanted answers, and he, unfortunately, didn't have many. Being the bearer of bad news had a historically poor rating.

The ranking officer in the room, Army Chief of Staff General Morris, listened to the confusion for five minutes before he cut to the heart of the matter. "Gentlemen, we have to accept the fact that there are bombs down there and there is nothing we can presently do to make that knowledge disappear. Given that, there are two courses of action we have to pursue.

"Our primary concern must be to secure the bombs. I say that is primary because of the potential physical threat they represent. Our secondary concern is to find out where these bombs came from and how they ended up at this base. Attached to that second concern is to find out why and how this Citadel was built."

Morris looked about the room to make sure everyone, particularly the President's National Security Advisor, was following him. With the Chairman of the Joint Chiefs in the Middle East, this problem was his problem. "In line with the first, I am going to have certain military forces alerted and deployed to the Antarctic to secure the weapons and remove them."

"Won't that violate the Antarctic accord?" an Air Force general asked.

Morris bit off a sarcastic reply. "The accord has already been violated. It is now time for damage control, and we have to get those bombs out of there.

"To help solve the second problem, the various intelligence organizations have all been notified and are investigating the situation." He swung his gaze to the ISA director. "I want your sources to find out everything they have on this. I also want everything you've received from the personnel you've already detained in connection with this incident." Morris fixed a full colonel at the end of the table with his gaze. "What do we have that can get there ASAP to secure those weapons?"

The colonel looked at the large map at the end of the room. "To be honest, not much, sir. I think the closest ground forces would come from either Panama or Hawaii. Elements of the 7th Fleet are operating off of Australia. The big problem is that we have no way to deploy forces by air there without an in-flight refuel. That's the most isolated place in the world—you have a minimum of a two-thousand-mile flight from the nearest land."

"I don't want problems. I want results."

"Yes, sir."

Antarctica

Kim laid the satchel charge in the middle aisle of the Earth First plane. They'd just found it, parked four hundred meters away from the base, and Major Min had directed him to destroy it. He estimated that thirty pounds of explosive would more than do the job. Kim pulled the fuse igniter and hopped out the door. He ran back to the SUSV and clambered into the cab, next to Min. The driver immediately threw it into gear, and they headed away.

Three minutes later the dull crack of the explosion sounded through the blowing snow, but the flash was lost in the white fog. Thirty miles directly ahead lay the coast.

"I wonder why they haven't cut off the power?" Brothers asked.

"Maybe they don't care if we're hiding in here," Vaughn suggested.

"Maybe they've already left;" Logan added. "Surely they wouldn't want to hang around any longer than they have to."

The five of them were sitting in a semicircle, facing the hatch. There had been no noise for quite a while. Tai had to admit to herself that she was surprised the power was still on and that the North Koreans hadn't tried to finish them off. The more she thought about it, the more it didn't make much sense.

She nudged Vaughn. "What do you think?"

He considered his reply for a few seconds. They

were all deferring to him since he was the only one who'd had some sort of plan, which was why they were alive now. "This whole thing doesn't make sense. Skipping the issue of why the Koreans—be they South or North—would want two nuclear bombs, we're left with the question of how they think they can get away with this.

"Even if they had wiped us all out here and tried to make it look like an accident—say a fire destroying the base and all the bodies—they've got to know that someone else knows about the bombs. The U.S. would then send a team down here to search for the bombs, and when they didn't find them, the heat would be on."

"Maybe they were hoping there would be enough of a time delay before that was discovered, that they could get away," Tai offered.

"True," Vaughn agreed. "But then they would have had to kill all of us." He shook his head, which was beginning to throb with a splitting headache. "They've got a long trip back to Korea with those things, and then what are they going to do with them once they get there?"

"Whatever happens," Logan said, "the United States government is going to look pretty stupid. How could they have put nuclear weapons down here and then just forgotten about them?"

Vaughn had spent quite a bit of time thinking about that. "There's a lot of ways that could have happened. You all probably don't realize the shear number of atomic weapons the U.S. has. If I remember rightly, there were over three thousand of these MK/B 61s built. And that's just one of several types of weapon in the inventory. There's easily over ten thousand weapons in various places all over the world, and that's just the U.S.'s. Add in the former Soviet Union's and it's a wonder no one has had some stolen or turn up in the wrong hands before this."

"Well, let's pray that these two never get used," Tai said.

"Amen to that," Brothers added.

Logan abruptly stood up. "I can't sit here any longer and just allow this to happen."

"What are you going to do?" Vaughn asked.

"You're probably right," Logan said to Vaughn, "the access tunnel is most likely booby-trapped." He pointed to the ceiling. "I say we go up to the surface and come back down the main shaft. They won't expect us coming that way—that's if they're still here. Or we go for the plane."

Brothers, Tai, and Burke all turned to Vaughn, for his opinion. "Well, we're going to have to get out of here sooner or later," he said, "but I would prefer to wait for later and let someone come to us. If we get out and the weather still isn't good enough to take off, then we're stuck out on the surface. Plus, I think the Koreans have probably destroyed the plane. I would if I was them."

"Someone won't come here looking for us for several days at least," Logan countered.

"I still think we ought to wait," Vaughn quietly replied. "You don't have a plan beyond getting to the surface."

"Let's at least see if the shaft is blocked," Tai offered.

Vaughn couldn't find any way to refuse that request. "All right." He grabbed one of the chairs and slid it underneath the trapdoor in the ceiling. The door was held in place by two latches. The first one came free easily enough, but the second was more stubborn, resisting his efforts for a few minutes. Brothers took his place and tried. After three attempts the latch slid free and the door swung down, sending Brothers sprawling on the floor.

"You all right?" Vaughn asked.

"Aye, mate."

Vaughn stepped up and shined his flashlight into the shaft. It was clear for five feet, then another hatch blocked the way. "They sure believed in putting a lot of doors in this place," he remarked.

Logan explained that. "That's to keep the radiation in once they powered the plant up. It's the same reason this place is set a quarter mile from the main base and the tunnel has those turns in it. They shielded the reactor not only with these walls but also with all the ice in between here and the main base. They probably planned on using this room only for occasional maintenance checks."

Vaughn grabbed the inside lip of the first door with his gloved fingers and lifted himself up. There were rungs in the wall, and he could stand on the six inches of frame that extended all the way around the first door. The second door was similar to the first, and he went to work on the latches.

Both moved relatively easily, and he knelt down to let the door swing open over his head. Shining the light up, he wasn't surprised to see the shaft blocked by ice, about ten feet above his head. He carefully dropped back down into the reactor room.

"It's filled with ice. I'm not sure how much of it is blocked." He looked at Logan. "How far below the surface do you think we are?"

Logan shrugged. "Hard to say. If we're on line with the main compound, then I'd say about thirty feet under. But I got the sense going through the access tunnel that it sloped down a little bit, which makes sense, as they would want to have enough ice on top to help shield it. I'd say we might be as deep as fifty or sixty feet below the surface."

Vaughn didn't fancy the idea of digging through thirty feet of ice if the entire shaft was blocked. On the other hand, the plug might only be a few feet thick. "I'll take the first shift digging." He looked around. "I'll knock the ice down, and you all pile it up in that corner."

He took the entrenching tool from his ruck and tucked it inside his parka. He also unsnapped a twelve-foot length of nylon rope attached to the outside of his ruck. He wrapped the rope about his waist and through his legs, making an expedient climbing harness, tied two loops in the ends and connected them with the snap link that had held the rope to his ruck. Then he clambered back up into the shaft and used the rungs to climb up.

Reaching the ice, Vaughn clicked the snap link on a rung and sat back in the harness. He reached inside his parka, pulled out the e-tool and unfolded it. Carefully pulling his hood over his head, he used the point of the shovel to break chunks of ice free, letting them fall down the shaft to the floor. He worked mostly by feel, as the reflected light from the room below barely lit the shaft.

It was the sort of mindless work that Vaughn enjoyed doing. It took his mind off the sight of Smithers lying in the corridor, bullets slamming into his body. He hadn't allowed himself to think about the fact that he had killed again today, and he knew now wasn't the time. There would be plenty of time for thinking after they got out of here.

Howard Air Force Base, Panama

Major Frank Bellamy watched the confusion in his men's faces as they were handed the cold-weather clothing that the battalion sergeant major had scrounged out of the central issue facility. The fact that the facility even had cold-weather gear was a little surprising, but they were Special Forces, after all—ready to go anywhere in the world at a moment's notice. Just because they were stationed in Panama didn't mean they wouldn't be sent to someplace less temperate.

Bellamy grabbed the red webbing that served as seats on the side of the MC-130 Combat Talon as the plane suddenly stopped on the runway and then slowly turned, the roar of the engines easily penetrating the metal skin.

The loadmaster was yelling at Bellamy to get his men seated for takeoff. Bellamy ignored him—the Air Force always acted like they were the most important thing in the world and the other services were just training aids to support them. What difference would it make if his men were seated on the web seats or standing in the middle of the plane if it crashed on takeoff? They'd be dead either way.

Bellamy was the company commander for C Company, 3rd Battalion, 7th Special Forces Group (Airborne) stationed in Panama. He'd received the alert direct from Special Operations Command forty minutes ago, and in that time had gathered together the two of his teams that weren't out training and gotten them and their gear loaded onto this aircraft. The twenty-six men were now crowded in the rear of the aircraft, trying to sort through the rapidly loaded equipment. Halfway up the cargo bay, a large black curtain blocked the view forward. Bellamy knew that behind that curtain were banks of electronic equipment manned by Air Force personnel. With a slight bump, the brakes were released and the plane rumbled down the runway.

His XO, Captain Manchester, sat next to him and yelled into his ear, "Where are we going?"

"Antarctica!" Bellamy shouted back.

Manchester took that news in stride. "What for?"

"Fuck if I know," Bellamy replied. "All the alert said was to get our butt in gear. I'm supposed to get filled in once we're airborne and SOCOM gets its shit together and calls."

Manchester nodded and leaned back in his seat, closing his eyes. No sense worrying about what they didn't know. Bellamy had the same attitude. He bunched up a poncho liner behind his head and was asleep less than ten minutes after takeoff.

8th Army Headquarters, Yongsan, South Korea

The U.S. 8th Army Commander, General Patterson, steepled his fingers and contemplated his staff G-2. The G-2 was the officer responsible for intelligence, and it was at his request that the other primary staff members of Patterson's headquarters were gathered here at almost eleven at night in the situation room. The G-2 had just spent twenty minutes going over his recent intelligence data and had finished only a minute ago. The rest of the room was waiting on Patterson's reaction.

"Okay. Let me see if I have this straight. All these indicators that you've just briefed add up to level four activity across the border. Am I correct?"

Contrary to what many nonmilitary people thought, it was impossible to launch a large-scale military campaign without certain preparations. These preparations were the keys that the intelligence agencies of all the armed forces in the world watched for in their potential enemies. Noting some of those activities across the border in North Korea had led the G-2 to become concerned and call this meeting.

"Yes, sir."

"How many times have you seen this?" Patterson asked.

"We saw it during Team Spirit back in March. The North went up to level two then, but that was expected, as they do it every year during that exercise. We haven't seen an unexpected four like this in the past eight months that I've been here. This level four activity could just be part of movements among the various factions that want to take over next.

"However, I must point out that the activity seems to be southern directed." The G-2 gestured at the map on the wall behind him. "The satellite imagery definitely shows the V and II PKA Corps moving to forward assault positions along the border."

"They may be doing this just to get us to deploy our forward elements into their battle positions so they can ID them," the operations officer, G-3, said. "They can pull those units back just as quickly as they move them forward."

"Our sensing equipment is also picking up some tunneling activity in the DMZ," the G-2 pointed out. "We haven't pinpointed it yet, but it's the most extensive we've heard in a long time."

Over the years, three tunnels had been discovered and neutralized coming from the North under the DMZ. It was estimated that there were at least eighteen more tunnels in place that had yet to be found. Each of these tunnels was large enough to pass an estimated 8,000 troops an hour through.

Patterson frowned. Level four was the first stage of intelligence alert to possible invasion from the North. By itself, it required no action on his part other than to inform subordinate commanders. Level three—if it came to that—required the restriction of all personnel to base and a one-hour alert status for every unit. Level two required forward movement to defensive positions and the initiation of movement of reinforcements from U.S. bases outside of the Korean peninsula—the real version of the Team Spirit exercise that was conducted every year. Level one meant war was possible with less than a ten-minute warning.

All that was fine and well, but they were alerts that had been designed before the invasion of Iraq and Afghanistan. Patterson had been trying to coordinate with the Pentagon to update the alert system based on the reality that many of the reinforcements traditionally earmarked for South Korea in time of war were already at war in Iraq. And even a brigade of his own forces from the 2d Infantry Division had deployed just four months ago from South Korea to Iraq.

"How far out are they from reaching level one?" Patterson asked.

The G-2 bit his lower lip. "I'd say minimum of seventy-two hours, sir, if they're committed to it. More likely a week. If we get any of several intelligence nodes passed in the next eight to twelve hours we will be at level three."

Patterson nodded. "All right. Inform me immediately if I have to go to level three alert. I want all major subordinate commanders alerted about the level four. That includes all reinforcing units. I'm going to personally call the commanding general of the 25th in Hawaii and update him. I'll also call the war room in the Pentagon." He turned to his Air Force and naval commanders. "Please notify your respective personnel to go to level four alert."

"Yes, sir."

Antarctica

Tai had watched the steady stream of ice splatter down the chute for the past fifteen minutes. Now Vaughn's feet appeared as he hopped down. "Who's next?" he asked as he shook ice flakes off his parka.

Logan zipped up his jacket. "I'll go."

Brothers stood. "No. I'll go. I need the exercise to warm up. You take the next shift."

As Vaughn took the rope off his own waist and wrapped it around the pilot, he filled in the rest of the group on his progress. "I made about four or five feet in. Most of the metal tubing is still good. It almost looks like the ice either came in from the top or we haven't reached the break in the wall yet. Let's hope the ice didn't crush the metal together."

Brothers cinched the rope around his waist. "All set."

Vaughn pointed. "I hung the shovel on the top rung."

"Okay." With a weary smile, Brothers reached up and pulled himself into the tube.

The temperature in the reactor room had dropped considerably due to the open hatch and the slowly melting pile of ice in the far corner. Tai had gone through the supplies Vaughn had piled in the room and put together a cold meal of crackers and canned fruit cocktail. She handed a can to Vaughn as he sat down on his ruck.

"Thanks." Vaughn smiled and held up a can of fruit. "C-rations. I haven't seen these in a long time."

Tai glanced over at Logan. He looked worn and scared. His sudden desire for action bothered her. They ate in silence, interrupted only by the sprinkle of ice from the hatch as Brothers continued to dig away.

She was surprised when Vaughn slid over until their legs were touching. "This was a cluster-fuck of a mission," he said.

Tai nodded. "Royce is shooting in the dark, hoping to hit something."

"And we're the bullets," Vaughn said.

"And we have little idea what the target is," Tai noted. "I'm starting to think you might be—" She never finished analyzing those feelings as her world went upside down. It was as if a large hand grasped the reactor room and lifted it, tumbling everyone to the floor. The lights went out and a tremendous roar, sounding like thousands of locomotives roaring by, shook her ears. Her last thought as she was thrown across the room was regret that she and Vaughn hadn't talked sooner.

CHAPTER 13

Antarctica

The fact that the epicenter of the blast was underground muffled the kinetic effect of the explosion but utterly disintegrated the Citadel, producing a puckered crater in the ice over a quarter mile wide. The fireball lashed across the surface, the heat finding nothing to sink its teeth into but searing the surface for over two kilometers in every direction. The immediate refreezing of the briefly melted ice produced a landscape that resembled sheets of glistening glass.

The immediate radiation was absorbed by the ice in a relatively short distance. The delayed radiation in the form of Strontium 90, Cesium 137, Iodine 131, and Carbon 14, was grabbed by the howling winds, and as the elements rose in the atmosphere, the radiation began spreading over a large area.

* * *

The flash and thermal energy washed by the convoy, bathing the snowy plain in dulled white light—the swirling snow having lessened the effect—the heat at a bearable level here over fifteen miles away from the epicenter of the blast. Min had turned the vehicle so the rear pointed directly back toward the base, five minutes prior to the hour, but still the shock wave split through the storm and slammed into the back of the SUSV with gale force. The vehicle actually lifted a foot off its rear tracks before rocking back down and continuing on its way.

McMurdo Station, Antarctica

Over five hundred miles to the west of the Citadel, needles on seismographs flickered briefly and then were still. Scientists scratched their heads, perplexed at the cause for the burp in their machines. Dutifully they recorded the data and forwarded it back to the United States. Over the next twenty minutes other Antarctic stations forwarded the same data as their machines registered it.

The two favorite theories bandied about at the various U.S. stations were either an earthquake or a massive split of ice off the ice shelf falling into the ocean. They were both wrong.

Russkaya Station, Antarctica

The senior scientist at the Russkaya Station looked at the various reports on the seismic disturbance and combined that with the severe electromagnetic pulse that had washed over his station ten minutes ago. The former might be explained by an earthquake or ice breaking—the latter by a severe sunspot. Together they added up to only one answer—a nuclear explosion. But how? Why? And most important of all, who?

Ah well, the scientist shrugged. That was for people much more important than him to worry about. He wrote up a report and had his radioman send it over the one transmitter that had survived the EMP pulse—an old tube radio that had been here since the base opened. All the modern solid-state circuitry radios had been fused by the EMP.

Vicinity of the Citadel, Antarctica

Tai checked her body, starting from head to foot, making sure all the parts were still functioning. Everything seemed all right. She sat up and turned her head from side to side, listening. Someone was moving nearby.

The total dark was the worst. Eyes wide open, she could see nothing. Then a small light flared out next to her and, in the glow, she saw Vaughn holding his flashlight.

"You okay?"

Tai nodded. "I think so."

Vaughn swiftly ran the light around the room. Logan appeared to be unconscious, with several boxes of supplies piled on top of him. Burke was groggily moving, hands on his head.

Vaughn ignored both of them as he jumped to his feet. He shined his light up into the shaft. A pair of feet disappearing into ice were all that he could see twenty feet above. He turned to Tai. "Hold the light for me. Brothers's buried." He rapidly climbed up.

Reaching the feet, Vaughn hooked one arm through a rung and squeezed one of the feet with his free hand, just to let Brothers know help was here. He hooked his fingers and tore at the ice, pulling away chunks. The cold helped to numb the pain as he tore fingernails loose. Vaughn worked by feel, the glow from the light in Tai's hand doing little good this far up.

"Is he all right?"

Vaughn kept working. He had yet to get any sort of reaction from Brothers. "I need help. Get up here."

Tai climbed up to just below him.

"When I get him free I need your help to lower him down. He's unconscious." He shoved his arm up along Brothers's chest and pulled hard. A large chunk of ice broke free, bounced off Vaughn and tumbled below. He felt Brothers's body shift and quickly grabbed the rope that was still hooked to a rung, easing the body down.

"Get him!" he yelled as he tried to unhook the snap link with numbed fingers. Tai had one arm wrapped around Brothers's body, but Vaughn couldn't unsnap the anchor. "Fuck it," he muttered and pulled out his knife. The razor sharp blade parted the rope with one swipe.

Vaughn dropped the knife and reached down to help Tai lower Brothers. Together they got the body down to the reactor floor. Vaughn jumped down out of the shaft as Tai pointed the flashlight at the man's face. The eyes were closed. Vaughn used his good hand to feel Brothers's neck as he leaned over and placed his cheek next to his mouth to see if he could pick up any breath. No breath, no pulse.

Vaughn tilted Brothers's head back and quickly blew three quick breaths in. He linked his fingers together and pressed down through the bulky clothes on the chest. Within ten seconds he was into the CPR rhythm.

He didn't know how long he'd been at it when Tai slid in on the other side and relieved him. Vaughn sank back on his haunches, his arms and shoulders burning with exhaustion. The pain from his hand was now a deep throbbing.

Vaughn gave Tai an estimated five minutes, then he took over again. Still no movement or sign of life. He shut down his mind and concentrated on the routine.

"He's dead." Tai's voice barely penetrated Vaughn's mind. He kept on. Finally he felt Tai's arms wrapping around him from behind. "He's dead, Vaughn. You can't bring him back. He was up there too long without air." Vaughn allowed the arms to pull him back away from the body.

"How're Logan and Burke?" Vaughn asked as he finally accepted the reality of Brothers's death.

Tai took the light across the room. "How are you?" she quietly asked.

Logan lifted up a haggard face. "What happened? Earthquake?"

"I don't know." She looked at Burke, whose eyes were now open. "Are you okay?"

"I think so."

Tai turned back to Vaughn and echoed Logan's question. "What happened?"

Vaughn wanted to laugh, but the feeling died just as quickly as it came. They were past that now—way past that. "One of the bombs went off."

Tai's eyes opened wide. "How could we have survived?"

Vaughn answered succinctly. "A quarter mile of ice between us and the blast center. The low yield, ten kilotons. An underground burst, which helped contain much of the energy. Being in this reactor, which was built to contain radiation and heavily shielded. And a lot of luck."

"Why did they set the bomb off?" Logan asked.

"To leave no trace," Vaughn replied. "There's nothing left of the Citadel now except this place. They have the other bomb free and clear and no one will ever know."

"There's us," Tai countered.

Vaughn conceded that point. "They probably underestimated the protection the reactor gave us. As far as the Koreans are concerned, we're history." Vaughn thought about what he had just said. "We may well be history too, if we don't get up to the surface." He looked around in the dim glow cast by the mag light. "We can talk about it when we get out. If we stay here, we die."

Pentagon

General Morris looked up as General Hodges rapidly entered the situation room. He didn't like the look on his subordinate's face.

Hodges wasted no time getting to the point. "Sir, several research facilities in Antarctica have picked up a seismic disturbance. We've analyzed the reports." Hodges swallowed. "Sir, based on the triangulation and the size of the shock wave, we believe there has been an approximately ten-kiloton nuclear explosion at the location we have been given for this Citadel."

"What about imagery?" Morris asked.

"We've taken some satellite shots, but nothing can be made out through the cloud cover. That large storm front still covers most of Antarctica."

"What's the status on our unit heading down there?"

"We've alerted a Special Forces unit in Panama. They're heading down there on board a Combat Talon. Estimated time of arrival is 0500 zulu tomorrow."

Morris turned to the situation room's operations officer. "What fleet assets do we have that might be in that area?"

The officer looked up at the large world map that encompassed the entire far wall. "Nothing in the immediate area. The 7th Fleet has a carrier group near Australia."

"Order them to head south as quickly as possible."

"Yes, sir."

Morris turned back to Hodges. "What will the fallout be?"

"Should be minimal, sir. The winds will sweep it out into the South Pacific. As I said, it was a very low yield."

That didn't make Morris feel that much better. "What about the Russians? Have they picked it up?"

Hodges sighed. "They must have, sir. They have a research station less than three hundred miles from the Citadel location. General Kolstov has been notified."

Morris took a moment to collect his thoughts. "All right. I have to contact the President."

South Pacific

Fatima woke Araki. "We intercepted a report out of McMurdo Station. Seismic detectors have picked up a disturbance in the vicinity of the Citadel. They're not sure what has happened, although they suspect an earthquake."

Araki blinked the sleep out of her eyes. "An earthquake?"

Fatima stared at her. "An earthquake would be rather convenient, don't you think?"

"What else—" Araki blanched. "Nuclear blast?"

Fatima shrugged. "Perhaps. Which would mean either the North Koreans did it or someone else got down there."

"But why would someone detonate a nuclear weapon?" Araki asked.

"Destroying evidence by using the evidence," Fatima said.

"How far out are we from the rendezvous?" Araki asked.

"Just over twenty-four hours."

Antarctica

Vaughn felt at home in the dark. Gravity told him which way was up, and that was all he needed. He'd found the shovel still lodged in the ice where Brothers had been digging and he continued the work. It almost seemed as if the explosion had loosened the ice, as it broke free easier now. Vaughn estimated he had made almost fifteen feet so far. The surface couldn't be far ahead.

Thirty feet below, the mag light made the tiniest glow as Logan, Burke, and Tai cleared away the ice he let fall. Vaughn shoved the steel tip of the shovel upward and a large block broke free. Vaughn swung up again, and sparks flew as steel hit steel.

"I need the light," he yelled. A small pinprick of brightness appeared below and grew stronger as Tai climbed up to join him. Vaughn reached down, took the light out of her hands and examined the ceiling. It was apparent now why the shaft had filled with ice. The hatch was breached, half open. Vaughn played the light around. Both hinges on the far side of the hatch had succumbed to time and pressure and popped. The problem was, the opening was on the far side of the shaft, and Vaughn had no idea how much ice was on top of the hatch. He handed the light back to Tai.

He unhooked himself from the rung and, after warning Tai, stepped down one rung and then pushed his feet against the near wall and allowed himself to fall across the three-foot-wide tube. He was braced now, in the classic chimney climb position. Inch by inch, Vaughn edged himself up until the edge of the hatch was at eye level. Cautiously, he kept his balance with one hand while he used the other to probe through the foot and a half opening into the ice. Small pieces fell out, bounced off his stomach and tumbled below.

"I'm going back down," Tai called out as she beat a hasty retreat.

After five minutes Vaughn was in a position where he could brace his feet on the hatch itself. It took him a few more minutes to realize that he could dimly see. There was light from above, penetrating the ice.

Tasman Sea

The *Kitty Hawk* is not only the oldest aircraft carrier still on active duty with the U.S. Navy, it is the oldest warship still active. Built in the early sixties, it had been extensively refitted in 1991 and then assigned to the 7th Fleet operating out of Pearl Harbor. It was presently steaming east in the center of Battle Group 72, a collection of the *Kitty Hawk*, two Aegis cruisers, two destroyers, four frigates, two resupply ships, and two submarines hidden underneath the waves.

They'd just completed a joint training exercise with the Australian navy, and Admiral Klieg, the battle group commander, was taking this opportunity to correct several of the deficiencies he'd detected in some of his ships during the exercise.

This early in the morning, he was on the bridge of the *Kitty Hawk*, watching as his ships reacted to a practice alert, when his staff operations officer brought him a classified message for his eyes only.

Klieg examined the message under the red glow of the battle station's lights. He took a minute to think and then addressed the waiting operations officer. "Call off the present training exercise. All ships, battle cruising formation. Flank speed."

"Heading, sir?"

"Due south."

Ford Mountain Range, Antarctica

The SUSV was two and half hours out from the Citadel and had traversed twenty-two miles in that time. Since the explosion forty-five minutes ago, the cab had been silent, each man lost in his own thoughts and worries. It was Kim who broke the silence.

"Sir, you said I would know the plan when I needed to. Could you tell me when that will be? We have already lost half our party. If we lose you, I will not know what course of action to take. Nor will I know what to do with that." Kim nodded over his shoulder at the sled bobbing along in their icy wake.

Min's real reason for not informing Kim about all of the plan's details was that he hadn't believed the plan would work, and he knew his XO would have thought the same thing. In fact, Min still didn't believe they would be able to accomplish the entire mission despite the fact that they had been successful so far, albeit with the loss of five men—seven, if he included Captain Hyun and his copilot.

But now Min realized he had to brief Kim. They were committed, and there was definitely no turning back. And for the first time, he felt they had a chance to succeed.

"We are on our way to a rendezvous with a freighter that will pick us up off the coast. We will determine the exact location of pickup when we reach the shore and can establish radio contact with the vessel. The frequency to make contact is 62.32. Our call sign is Tiger; theirs is Wolf.

"We will load aboard the ship and immediately head for our target. It is estimated that it will take us another couple of days of sailing to make it to the target."

"Which is?" Kim pressed.

"Pearl Harbor."

Kim blinked. "The 7th Fleet!"

Min gave a weary smile. "We are not to destroy the target. At least not at first. The plan is that the mere threat that we are in position to do so will allow our government to blackmail the United States government to do—or perhaps rather I should say, not do—two things. One is not to deploy their reinforcing units to South Korea in the face of higher levels of readiness. The second is not to use nuclear weapons once the border has been breached."

Kim thought about it. "Do you believe the United States would accede to such blackmail?"

Min shrugged. "The United States stood still when

a handful of their citizens were taken hostage. The threat of tens of thousands of their people killed in a nuclear explosion might make them change their mind and question the worth of their allegiance to the South. Even if it doesn't, destroying their facilities at Pearl Harbor, now that Subic Bay is closed, will greatly reduce their ability to project forces into the Pacific."

"But how are we supposed to smuggle this bomb into Hawaii? How are we supposed to hide? Especially once the threat is made?"

Min shrugged. "According to the operations plan, that is up to our initiative. If we can get close enough to the Hawaiian Islands, we can make it.

"We do have the advantage that the Americans do not know we have the bomb. They will think the explosion was an accident. They will not be looking for us until we are already in position. That is to our advantage."

"How will they believe we have the one bomb, then?"

"Once we are in position, our government will give them the PAL code that arms the bomb, along with its serial number. They will believe that."

Kim leaned back on the rocking bench they were seated on and regarded his commander. "They are going to invade the South?"

Min nodded. "I would assume they are already mobilizing to do so."

"Do they really think we can succeed?"

"We have so far," Min answered evenly.

Kim shook his head. "But it is a long way from here to Hawaii. And then—"

"I know," Min said, cutting his XO off. "I know all that. But it is too late to question anything. We must do as ordered."

Vicinity of the Citadel, Antarctica

"What about radiation?" Tai asked. The crater that had been the Citadel lay two hundred feet away. The edges of the crater were jagged, and Vaughn had no desire to get any closer. Not only was the Citadel gone, but also all the bodies and evidence of the base. Along with the portion of the Golden Lily that had been secreted there. And the nerve agent and other weapons of mass destruction.

Vaughn was tightening down the straps on his rucksack. "We escaped the initial radiation because of the shielding of the reactor room. Residual is already up in the atmosphere and will follow the winds. We're all right."

Finished with his pack, Vaughn checked the others, making sure they were ready to go. Go where? was the key question, Vaughn realized. He'd been so happy to make it out of that dark hole that he'd thought of little else. Now, with the wind lashing his face and the cold latching onto his bones, he tried to figure out a course of action. "Let's see if the plane might have escaped the blast." He pointed at the white fog on the other side of the crater. "We'll walk around."

"But none of us can fly," Logan protested.

"I'm not thinking of flying," Vaughn replied. "I want to see if the radio is still intact. It's most likely the EMP has destroyed its circuits, but it's worth taking a look." He looked at the three of them. "Are you ready?"

They set out. It took fifteen minutes to circumnavigate the crater with a good two hundred meters of safety margin. Vaughn was surprised at how easy it was to walk on the ice. A thin layer of blown snow covered the ice cap, and he felt like he was just sliding along, the brittle snow barely covering the toes of his boots. The problem was the wind and the snow that blew with it. He had to keep his head bowed and the hood of the parka pulled in close. He was walking like that when he spotted where the plane had been parked.

"Shit," he muttered. "Sons of bitches. They blew the goddamn plane. Either that or the bomb blast did this. Either way it doesn't matter."

He lifted the edge of the plane's hood. There was little to indicate that a plane had even been here. Scattered pieces of metal littered the ice.

"Where now?" Tai asked.

Vaughn didn't say a word, and it was Logan who answered. "The nearest base is Russkaya, about seventy miles to the northeast."

"Let's get going then," Tai said.

"No." It was all coming together for Vaughn now. "No. We go after them."

"After who?" Logan asked, but Tai already knew the answer.

"The Koreans."

"But how?" Tai asked. "We don't know which way they've gone."

Vaughn considered that for a few seconds. His advice that they stay in the reactor room had both saved them and almost doomed them. "They're heading for the coast," he finally answered.

"How do you know that?" Logan wanted to know.

"Because that's where I would go. It's their only option. They didn't land a plane in that storm even if they did jump in." He pointed at the ground. "And that's the direction their tracks go in."

Tai turned and saw the tread marks leading off to the north.

"But they're probably very far ahead of us." Logan protested. "And they've got a vehicle."

Vaughn agreed. "They must have taken one or two of the over-snow vehicles from the storage shed. They're certainly not pulling that bomb with manpower. They had a big head start and are moving much faster than we can on foot. Nevertheless we have to go after them. If they're heading for the coast, that's the direction we need to go."

"What do you mean 'need'?" Logan asked.

"They've already shown they are willing to use the bomb," Vaughn pointed out. "That changes things. We have to assume they have the other and plan to use it. It's up to us to stop them."

Logan turned away from the two of them. Vaughn looked at Tai. "How do you feel? The three of you could stay here. The weather seems a little better. I'm sure they'll be flying someone out here in the next twenty-four hours."

"I'm with you," Tai quietly said as she stepped out to Vaughn's side.

"I am too," Burke said, moving beside her.

Logan waved his arms, gesturing toward the terrain around. "It's crazy. We could pass a quarter mile away from them and miss them. And what will we do if we do find them?"

"We stop them," Vaughn answered, slinging the rifle over his shoulder.

Logan looked into Vaughn's eyes. "I say we stay here. We go wandering out there on the ice cap, we might never make it alive, regardless of whether we run into the Koreans or not."

"What happened to the guy who wanted to attack them in the base?" Vaughn asked.

"That was before they fired off a nuke," Logan argued. "These guys are crazy."

Vaughn put his pack on. "You make your decision now."

"Tai, Burke, please stay here." Logan pleaded.

Tai picked up her pack. "We need to try, Logan."

Logan reluctantly shouldered his pack.

Vaughn's voice was flat. "All right. We go after them. But you three have to listen to me and do what I say without asking questions. This is my area of expertise."

They all nodded.

Vaughn pointed. "This way." With long strides he was off into the blowing snow, Tai at his side, Burke and Logan falling in behind.

CHAPTER 14

Pentagon

General Morris rubbed his forehead as Hodges came into the situation room. His conversation with the President had not gone well. The Secretary of Defense was on his way back from the West Coast to take over the operation here, but in the meantime the monkey was on Morris's back.

"We have the signature of the blast, sir. Fits the profile for a nuclear weapon."

"So how the hell did they end up at this place?" Morris demanded. "Who put them there?"

"I assume the same person who built the base, sir," Hodges replied.

"Anything from your guest?"

"Not yet, sir, but we'll get something. We're close. From what we've received so far, I would say that it appears the Citadel was a privately funded enterprise using government support."

Morris closed his eyes. He didn't doubt that for a moment. Billions of dollars a year were spent by the government on various secret projects. Who was to say that some influential civilian couldn't do the same thing, especially if that civilian had the proper connections in the military industrial complex? "I want a name."

"Yes, sir."

Morris opened his eyes as the door opened, and an imposing figure in a medal-bedecked uniform stomped in.

Morris stood. "General Kolstov. Welcome."

The Russian general wasted no time on a greeting. "I understand there is a problem. A nuclear one."

Since the President had informed the Kremlin of the source of the nuclear explosion that the Russians had also picked up, a liaison officer from the embassy representing all of the Confederation of Independent States of the former Soviet Union—commonly referred to simply as the CIS—had been assigned to the Pentagon to monitor the situation. It was part of the nuclear disarmament and control treaty both countries had signed the previous year: any incident involving nuclear weapons was to be monitored by both the U.S. and the CIS to ensure that there was no confusion or misunderstandings that might lead to unfortunate consequences.

Morris wasn't sure which he hated worse—having a civilian superior riding herd on him or the presence of General Kolstov in the Pentagon War Room. Still, he had to admit it was a good idea. He knew that if his people had picked up an unknown nuclear explosion in Antarctica that the Russians said was an accident—especially an accident that so far had very little logical explanation—he'd sure as shit want to have someone sitting in on their investigation of it. Morris wasn't sure he'd buy the story of two bombs lost overboard and now suddenly reappearing at a mysterious base. He wasn't sure General Kolstov was going to buy it either.

Ford Mountain Range, Antarctica

The SUSV stuttered, pivoting to the right and not moving forward. Min grabbed the dashboard and turned a quizzical look at his driver. "What is wrong?"

"I don't know, sir. It is not responding."

"Stop." Min zipped his coat up and then opened his door. He climbed down to the snow. The answer stared him in the face. The track on the right side was gone. Min peered back. It was thirty feet to the rear, laid out in the snow like a long, thick metal snake. One of the linchpins holding it together had snapped in the bitter cold.

Kim joined him. "What now, sir?"

Min's reply was short. "We walk."

Kim didn't question. He rapped on the door to the rear cargo compartment and yelled in his instructions. Ho and Sun threw gear out. Lee came out of the driver's seat and joined them around the sled. They unhooked the tow rope and rigged it to be pulled by men.

Kim used his last satchel on the SUSV. The party moved out to the north, all men straining in the harness. Twenty minutes out a sharp crack from behind told of the destruction of the vehicle.

Vaughn's anger had started, low in his gut, from the minute he'd watched Smithers get shot. He'd been on the other side of the kind of ruthlessness the Koreans were displaying, but it had been for a better cause then. Or at least he'd thought it had been a better cause.

He was channeling his anger into his legs, pumping them as the miles passed beneath them. He was more than willing to go on without rest, but he knew that wasn't smart. His plan was to halt the party every fifty minutes for ten minutes of rest. Every other hour he would break out his small stove and cook up something hot—soup or coffee. Initially they would go slower that way, but in the long run they would cover more miles. Years of bitter experience in Special Forces with the merciless weight of a rucksack on his back had taught him that. It was the long haul that was important here.

They'd continued to follow the trace of tracks in the snow: two treads and a deep impression in the middle. Occasionally the trail would disappear as blown snow obscured the ice, but it was easy to pick up again. The Koreans were heading due north as quickly as the terrain would allow. Vaughn didn't allow himself to dwell on the fact that they were probably moving two to three times faster than he was.

"Does the sun shine all the time?" Kim asked as the five men huddled together next to the large sled, trying to share some warmth during the short break Min gave them every so often.

Min looked up. The storm had lessened two hours ago, and visibility had increased to almost a mile. "We will have no night." Min's best estimate was that they were less than five miles from the coast. The only map he had was one he'd torn out of a world atlas stolen from a schoolroom prior to their departure from Indonesia. It was totally useless for navigating. He was

offsetting his compass based on where the map said
magnetic south was, but wasn't totally confident that
he was taking the quickest possible route.

His main goal was to head north—as best he could
tell—and also stay on the lowest possible ground, skirt-
ing around mountains. Despite the bomb's weight, the
sled pulled easily behind the five men—as long as they
were on level ground. They'd just spent the past forty-
five minutes traversing back and forth, getting the sled
up and over a large foothill— making only two hundred horizontal meters in the process.

Min directed them to the left, along the edge of a
massive wall of ice that shot up into the sky, where
the polar ice cap had ruptured itself against rock. He
hoped they could continue bypassing such formations
and make it to the coast. They'd already lost quite a bit
of time hauling the sled.

"Let's move," he ordered.

The five men staggered to their feet and placed themselves in harness.

Airspace, Pacific Ocean

"I'm awfully thirsty down here, big brother."

"Roger. I've got what you need."

The KC-10 stratotanker dwarfed the MC-130 Combat Talon as it jockeyed into position, closing in, less
than forty feet above and to the front of the smaller aircraft. In the rear of the tanker, seated in a glass bubble,
the boom operator toyed with his controls, directing
the drogue boom toward the refuel probe on the nose
of the Combat Talon. As the cup fit, he flicked a button
on his yoke, locking the seal.

"We're in," he said into his mike, verbally confirming what the pilot 120 feet in front in the cockpit could already see on his control panel. "Pumping."

The two planes were at 25,000 feet, cruising at 350 miles per hour, yet maintaining their relative relationship with less than a two-foot variance at any moment. Jet fuel surged through the hose, filling up the almost dry tanks of the Combat Talon. The umbilical cord stayed in place for two minutes.

"I'm full down here, big brother."

"Roger. That'll be fourteen ninety-five." The drogue separated, and the KC-10 started gaining altitude, pulling away.

"Roger. Do you take checks?"

The stratotanker banked hard right, turning back toward home. "Your credit is good. Good luck and good hunting."

Surprised, the pilots in the cockpit of the MC-130 looked at each other. "Good hunting" was the traditional Air Force war cry for fighter pilots, not transport aircraft. But they realized the pilot of the KC-10 knew the same thing they did: their weapons were the men in the back half of the cargo hold. The 130 pilot keyed his mike. "I'll pass that on. Out."

Ford Mountain Range, Antarctica

Vaughn worked the bolt of the M-1, checking that it hadn't frozen. He pushed down on the top bullet, making sure the spring was still functioning correctly. Looking up, he noticed Tai watching him, her eyes framed by the frosted edge of her hood.

"Do you think we'll catch them?" she asked. He could see that she was shivering. That was bad—he needed to balance the rests with the loss of heat better.

It was hard for him to factor in the others' needs with his desire to catch the Koreans. Logan and Burke were wrapped together in a sleeping bag, trying to conserve their warmth.

"Not unless we get lucky."

"Then why do you want to go after them?" The words puffed out.

Vaughn laid the rifle across his knees. His face hurt from the cold, and the skin on his cheek felt like crinkled paper as he spoke. "Several reasons. I didn't see much sense in doing anything before—I figured we'd get out alive if we did nothing, and I also figured these guys would get caught. I was wrong on both counts: we're lucky to be alive, and these people are getting away. That's two mistakes, and I don't want to go for number three."

"But what can we do if we catch them?"

"I'll figure that out when we get there," Vaughn replied, which quite frankly was the truth. "We have to catch them first." He got to his feet. "All right. Let's move out."

"We're never going to catch them," Logan said, peering out from his bag. "I say we stay still—we're losing too much energy walking."

Vaughn held back his anger. "Listen. If you want to, you can head back to the Citadel and camp out in the reactor room. Or you can head for the Russian base. Or you can stay here. I don't care. You do whatever you want to." He stood. "Time to move out." Tai stood and started putting her gear in her backpack. Burke slid out of the sleeping bag.

Surprisingly, it was Burke who talked to Logan. "We can't split up now. It would be too dangerous. Come on, Logan, let's go."

"We should have gone after them at the base like I wanted to," Logan complained. "We'll never catch them here. We need a break. We've been moving for over eight hours now."

Vaughn started walking along the track, and Tai moved with him. After twenty meters he looked over his shoulder. Burke was talking to Logan, his head bent close next to him. Vaughn went another twenty meters and looked again. They were following.

Airspace, South Pacific Ocean

Major Bellamy listened through the headset as the pilot updated him on the situation. "The weather over the target is still too rough for you all to jump in. We're going to head to McMurdo Station and let you all jump there—the winds are much lower. We've received word that there will be a platform there that you will load onto, and that will take you out to the target."

"What kind of platform?" Bellamy asked.

"Unknown. That's all I've got."

"Roger."

Bellamy put the headset down. They'd received the news about the nuclear explosion several hours ago, and Bellamy hadn't been thrilled with the idea of jumping right in on top of that. As far as he knew, he was supposed to just secure the site, but the information he was getting over the radio was confusing. The biggest unanswered question was why had the bomb gone off?

Antarctic

Walking along with her head bowed, eyes following the trail, Tai almost tripped over the tread lying there.

She looked up and saw the circle of debris from the tractor twenty meters ahead.

"What happened?" she asked. "Did they have an accident?"

"Looks like they threw a track," Vaughn answered. "They must have destroyed the tractor, and they're on foot now, pulling the bomb."

"We might catch them, then," Tai said, feeling a surge of adrenaline.

"Yes." Vaughn didn't even bother to look at the others. He walked past the wreckage and found the furrow on the other side formed by the sled the bomb was on. He set out at an even quicker pace.

8th Army Headquarters, Seoul, South Korea

The staff was assembled for the daily 1000 briefing. The mood in the war room was deadly serious as the speaker approached the podium. General Patterson sat in the first row, facing the front. The G-2 was the lead briefer, as always, and today he had a rapt audience.

"Sir, unless there is a drastic change in data trends, we are currently less than two hours from going to level three threat. Our intelligence indicates the entire Korean People's Army is mobilizing. There are also unconfirmed reports that first and second stage reserves are being given their mobilization orders. The South Korean 4th Infantry Division has destroyed one infiltration tunnel in their sector of the DMZ north of Kumsong when the exit was opened." The G-2's pointer slapped the map. "No report on ROK or PKA losses."

Patterson ran a hand through his thinning gray hair. Since taking command of the 8th Army a year ago, he'd known he was in the most volatile military theater in the world that wasn't yet hot. The two countries were still technically at war, over fifty years after most people thought the Korean War had ended. In those fifty-odd years, thousands of people—Korean and American—had died in what the politicians liked to term "incidents." But what was brewing now was no incident.

The accord that the two countries had signed in '92, promising better relations, had barely been worth the paper it was printed on. As long as Kim Il Sung ruled, there would be no united Korea other than under their rule.

"No indication of any drawback?" the G-3 asked.

"No, sir."

Patterson wasn't willing to wait two hours. Most of his combat troops were based less than an hour's flight time from the border, vulnerable to a quick air strike. While the carefully mapped intelligence plan for North Korean mobilization and preparation for war was accurate, Patterson also knew that there had been a very good intelligence plan in 1941 in Hawaii too. It hadn't worked too well.

Patterson had authority to go to level three. Two required presidential approval. He had been here long enough to know one thing. The North Koreans were determined to go through with this, especially if Kim Il Sung was dying.

"All U.S. forces will go to level three. I will inform my South Korean counterpart and the Pentagon."

Ford Mountain Range, Antarctica

"Hold on!" Min yelled as he felt the rope give way through his gloves. Lieutenant Kim and Corporal

Lee—at the tail end of the sled—wedged their bodies behind it to keep it from sliding back down the hundred-foot incline they had just laboriously negotiated.

"Pull," Min exhorted Sun and Ho, and they tried to get a better grip on the icy rope in the front. Ho slipped, and that did it—the rope burned out of Min's grip, its entire weight bearing down on the two men on the rear. Lee screamed as the eight hundred pounds of weight snapped the leg he'd wedged up against the lip of the sled. Kim threw himself out of the way, and the sled ran over Lee's twisted leg and rocketed to the bottom of the incline before finally turning over.

Min slid his way down the hill to Lee. He didn't need to probe for the injury in Lee's thigh—white bone had pierced through the many layers of clothes and was exposed to the brutal cold.

Kim joined him, and they looked at each other over the injury. Lee's face was twisted as he forced himself not to scream again.

"We can pull him on the sled," Kim weakly suggested.

Min was angry at his executive officer for even saying that. With five men they had barely been able to keep pulling the sled. Now they were down to four.

Min slowly stood and took a deep breath.

"I will take care of it, sir," Kim said, obviously realizing the foolishness of his earlier comment.

"No." Min put his mittened hand on Kim's shoulder. "I am the leader. It is my responsibility." He looked down. "Do you wish for some time?"

Lee shook his head and closed his eyes. Min pulled his AK-47 up from where it hung across his back and slipped his index finger into the trigger finger in his mitten. He fired twice, both in the head, then turned and walked away. Behind him, Kim pulled two thermite grenades off his harness. He grabbed Lee's weapon, then placed one grenade on top of where Lee's face had been prior to the shots and one on his chest. He pulled both pins and followed his commander.

They went to the bottom of the hill. The puff and glow from the thermite grenades flickered on the incline above them as they struggled to right the sled. The fire had long burned out by the time they accomplished that and started the sled back up the hill, using longer traverses this time to prevent a repeat of the accident.

South Pacific Ocean

The flight deck of the *Kitty Hawk* was packed with rows of aircraft. F-14 Tomcats, E-2 Hawkeyes, S-3A Vikings, and F-18 Hornets competed for valuable parking space. On the port side of that crowded deck, the elevator from the first level hangar lifted into place smoothly, bringing up the only aircraft the carrier had just one of.

The most unusual thing immediately noticeable about the aircraft as it reached deck level was that the two engines at the end of each wing were pointing straight up, with massive propellers horizontal to the gray steel deck. The aircraft remained on the elevator as it came to a halt. Slowly, the two blades began turning in opposite directions.

After a minute of run-up, the aircraft shuddered and the wheels separated from the deck. Sliding slightly left, the aircraft gained altitude as the swiftly moving ship passed beneath. At sufficient height, the propellers slowly began switching orientation, moving from horizontal to vertical as the entire engine rotated and the airframe switched from helicopter mode to airplane. When the engine nacelles on the wingtips locked in place facing forward, the CV-22 Osprey caught up with the *Kitty Hawk* and passed it, racing ahead for Antarctica, 1,900 miles away.

The tilt rotor operation of the Osprey made it the most valuable and unique transport aircraft ever built. Congressional budget cuts and interservice squabbling had killed the program back in 1990, but this particular aircraft was one of eight that had been produced by Bell-Boeing during the original prototype construction. The eight had been deployed to the various carrier groups, flown by Marine Corps pilots, to allow maximum flexibility of use. That innovative deployment idea for an original plane was now paying dividends.

Ford Mountain Range, Antarctica

Tai sensed something different and halted. She peered ahead, trying to figure out what it was that had alerted her when she realized that it was the lack of something, rather than the presence, that had caught her attention. She turned around and looked back—Burke and Logan were almost a hundred meters behind them and moving very slowly. She had no idea how long she and Vaughn had been pulling away from them. It had been the lack of the sound of their shuffling feet on the ice that she had finally missed in her single-minded efforts to keep up with Vaughn.

"Hold it," she called out to Vaughn.

He turned. "What?"

Tai pointed, and together they retraced their tracks.

"What's the matter?" Tai asked Burke when they came up to them.

He pointed at Logan, who was shivering uncontrollably. "He says he can't feel his feet."

"Sit down," Vaughn ordered Logan.

Vaughn shrugged off his backpack and knelt down next to him. Logan's skin was white, and he was not fully aware of his environment. His lips were pale blue and he was shivering uncontrollably: the early symptoms of hypothermia. If allowed to progress much further, Logan would go into true hypothermia, and Vaughn knew he couldn't do anything then—not in this environment.

"Get in your sleeping bag," Vaughn ordered Burke. "Zip your bag with his and try to get him warmed up."

Logan looked right through him. He started walking off, back in the direction they had come from. Vaughn stood and caught up with him. "What are you doing?"

"I'm going to get help," was the barely coherent reply.

Vaughn grabbed his arm and dragged him back. He took Logan's backpack off and pulled out the sleeping bag. "Get in this. You're not in any shape to go looking for help."

He quickly dug through Logan's backpack and pulled out his bag and sleeping pad. He laid them out, unzipped the bag as well as Burke's, and helped them into it. Then he pulled out his portable stove as Tai crawled into her own bag to keep warm. He pumped it up, squeezed starter gel around the nozzle and lit it. After getting it running smoothly, he pulled his canteen from the vest pocket of his parka and poured water into his canteen cup.

Vaughn made a cup of instant soup and split it between Logan and Burke. He forced it down Logan's throat, getting the warm liquid to his stomach. The early stages of hypothermia consisted of circulation to the hands and feet being reduced as the body tried to maintain temperature in the vital organs. Vaughn knew that no matter how well insulated those extremities now were, they would not keep warm unless the central core of the body was warmed. He also knew that it wasn't the cold that had precipitated this, but lack of fluid intake.

It was now a grim equation—they had to raise Logan's heat production higher than his heat loss using body warmth. "Keep him warm," Vaughn ordered Burke. The large black man nodded from within the sleeping bags. Vaughn himself could feel the cold gnawing through his joints, so he placed his bag next to Tai's and crawled in. They had to give up an hour or two of traveling to ensure that they could keep going.

"What are you doing?" Tai mumbled as Vaughn pressed up against her.

He didn't say anything, wrapping his body around hers, and with great difficulty he managed to get the two bags zipped together. He could feel her drawing off his warmth like a heat vampire.

"You need to stay awake for a little while," he exhorted her. "At least until we get your blood circulating properly. You're not too far away from going hypothermic yourself. Then you can rest."

"Too tired," she mumbled.

Vaughn considered the situation. They needed to get their core body temperatures stable before they could move again. Despite the time pressure of wanting to catch up to the North Koreans, he accepted the reality that they had to stop for a while.

Vaughn forced himself to spoon around Tai and wait. After half an hour he knew she was over the worst of it,

and he felt the desire to get moving again. They needed
to leave Burke and Logan behind and move ahead on
their own. Vaughn could feel the time clock going.
How far ahead were the Koreans?

But taking over from all that resolve was his exhaustion. He knew that he himself wasn't too far away from
going hypothermic. His hands were already flirting
with frostbite. Aw fuck it, he decided, even while another part of his mind screamed *no*—an hour or two
of rest would be worth it if he could move faster. He
hugged Tai closer, closed his eyes and felt her head
nestle against his shoulder.

Pentagon

Secretary of Defense Torreta did not appear to be
pleased to be sitting in the situation room at ten at night
after a nonstop flight back from the West Coast. General Morris ran a hand along the stubble of his beard
as the Secretary gestured for him to continue with his
situation update.

"The Combat Talon is three hours out from Mc-
Murdo Base. The Osprey has just taken off from the
Kitty Hawk. It will arrive at McMurdo in five hours.
The Special Forces soldiers will cross-load to the Os-
prey and fly out to the target site."

"We still have no imagery of what happened there?"
Torreta inquired.

"No, sir. The weather is clearing, but the site itself is
still cloud covered. We only have a viewing opportunity by satellite every three hours as it passes over."

Torreta glanced at the notes his aide had prepared for
him. "What's the problem in Korea?"

Morris frowned at the change in subject. "Intelligence has picked up enough North Korean activity to justify going to a level three alert."

"Yes, yes, I know that." Torreta replied testily. "But what's this message about the *Kitty Hawk* Carrier Group from the 8th Army commander?"

Morris hated airing conflicts in front of civilians. "General Patterson wants the group to move north in order to be in better position to support him if something occurs in the peninsula."

"Does the man understand we have a nuclear problem?" Torreta demanded.

"No, sir. That information is under a need-to-know basis."

"Well, I don't want to see any more messages like this. One problem at a time. The President is not happy. He's already had to talk to the CIS president about this incident, and that has proved to be somewhat embarrassing as he doesn't have all the answers himself. I want this mess secured and cleaned up. Do I make myself clear?"

"Yes, sir." Morris had long ago learned not to argue with his civilian superiors, but he disagreed with the present prioritizing of events. This Korean thing was much more significant than Torreta was giving it credit. Since the war in Iraq he felt people were getting much too focused on the wrong things and complacent about the potential for war in other locations. Korea had been hot for over fifty years, and sooner or later the simmering would break out into flames.

Morris looked over his shoulder at the electronic wall map that represented significant military—U.S. and foreign—deployments throughout the world. He had a feeling he was missing something very important.

Ice Pack, 20 Miles Off the Ruppert Coast, Antarctica

The freighter picked its way through the ice, barely crawling at three knots. Every so often it had to back its way out of a dead end and try to slip left or right. The captain was in constant communication with his shivering lookout eighty feet above the bridge in the crow's nest, trying to find a route through the piles of ice. Occasionally, the captain would use the reinforced bow of the ship to smash through thinner ice, but large chunks, some hundreds of meters in width, were more than a match for his steel ship. Those had to be bypassed.

The horizon far ahead was a mass of clouds, but the captain knew that if the clouds lifted, he would soon be able to see the shore. So far his radio operator had not heard a single transmission on the designated frequency. The captain hoped that the people he was to pick up were ready for him because he did not want to sit in the ice pack waiting for them. Ships had been crushed as the ice froze around them. He wanted to move in and out as quickly as possible and get this mission over with.

Ford Mountain Range, Antarctica

Vaughn opened his eyes and tried to orient himself. He felt strangely warm, which was a very nice feeling. He twitched his fingers and was surprised to find them wrapped around a body. Then it all came back to him—stopping, climbing in the bag with Tai to warm her up, talking. He must have dozed off. The thought of giving up the warmth of the bag was extremely discouraging.

Vaughn unzipped the bag and crawled out. His movements woke Tai, who blearily opened her eyes.

"What's up?"

"Get your boots on before they freeze up," he told her. "They're in the waterproof bag near your stomach. We need to get moving."

He peered up—the sky was clearing. The sun hadn't broken through yet, but the clouds were much higher, and he could see farther along the ice than at any period since the storm had started. The wind had also died down. Vaughn checked his watch. They'd been out for almost two hours. He wasn't happy about losing that time, but he'd had no choice.

He glanced over to the other sleeping bag lying there on the ice. There was no movement from Logan or Burke.

"Wake up!" he called out as he started packing his stuff up.

"Oh my God!" Burke cried out as he scrambled out of the bag.

Vaughn rushed over. Logan wasn't moving. His eyes were staring at him wide-open, and it took Vaughn a second before he realized they were totally unfocused and glassy. The pupils in the center were black orbs looking into the depths of wherever Logan had allowed himself to be dragged.

Vaughn looked up with a grim face. "He's dead."

Burke was shaking, but not from the cold. "You mean he died there right next to me?"

Vaughn zipped up the sleeping bag, closing it over Logan's face. "Yes," he replied, and looked at the inert sleeping bag. There was only one way they could atone for this. "Let's go."

Burke looked at him with wide eyes. "We're just going to leave him here?"

Vaughn finished stuffing his sleeping bag into his backpack. "There's nothing else we can do. We can't haul the body."

The increasing visibility made Min pessimistic about making it to the coast, as it revealed a massive ridge lying directly across their path. There was no way around it. The ice rose in moderately steep waves, up over a thousand feet for the next three kilometers.

He had given his men a one-hour break earlier, but it had done little to restore the energy they were burning pulling the sled and fighting off the cold. He could sense his men looking at him and the ridge, their eyes shifting from one to the other. Not a word was said.

Min leaned forward, the rope around his waist pulling tight, and the other men joined and began to traverse to the right, angling their way uphill.

Airspace, McMurdo Station

The MC-130 Combat Talon leveled out over the Ross Ice Shelf, boring straight in for Mount Erebus, twenty miles away. In the rear, Major Bellamy checked the rigging of the static lines for the two bundles, one hooked to each cable. The bundles were tied down on the back ramp, and Bellamy's men were standing now, parachutes on their back, just short of the edge of the ramp.

They all felt the plane slow down, and the loadmaster looked at Bellamy. "Three minutes out."

A gap appeared up in the top part of the rear of the aircraft, and freezing air swirled in. The back ramp leveled off, while the top part ascended up into the tail, leaving a large open space. Bellamy stared out. The view was spectacular, with the entire Ross Ice Shelf laid out below to the east.

"One minute!" the loadmaster yelled through the scarf wrapped about his face, trying to be heard above the roar of engines and air.

"One minute," Bellamy relayed to his men, all hooked up to the left cable. He edged out, right behind the bundle. The red light glowed up in the darkness of the upper tail structure.

"Stand by!" the loadmaster yelled as he leaned over one of the bundles with a knife in his hand as another Air Force man did the same on the other side.

The light flashed green, and the loadmaster severed the nylon band holding the bundle down. It immediately was sucked out the rear of the plane. The other bundle went out at almost the same time. Bellamy waddled out after it, hands over his reserve, chin tucked into his chest.

He felt like he was passing straight through the static line and deployment bag of the bundle as he stepped off the edge of the ramp. Three seconds of free fall were followed by the snap of the chute deploying.

Bellamy guided himself by the two bright red parachutes of the bundles as he descended. As the ice rushed up, he stared straight out at the horizon and bent his knees. With a grunt he hit the ice.

Gathering in his chute, Bellamy watched as the rest of his men hit in a long line of white parachutes along the track of the aircraft. He could also see a large snow tractor rumbling toward him, pulling a sled. The tractor pulled up, and two men hopped off, one wearing an Air Force parka and the other in civilian garb, sporting a large beard.

The military man introduced himself first. "I'm Lieutenant Colonel Larkin, and this is Dr. O'Shaugnesy, McMurdo Station leader. We—"

"What is your purpose here?" O'Shaugnesy interrupted.

Bellamy blinked and looked at the civilian, then at Colonel Larkin. "Didn't you brief him?"

Larkin wearily nodded. "I briefed him."

"If you expect me to believe you and your men are conducting rescue practice, then you must take me for a fool," O'Shaugnesy snorted. "Do you have any weapons with you?"

Bellamy spread his empty hands wide. "Of course not." Asshole, he thought. O'Shaugnesy and the entire scientific community at McMurdo were almost totally dependent on support from the U.S. military, yet they acted as if they owned the place. Bellamy had not been thrilled about putting all his weapons in the bundles, but had followed his orders. One of these days public relations was going to destroy a mission.

Larkin interposed himself between the two. "Your other aircraft is en route, Major. It should arrive in about four hours. In the meanwhile, we'll put you up in the airstrip control tower." He turned to O'Shaugnesy. "Doctor, I did you a courtesy by obliging your request and bringing you out here. I ask that you not harass Major Bellamy and his men. They will be out of your station as soon as possible."

Under the distrusting eye of O'Shaugnesy, Bellamy's team gathered together and loaded the two bundles on the sled. The men jumped on board, and then they all moved out for the main base, three miles away.

Ice Pack, 8 Miles off the Ruppert Coast, Antarctica

"This is as far as we can go," the captain informed Fatima. The bow of the freighter was securely wedged in ice, and less than a hundred meters to the front a large block of ice that had broken off a glacier last season and slowly made its way out into the ocean blocked the way.

The captain knew he could probably do some more maneuvering—trying to find the thin ice—but he also had to be able to get back out, and he felt he was as far in as he could go and still be able turn around.

Fatima stood next to him, peering out the glass of the bridge at the mountains that now loomed in the near distance. They looked less than a mile away, but the captain knew they were farther—he just didn't tell Fatima that. A large glacier, probably the same one that had spawned the block just in front of them, split the mountains to the right front.

"All right. We wait." Fatima turned and went back to his cabin.

Far South Pacific Ocean

With the assistance of the hydraulic catapult, the E-2 Hawkeye roared off the deck of the *Kitty Hawk* and dipped down below deck level, then rapidly gained altitude as it headed southeast. Upon reaching 10,000 feet altitude, the twenty-four-foot diameter radome that sat on the top of the fuselage began turning, at a rate of six revolutions per minute. Inside the fuselage, the three controllers watched their screens as an area three hundred miles out in all directions from the aircraft was displayed before them. In three hours the Citadel would be in range.

Vicinity Ruppert Coast, Antarctica

They were three-quarters of the way up the ridge when Min finally called a halt. It was only another kilometer straight-line distance to the top, but the wide traverses would more than triple that distance.

"Rest," Min ordered. "I will be back shortly." He had to know whether they were at the coast or not. He could tell that dedication to duty only went so far. His men were at the limits of their capabilities. They needed some positive news.

Leaving his three men huddled together next to the sled, Min untied the rope from his waist and headed straight up the ridge, ignoring the screaming pain of exhaustion in his thighs. His breath crackled in the brittle air as he made his way to the top.

As he climbed, his thoughts turned to home, a place he had a feeling he would never see again. Even if they made it to the freighter—if the ship was there—and the ship made it to Hawaii … and they managed to infiltrate with the bomb … and—

Min stopped that train of thought. He thought of his mother and regretted never having married so his mother would have a daughter-in-law to take care of her in her old age. As an only son, his dedication to country had taken him away from his family, leaving his parents alone.

The top was not much farther. Min slipped and fell, almost tumbling back down the way he had come, but he dug the metal folding stock of his AK-47 into the ice and stopped himself. Getting to his feet, he covered the remaining distance.

Cresting the ridge, he stopped and stared, his heart lifting. The ocean—at least he assumed it was the ocean under all that ice—was less than four kilometers away. Sweeping in from his left and descending to the ocean was a large glacier.

Min stared for a long time, then his eyes focused in on a black speck just to the side of a large iceberg. The ship! It was far out on the ice sheet but within sight. He turned and headed back down the slope.

Vicinity Ruppert Coast, Antarctica

"Look!" Vaughn exclaimed.

Tai squinted and peered through red-rimmed eyes. She had no idea what he was pointing at. In fact, she had a feeling she was in a dream—a very bad one at that. She wished she could dream of warmth and comfort and lying in front of a fireplace with—

"There." Vaughn grabbed her and pointed again. "Near the top of the ridge of ice."

Tai seemed to remember lying safe and warm in a pair of strong arms. Was that a dream too? Or had that been reality and this a dream? Which was which? Then she saw it too. Tiny black figures against the white background, just below the top. An oblong shape on the ice to their left rear. Reality came flooding back.

"Is it them?"

"Yes." Vaughn's voice held an edge she had never heard before.

"How far away do you think they are?"

"It's hard to tell. Maybe four, five miles."

It had seemed closer than that to Tai. Four or five miles sounded like forever. "Can we catch them?"

"It depends on how far away the coast is," Vaughn replied. "They've got the high ground on us." Instead of immediately running off toward the Koreans like she expected him to, he turned and looked at her. "Are you all right?"

"I'm tired and I'm cold. But I can make it." Tai was surprised as soon as she said it, but it was true.

Vaughn's face was wind-burned, and the stubble of a two-day beard competed with the raw flesh for surface area. When he smiled at her, the lines around his eyes and cheeks cut deep divots. He glanced at Burke, who nodded his assent. "All right. Let's go."

They moved out, and the Koreans disappeared from sight as the two approached a small ice ridge. Vaughn was leading the way up when he caught sight of something black off to the right. He headed in that direction.

"What's that in the snow?" Tai asked as she also spotted the unnatural object.

"Wait here," Vaughn told her. He walked forward and stared down for a few brief seconds until he recognized what he was looking at, then quickly turned and bumped into Tai, with Burke standing next to her.

"I told you to wait back there."

"I'm not a child that you can tell what to do and what not to do." Tai looked over his shoulder. "What is that?"

"One of the Koreans. Or what's left of one of them," he replied.

Now she could recognize the pieces of white as bone and the charred flesh. Thankfully, there was no smell. "What could have done that to him?"

"I don't know how he died, but someone put a couple of thermal grenades on the body so it couldn't be identified." Vaughn tapped her on the shoulder. "Let's keep going. This means they'll be moving even slower."

* * *

Min collapsed. Getting to the top of this ridge, pulling the sled, was the hardest thing he had ever done in
his life. His entire body reverberated with pain overlaid
with exhaustion. He lay there panting, feeling the sweat
freeze on his skin. He knew he needed to do something,
but he couldn't. Not now. He wanted to be home again,
lying on the tiled floor of his parents house, feeling the
heat rising through the floor from the burning coal he
had to load every evening, hearing his mother in the
kitchen pounding cabbage, preparing kimchee.

Min roused himself. "The radio," he called out. Ho
pulled a package off the sled and handed it to him. With
fumbling fingers inside his mittens, Min unwrapped
the radio. He hoped it worked. They had wrapped it
in metal foil to protect it from the EMP blast of the
bomb, but he had little faith in the recommendations
of scientists.

He threw the antenna out on the ice. Taking his mittens off, Min swiftly dialed in the correct frequency
and turned the radio on. By the time he put his gloves
back on, he had lost the feeling in all his fingers. A distant part of his mind told him that was bad, very bad.

Using both hands, he pushed the Send on the hand-
set with a palm. "Tiger, this is Wolf. Over."

As each second of silence ticked by, Min's heart fell.

"Tiger, this is Wolf. Over."

"Wolf, this is Tiger. Over."

Min felt a wave of relief. "This is Wolf. We are
within sight. Over."

"Roger." There was a brief break of squelch as if
the other station went off the air. Then the voice came
back. "Do you have the package? Over."

"Yes. Over."

"Roger. We will wait for you. Out."

Airspace, Ross Sea, Antarctica

"What language does that sound like?" the Signal Intelligence operator aboard the E-2 Hawkeye asked the other four men on board as he played back the message he had just intercepted.

He received negative replies from all, although the pilot suggested it was Asian. "Where'd you pick it up from?"

"Low power, high frequency radio coming from the southeast."

"Airborne platform?" the pilot asked.

"Negative. I don't think so—the signal was fixed," the SIGINT operator replied.

"I've got zip on the scope," the radar operator replied. "We're the only thing in the air other than the blip down near McMurdo."

"Relay it back to the ship, maybe they can figure it out," the pilot ordered.

"Roger."

McMurdo Station, Antarctica

The Osprey slowed as its engines switched from horizontal to vertical. Major Bellamy watched as the aircraft slowly settled down in a whirlwind of snow.

"Let's go," he yelled as his men followed him, hauling their two as-yet unopened bundles with them. They crowded into the cargo bay as the crew chief ran out and coordinated the refueling. Hoses were run from the fuel blisters, and JP-4 fuel was pumped in as Bellamy's men settled in. Bellamy went forward into the cockpit.

The pilot looked over his shoulder as Bellamy poked

his head in. "Captain Jones." He nodded at the copilot. "As soon as we're topped off we'll be lifting."

"Have you heard anything about the target site?" Bellamy asked.

The pilot shook his head. "Nothing. We've got a Hawkeye in the air, and it should be in radar range of the site soon. I'm not sure if that will give us anything, but at least we'll know if we're the only ones in the sky."

Bellamy frowned. He'd expected something more.

"We're full," the pilot announced.

Bellamy made his way back to the rear. His men had opened the bundles and were passing out the weapons, each man receiving his according to his specialty and talents: silenced MP-5SD submachine guns, PM sniper rifles, SPAS 12 shotguns, M249 Squad Automatic Weapons (SAW), LAW 80 rocket launchers, and sidearms. If there was anybody left alive at the target site and they were antagonistic, Bellamy's men were ready.

Airspace, Ross Sea, Antarctica

The radar operator stared at his screen. "Shit, there's still nothing out here," he muttered to the man on his left. He'd never seen such a blank screen. Not a single aircraft in a six-hundred-mile radius, the Osprey having disappeared as it landed at McMurdo.

He flipped a switch and the radar went from air to surface. This was a different story. He stared at the screen, trying to make sense out of the jumbled mess. The surface bounce-back was very confusing, even where the sea should be. He was used to a flat reflection where ships stood out in stark relief to the ocean.

Here, ice formations broke that image up into a confusing disarray.

The naval officer slowly started sorting the screen out, trying to see if there was anything identifiable. He fiddled with his controls, adjusting and tuning, like a kid playing a computer game.

"Hey, I've got something here," he told the SIGINT operator. Keying his mike, he relayed his report back to the *Kitty Hawk.* "Big Boot, this is Eye One. We have a surface target, bearing 093 degrees true. Distance, 273 miles. Speed zero. Over."

CHAPTER 15

Ruppert Coast, Antarctica

Min had been tempted to pile his survivors on board the sled and ride the glacier down, but wisdom had prevailed, and they lashed themselves as a human brake to the rear of the sled, keeping the bomb from getting away from them only with great difficulty.

They'd gotten off the glacier less than ten minutes ago, and now they were on top of the ocean, making their way across the ice. In most places it was so thick they couldn't tell the difference between it and the polar cap they'd been on, but in other places the ice thinned out and, with the snow scraped off by the wind, the ocean could be seen below. It was these areas that Min had his men skirt around. He estimated another four to six hours until they arrived at the freighter, which was now hidden by the surface ice.

Pentagon, Alexandria, Virginia

General Morris listened to the intercepted message as he tried to shake the cobwebs of sleep out of his brain. "That language sounds familiar," he remarked as the short exchange played out.

"It's Han Gul—Korean," Hodges informed him.

Morris felt a chill hand caress his spine. "Where did the Hawkeye say this originated from?"

Hodges tapped the map. "Here along the coast due north of the Citadel. It was someone on the shore communicating with a ship the Hawkeye has located as fixed in the ice pack right here, eight miles off the coast."

"Do you have a translation of the message?" Morris asked.

"Yes, sir." Hodges pressed a button on a tape player, and an unemotional voice spoke in English:

Station One: "Tiger, this is Wolf. Over."

Station One: "Tiger, this is Wolf. Over."

Station Two: "Wolf, this is Tiger. Over."

Station One: "This is Wolf. We are within sight. Over."

Station Two: "Roger. Do you have the package? Over."

Station One: "Yes. Over."

Station Two: "Roger. We will wait for you. Out."

"Oh, sweet Jesus," Morris muttered to himself. Then he spoke up: "Do you have an ID on the ship?"

"No, sir. The E-2 is over two hundred miles away and at its fuel limit range. They just have a radar image. They're launching another E-2 right now to replace it and it will be able to get in a bit closer."

Morris turned to the duty officer. "Get the SecDef and General Kolstov here ASAP."

He looked at the situation map. The *Kitty Hawk* was still 1,100 miles from the Citadel, over 1,000 from the freighter. "What's the range on your attack aircraft from the carrier?" he asked the naval duty officer. "More specifically, do you have anything you can put on station over that ship?"

The naval officer didn't even have to consult his notes. "Not yet, sir."

"When, then?"

"We'll be able to launch some Tomcats in about three hours. They won't have much time on station— less than twenty minutes—and they'll have to carry a minimum armament load."

Morris stared at the situation map, the pieces falling in place even though he wasn't sure what they all meant. The North Koreans had one bomb and were still making for the ship. Once they made it on board, it was going to be a very ticklish situation. But it definitely fit in with the alerts they were hearing from the peninsula. Morris wondered what the North Koreans were going to do with one nuclear weapon, but he knew there were a variety of answers, none of them good.

If not for the alert from Area 51, the whole thing might have been overlooked, even the explosion, as no one would have initially thought of a nuclear weapon. The reaction here would have definitely been quite a bit slower. Damn, the sons of bitches almost got away with it, he thought. They still might, he reminded himself.

"How about the Osprey with the Special Forces men?" he asked.

"Just lifted from McMurdo. A little less than three hours out."

"Divert them directly to the coast."

"Yes, sir."

Morris looked up as Kolstov strode in. He idly wondered how the Soviet general managed to look so unruffled after being dragged out of his bunk down the hallway. The uniform was immaculate, and Kolstov's bald head gleamed under the overhead lights.

"I understand you have something new?" His English was perfect also.

"Yes." Morris quickly filled him in on the data picked up by the Hawkeye and then played the translation tape. He concluded with his best estimate of the situation. "I think this has something to do with the mobilization intelligence we are picking up in North Korea."

Kolstov raised an eyebrow. "You did not inform me of the situation in Korea."

"I didn't think it was applicable."

Kolstov nodded. "Yes. Hmm. Well, I was aware of the situation there from my own sources." Morris knew he meant the coded radio messages that poured in and out of the CIS Embassy. He had no doubt that the Russians kept a very close eye on the North Koreans.

"What are you going to do?" Kolstov asked.

"From the message, it appears that the ship is waiting for a party on foot that has one of the bombs. We're going to have to stop it."

"What if the party makes it on board the ship before you can stop it?" Kolstov was looking over Morris's shoulder at the situation board and could easily see that there were no U.S. forces in the immediate vicinity of the ship.

"Then we stop the ship," Morris coldly replied.

"Ah, my American friend. You have no right to stop that ship in international seas."

Morris bristled. He knew they never should have allowed the goddamn Russians in on this. This guy was going to give him bullshit arguments about freedom of navigation when a nuclear weapon was involved. "My job is to get that bomb back."

Kolstov appeared not to have heard. "In fact, my friend, you are not even certain that the package referred to in the message is your lost bomb. What if you attempt to board that ship and you are wrong?"

Morris bit his words off. "They've already detonated one bomb. That proves they are capable of doing it. I have no doubt they will not stop at detonating the second. I will not allow that ship anywhere near a potential target. I am not sure how this is tied in to what is presently happening in North Korea right now, but I am sure there is a connection.

"We have the potential here for all-out war on the Korean peninsula, and I believe your government is in agreement with mine that we don't want that. I am willing to take the chance that I am wrong to stop that ship."

"Ah," Kolstov said. "But what if your boarding that ship constitutes an act of war in the eyes of the North Koreans? What if they are drawing you into a trap?"

That hadn't occurred to Morris. This whole thing was so vague he wasn't sure which end was up. "Maybe," he conceded. "But we're going to make sure."

Kolstov held up a hand, palm out. "My friend, perhaps in the interest of world peace, I might be able to help you with your little problem."

Morris would rather have crawled naked over broken glass for a mile. But he forced a smile and said, "What do you have in mind, my friend?"

Ruppert Coast, Antarctica

"How are you feeling?" Vaughn asked as they all collapsed to their knees on the crest of the ridge.

"Tired," Tai replied.

"Ditto," Burke remarked.

"Are either of you sweating?"

"No."

"No."

"Good. Drink half your canteen. I'll melt some more water in a minute." Vaughn pulled his own canteen out of the flap pocket of his parka—the only place it could be carried and not freeze—and took a deep drink of the chilly water.

He peered down to the ocean, scanning in sections. "Look—out there!"

The ship lay like a black bug miles out in the ice pack.

"Where are the ones on foot? Have they reached it yet?" Tai asked.

"It doesn't appear to be moving, and I don't think they could make it that far this quickly." Vaughn brought his gaze in closer. After a minute he spotted them. "There. See that large square iceberg? To the left and in."

"They're halfway out there." Tai sounded resigned. "We'll never catch them."

The walk up the ridge had just about wiped out Vaughn. A quarter of the way up, seeing Tai occasionally stumbling with exhaustion, he'd taken her pack and strapped it on top of his own. For a little while she'd done all right, but he could tell she was at the limit of her resources.

"You stay here. I'll go after them alone." Vaughn knew if he didn't catch them before they got on the ship, the chase was in vain.

Tai shook her head. "I'll go with you. If it's a choice between being tired and being cold, I choose tired. As long as I keep moving I'll be all right."

"I'm not staying here alone," was Burke's only comment.

Vaughn was too numb to argue. He knew it was up to them to catch the Koreans or else they'd get away. He took the stove out and got it started. He emptied his canteen in the metal cup and placed it on top of the stove. Once the water was boiling, he scooped up ice and melted it, gradually filling his, Tai, and Burke's canteens as they rested.

"Are you ready?" he asked as he put the stove away.

Tai stood. "Do you think we can catch them?"

In reply, Vaughn took two snap links and slipped them through small loops at the end of his twelve-foot length of rope. He reached under Tai's parka and hooked one end to her belt. He hooked the other to Burke's and then himself to the center.

"What's this for?" Tai asked.

Vaughn pointed to the left, where the deceptively smooth surface of the glacier glistened a quarter mile away. "We're going to make up some time going down."

Ruppert Coast, Antarctica

"Ready?"

Tai looked up at Vaughn and weakly nodded. Burke had a death grip around her and didn't say anything. They were both wrapped in a nylon poncho, lying on their back inside a sleeping bag, heads cushioned with their backpack. Vaughn's M-1 was on Tai's chest, her hands wrapped around it.

Vaughn began walking, the rope tightening around

Tai's and Burke's waists, pulling them along on the ice. He accelerated to a jog, the slope helping increase their speed. Satisfied, he flopped down on his stomach, his Gore-Tex parka and pants sliding on the ice.

Linked together, the three tobogganed down the glacier, Vaughn trying to control speed and direction with the point of his entrenching tool. Tai had no doubt that they would be very black and blue if they survived this as they rattled over bumps in the ice.

They were three-quarters of the way down to the coast, Tai too numb to even feel anything anymore, when Vaughn broke through the ice into a crevasse. His yell gave Tai less than a second to react. She did the only thing she could, holding the M-1 up across her body as her feet slammed against the far side of the break. She started sliding down, the rope around her waist dragging her down, and desperately jammed the muzzle of the weapon into the ice. The poncho and sleeping bag fell off and disappeared into the depths. Tai came to a brief halt and then felt a tremendous jar as Vaughn reached the end of her rope and dangled below.

Suddenly there was no more weight on the rope. Tai was still, not believing she was alive. Her feet were pressed up against the far side ice wall, and the rifle, dug into the near side, kept her in a precarious balance in the mouth of the crevasse. Carefully, she looked down below. The crevasse widened and descended into a blue darkness as far as she could see. Vaughn was standing there, ten feet below on a narrow ledge of ice, looking up with wide eyes.

"Vaughn!" she cried out.

"Yeah. Are you all right?" The voice echoed off the walls.

"I can't move!" she replied.

"Hold still! I'm on a small ledge down here. Let me try to climb up. Burke?"

The reply from above echoed down. "Yeah?"

"Are you stable?" Vaughn asked.

"I got my feet dug in. I can hold, but I don't think I can get enough traction to pull the two of you up."

"All right, just hold on, then," Vaughn said.

Tai wasn't about to go anywhere. She could hear Vaughn working with his entrenching tool below her. The minutes passed, and she felt her feet shift on the ice, her heart going to her throat. How far would she fall if she slipped? she wondered. Would the fall kill her or would she lie down there broken but alive, the cold taking the final toll on the way to an icy grave, preserved forever here?

"Hang tough." She heard Vaughn's labored breathing, and out of the corner of her eye she could finally see him moving. He would reach up and dig out a hold in the ice with the shovel and haul himself up. It was a slow process, and she wasn't sure how long she could hold here, her numb hands wrapped around the rifle, all feeling in her feet already gone. She assumed her feet were still at the end of her legs. She knew they weren't moving only because she could feel her knees shivering inside her heavy pants.

Vaughn reached Tai's level, and she carefully turned her head to look at him. He gave her a forced smile. "Some ride, eh?"

He was now wedged like she was—his back and feet against the ice. She watched as he squirmed his way up until he could get over the lip. He disappeared over the forward side, then his head reappeared. "I'm anchored up here with Burke. Ready?"

Tai shook her head. "I can't feel my feet."

Vaughn puffed out a deep breath. "All right. We'll pull you up. When I yell, you pull your feet out. Okay?"

"Can you do it?"

"We'll do it." He was gone.

Tai anxiously waited.

"Ready?"

Tai briefly closed her eyes. "Yes."

"Let go."

Tai tucked her knees in and fell for an interminable split second, and then the rope tightened down on her waist, causing her to exhale sharply and stopping her. She scrabbled at the ice with her dead hands and feet, trying to help Vaughn and Burke as much as she could. Inch by inch she went up until she could slap an arm down on the surface. The pressure on the rope was maintained, and she continued up until she could get her waist over and roll onto the surface.

She lay there, savoring the sight of the open sky. Vaughn crawled up next to her and collapsed, throwing an arm over her and pulling her in tight. "You all right?" he asked.

"Yes," she whispered.

Vaughn leaned over her. "Do you want to go on?"

She got to her feet with great effort. "Yes."

Geneva

"We have the other eleven names," the Senior Assessor informed the High Counsel.

The names were projected on one of the large screens and on the High Counsel's own office screen. All eleven were either very high in the United States government or very rich men.

"They went international," the High Counsel noted as he read one of the names.

"Pablo Escovan," the Senior Assessor noted. "The head of the Mexican drug cartel. The richest man in Mexico."

"This is a mess," the High Counsel said. "Only three of those names are ours. Have you projected courses of action?"

"Yes, sir. With a sixty-four percent recommendation: wipe out Majestic-12."

The High Counsel sighed. "CARVE?" he asked, using an acronym they had developed.

"Criticality," the Senior Assessor began, reciting from the first letter of the acronym. "These men are the members of the group that established the Citadel and kept it secret from us all these years. They have been pursuing their own course of action for over fifty years. If they are gone, Majestic-12 is gone.

"Accessibility. It will be difficult to attack the remaining eleven at the same time under normal circumstances. Some of them are the most heavily guarded people on the planet. However, these are not normal circumstances. Our sources report that at least four that we know of are either en route or already at Area 51. The other seven we don't know about, but we should assume they also will be there shortly. An emergency meeting.

"Recuperability. These are not men who share with underlings. And since they have managed to keep the existence of Majestic-12 from us for this long, we have to assume they have extensive cutouts in place. Thus, if we cut off the head, it is a very high probability there will be no one to take their places.

"Vulnerability. Area 51 is a hard site. Their meeting place is deep underground. However, it is a United States military base. We have access to resources. We can do it.

"Effect. Extensive. Economic turmoil. Political fallout in Washington. We have already alerted our public relations people to prepare for it. The presence of Escovan certainly helps. It will be costly but manageable."

The Senior Assessor fell silent.

"Action is authorized," the High Counsel finally said.

Ruppert Coast, Antarctica

"Come on!" Min exhorted his three exhausted partners. "There is the ship."

The four leaned into the rope, and the sled creaked along the ice, making its way toward the ship, now less than two miles away.

"How close—do you—have to—get?" Tai asked in between puffs of breath as they crossed a high point where two sheets of ice had buckled together.

"A quarter mile at maximum. I'd like to get closer than that," Vaughn replied. They were at least three-quarters of a mile behind the Koreans, and his best estimate was that it was going to be close, very close.

There was also the additional problem of whether the ship, which lay ahead, had weapons on board. If it did, Vaughn had to assume that once he fired on the party pulling the sled, the ship would return fire. He didn't fancy the idea of being caught out on this ice in a running gun battle. That had only one foreseeable conclusion, which wasn't favorable for them.

As they went along, he noticed black spots on the ice, about three hundred meters to the left. He dropped and pulled Tai and Burke down with him, out of sight. An ambush? He peered at the figures until he realized what he was looking at: seals, lying on the ice, near a water hole they'd broken in the ice. It was the first sign of animal life they'd seen.

"There they are!" Fatima exclaimed, pointing off the starboard bow.

The captain trained his telescope in that direction. "There are four men, and they are pulling a sled with something on it."

"I want you to get together a party of men to go out there and help them."

The captain wasn't thrilled with that idea. His men were civilians, and he didn't want to risk them on the ice. As he turned to his executive officer to reluctantly relay the order, his eyes widened.

Seven hundred meters off the port side the ice was erupting, three long black shafts pushing through. The shafts abruptly widened, and a massive black conning tower appeared, tossing the ice aside like child's blocks. It continued to emerge, and the ice behind the tower split to reveal a long black deck that sloped down 150 feet behind the tower. The exposed portion of the vessel was almost as long as the freighter.

"What is that?" Fatima demanded.

"A submarine," the captain replied.

"I know that, you fool," she snapped. "Whose submarine? American?"

"I don't know."

"What should we do?"

The captain turned to look at her. "There is nothing we can do. We wait to see what they"—he nodded at the black hull—"do."

* * *

Min and his men halted, staring past the ship at the submarine. He knew in his heart it was all over. Even if they made it to the ship, the Americans would never let them sail away. He wondered how the plan had failed.

"Sir?" Kim turned to look at him for instructions.

Min turned to look back at his executive officer. "We go to the ship. Quickly."

Four men strained for the ship in a direct line as quickly as they could go.

Vaughn had started sprinting as soon as the submarine began to surface, leaving Tai and Burke behind, yelling at them to stay put. He passed four seals around a small circle of open water, and the distance was now down to five hundred meters. Another two hundred and he could fire.

The present Hawkeye on station was the third one rotated in, as the earlier ones had exhausted their fuel supplies down to what was needed to get back to the *Kitty Hawk*. The radar operator had picked up the sub as soon as the mast breached the ice. Now he was busy guiding in the two F-14 Tomcats from the *Kitty Hawk* and the Osprey, matching the glowing green dots representing the planes with those of the ship and submarine.

"Eagle One, this is Eye One. Assume heading eighty-seven degrees, range 150 kilometers and closing. You've got a sub on the surface, about seven hundred meters to the east of the ship. Over."

"Roger. Out," the pilot of the lead Tomcat acknowledged in the operator's left ear. In his right ear was the tactical center of the *Kitty Hawk,* demanding information.

"Eye One, this is Big Boot. Do you have an ID on the submarine yet? Over."

"Negative. Over."

"Eye One, what is Eagle's ETA? Over."

"ETA five minutes. Over."

Min was pulling at the front end of the rope when he felt the ice crackle beneath him. He halted and looked down in surprise. In his haste, he'd run onto a thinner portion. There was no way it would support the weight of the bomb, twenty feet behind him.

"To the left," he ordered Kim, Sun, and Ho.

As they turned, the thin ice exploded upward, and Min caught a glimpse of a massive black snout rising up into the air. The snout split in two, revealing two rows of glistening white teeth. Min could swear he saw a tiny black eye staring at him as the front half of the creature slammed down onto the ice, half out of the water, and the teeth closed on Kim.

The XO's scream was cut short as the killer whale slid back with its meal into the hole it had just made in the ice. Min pulled out his knife and desperately slashed at the rope around his waist as he was pulled toward the hole. He succeeded inches short of the freezing water. Ho and Sun weren't so fortunate. The men slid in, and Min had a last glimpse of Ho's pleading eyes as the rope that was still attached to Kim and Sun pulled him under the ice to a freezing death. Min slashed down with his knife and cut the rope from the sled, then scrambled away from the thin ice to the far side of the sled and its precious cargo.

"What happened?" Araki screamed.

"Killer whale," the captain curtly replied, saying

a mental prayer for the three men. "That's how they hunt seals." He removed his eye from the telescope and turned to look at the two women. "Men. Seals. Not much difference, is there? What do we do now?"

They all twisted their heads as two gray jets came roaring in low over the ice from the west.

"Big Boot, this is Eagle One. Over."

"This is Big Boot. Over."

"Roger. We've got a visual on the sub. You've got one Russian Delta-class boomer on ice. Over."

There was a pause. "Roger. Maintain station and await further instructions. Break. Viking Two, break from patrol and head for target site, maximum speed. Over."

"This is Viking Two. Roger. Out."

Aboard the E-2 the radar operator exchanged a worried look with the SIGINT operator. The Delta was the largest submarine in the world and carried twelve missile launch systems for multiple warhead ballistic missiles. What was it doing here?

The Viking the tactical operations center had diverted was the *Kitty Hawk*'s primary antisubmarine defense system—a plane totally dedicated to killing submarines, carrying both torpedoes and depth charges for that purpose.

The operator checked his screen. He estimated another fifty minutes before the Viking arrived. He had a feeling that whatever was being played out below would be over long before the Viking arrived.

His eyebrows rose at the next message from the *Kitty Hawk*. "Eagle One, this is Big Boot. Delta submarine is to be considered friendly. I say again, Delta submarine is to be considered friendly. Out."

* * *

Vaughn came to an abrupt screeching halt after witnessing the killer whale attack. He looked down and saw a dark shape down through the ice. He quickly sidled left to thicker ice, figuring that if he couldn't see the whale, it couldn't see him,

He twisted his head and watched as two planes with U.S. Navy markings flew by once more. About time, he thought. He moved forward slowly, aware that the lone man ahead could kill him as easily as the whales could.

Min glanced up as American planes flew by. He looked to the ship and beyond it to the submarine. He could not pull the bomb by himself. There was only one thing left to do. He reached inside his parka and pulled out a sheet of paper.

Min bent over the gray carcass of the bomb. He stripped off his gloves and ignored the knife of cold that stabbed into every joint. He flipped the latch open on the control access panel.

"The submarine is signaling us!" the ship's executive officer exclaimed.

The captain swung his telescope around to the port. A light on the conning tower was flashing international Morse code. "Copy!" the captain ordered. Something was going up on one of the tall black masts on the conning tower. The captain focused on that. He watched as it went up halfway, and then the wind caught it. It was the Russian flag.

The captain pulled back from the telescope and turned to his executive officer. "What does the message say?"

The XO ran a tongue over his lips and glanced at the political officer.

"Go ahead!" The captain insisted.

"Sir, it says: L-E-A-V-E-N-O-W."

The captain ran his eyes over the familiar lines of his ship. Slowly, he reached for the speaking tube. "Engine Room. Port Engine. One quarter, reverse."

"What are you doing?" Fatima demanded, grabbing the captain by his coat.

"I am going home," the captain replied.

"You cannot. I forbid it!"

The captain pointed out the window to the left. "The Russians are there and say leave." He pointed up. "The Americans are there, and I believe they want us to leave. We have no weapons." He pointed out to the ice. "He is alone out there. We cannot help him." The ship shuddered as the engines engaged for the first time in hours, and the newly formed ice cracked around the hull. "We leave."

Fatima looked around, taking in the scene. Then she reluctantly nodded. "We leave."

Vaughn picked his way along the ice, avoiding the sections where he could see the ocean, at the same time making sure he was out of sight of the Korean. There was no way the man could pull the bomb by himself.

Vaughn's head snapped up as he heard the throb of engines and the crack of ice. The civilian ship was turning very slowly away. He looked farther and saw the flag above the submarine. It didn't make sense, but he didn't care. It was over. He continued forward, going slower, making sure he didn't expose himself to a chance shot from the man trapped on the ice.

"Big Boot, this is Eagle One. The ship is leaving. Over."

"Roger. Break. Eye One, this is Big Boot. Status of Stinger? Over."

"Fifteen minutes out. Over."

"Roger. Break. Eagle One. Is there anything on the ice? Over."

"Wait one. Over."

Min winced as a jet screamed overhead again, barely thirty feet above the ice, but he didn't look up. His numbed fingers continued working.

"Big Boot, this is Eagle One." The naval flight officer in the backseat of the Tomcat glanced down at his video display and flicked controls. The TV automatic target identification system blanked and then showed what the camera had picked up on the previous pass in slow motion.

"Uh, this is Eagle One. We've got four figures on the ice. One with ... " The officer peered closer. "One with our object. It is not on board the ship. I say again, it is not on board the ship. Over."

"Roger, Eagle One. Go to altitude and maintain position. Stinger will take care of this when they arrive. Over."

"Roger. Out."

Vaughn did a quick peek over a block of ice, then stopped and took a slower look. The Korean was leaning over the bomb, a hundred meters away, and his arms were moving.

"Oh, shit!" he exclaimed, then stood up and began running.

CHAPTER 16

Ruppert Coast, Antarctica

With shaking fingers Min punched in the six-digit code, one by one. He cursed as his numbed fingertip slipped on the fifth digit and struck the wrong number on the numeric pad inside the access panel. The LED screen cleared, and Min took a deep breath. Once more he began.

Vaughn was less than fifty meters away. He threw the M-1 to his shoulder and stared down the iron sights. The head of the Korean wavered in them. Vaughn drew in a frigid breath and held it. The sights steadied and he pulled the trigger. The comforting recoil of the weapon was erased as the round made impact with the ice that had jammed into the barrel when Tai used it to break her fall. He felt the pain in his hands as the breach exploded.

Vaughn realized his error in a heartbeat as the Korean lifted his head at the sound of the small explosion and stared at him, their eyes locking over the bomb.

Where had he come from? Min wondered as he swung up his AK-47, pressing the metal folding stock into his shoulder. His eye never left the other man's as he lined up the front sight post with rear and pulled the trigger back.

The rounds roared out and streamed across the fifty meters, slamming into the man and throwing him out of sight down to the ice. Min put the weapon down and checked the piece of paper again. What number had he been on? His fatigued mind struggled to understand.

Vaughn's breath came in deep, painful gasps. His right side was on fire and he could feel the blood seeping into his layers of clothing. He knew he had to move. He put every ounce of energy into his legs. Nothing. He tried to scream, but a gasp was all he managed. He had to stop the Korean, or else the Russian sub would be destroyed and he would die.

Min tried to concentrate on the LED screen. Yes, he was up to the fourth. He held his finger over the numbered keys. He had no feeling in the hand anymore, so he guided it down by site. When the dead finger rested on the proper number, he pushed.

The fifth now. Min looked at the number on the code sheet. He matched it with the keyboard. His right hand would no longer hold steady. Min took his left hand and placed it over the right forearm, steadying it. He pushed down and glanced up at the LED screen. The

ENTER sign was still flashing on the top. Yes, the five were correct.

Min checked the sixth number. He forced his finger over and down. He hesitated as he thought of his family, so far away in Korea. Min sighed and pressed on. An inch away from the keyboard, stars exploded on the right side of Min's head. He rolled away from the bomb onto the ice and looked up, trying to see his attacker.

A figure loomed above. Min put his arms up to block the blow that came down on him. He felt his left forearm shatter as steel hit bone. The pain brought it all into focus. He was desperately reaching for his AK-47 on its sling along his right side as he stared into the greenest eyes he'd ever seen. A woman!

She swung the shovel again and he rolled away from the next blow. But he moved too far, and gravity took control as he began to slide.

Tai collapsed to her knees, dropping the bloody entrenching tool as the Korean fell into the hole in the ice. She started to stand when the man suddenly surged out of the water and grabbed her left forearm with his right hand.

The Korean pulled her down to the edge of the hole. He looked up at her, his dark eyes boring in. Tai felt herself drawn in by them as she bent over, her face lowering toward the almost frozen water.

The entrenching tool whirred by the side of her face and smashed into the Korean's head. His grip loosened on her arm and he slipped beneath the surface. Tai collapsed to the ice then, and Burke slid down beside her, dropping the e-tool.

Tai struggled to her feet. There was no sign of the

Korean. The bomb sat alone on the ice near them. Tai walked over to it. The cover on the control panel was off.

"Oh crap," she muttered. "Vaughn!"

Vaughn managed to crawl almost ten feet, leaving a trail of red on the ice before he could go no farther. A coldly logical part of his mind knew he was going into shock from the combination of loss of blood and the cold, but that didn't bother him much. It would only be moments before the Korean finished entering the code and the bomb went off, so oblivion wasn't far off either way.

As he retreated into the numbness, a persistent voice intruded. With great difficulty, he cracked his eyes and peered up. A stinging blow across his cheek barely elicited feeling from his frozen skin.

"Wake up, goddamnit!"

Vaughn found a scrap of energy and focused. "What?" he muttered.

"The Korean was messing with the bomb. We stopped him, but I need to know if he finished arming it." As Tai grabbed his arms, the pain brought Vaughn fully alert. He tried to help her and Burke drag him across the ice with little pushing movements of his feet.

"I can't land on the ice," the pilot said for the third time. "This aircraft needs fifty-six inches of solid ice to support it, and you can't tell that by looking out the window." The Osprey's engines were in the helicopter position, and they were cruising at forty knots above the ice.

Bellamy accepted the inevitable. "All right. Then give me a hover and we'll fast-rope out."

"Okay."

Bellamy turned to Captain Manchester and signaled. Manchester and an NCO began rigging the fast rope to bolts in the ceiling of the Osprey, while Bellamy looked out over the pilot's shoulder. He could see both the submarine and the ship that was slowly making its way out of the ice pack.

"Where's the bomb?" he asked.

The pilot did a gentle bank right. "There," he called out.

The sled was a long black spot on the ice. Bellamy noted the three figures, two dragging one, less than twenty feet away. He ran back to the rear of the plane as his team lined up on the rope.

"There're three people on the ice near the bomb. They make a move for it, take them out."

The first man nodded and slipped the selector switch on his MP-5 sub off safe. The plane came to a halt, and Manchester threw the door open, heaving the fast rope out.

Tai and Burke propped Vaughn up so he could look at the LED screen. He scanned it for ten long seconds and then shook his head. "He entered five of the six numbers on the PAL code. You stopped him before he could enter the last one."

They looked up as the Osprey came to a hover overhead and a thick rope uncoiled out the door. Vaughn watched the first man emerge with the MP-5 over his shoulder, quickly followed by a line of men, slithering down to the ice less than thirty feet away.

"Get me away from the bomb," he said to Tai. *"Now!"*

She grabbed his jacket and pulled him back onto the ice, the bomb between them and the men, just as bullets cracked by overhead.

"Cease fire!" someone was yelling. "We don't want to hit the bomb. Alpha team, fan right. Bravo, cover."

"I think we'd better surrender," Vaughn suggested. "Just keep your hands far away from your sides and start yelling in English."

"Don't shoot! Don't shoot!" Tai and Burke called out as four men rushed up, weapons at the ready.

"Freeze! You on the ground—hands away from your sides."

"He's wounded," Tai informed them.

"Step away." she was ordered. One of the man carefully rolled Vaughn over as another kept a weapon on him. "Shit," the man muttered as Vaughn's blood-encrusted jacket came into view.

"Berkman, get over here. We've got some work for you."

As the medic went to work on the wounded man, Major Bellamy checked the bomb. His heart gave a jump when he noted that five of the six numbers for the PAL code were entered. They'd made it just in time. He didn't understand what had happened and who these three people were. His job was to secure everything. It would be up to the powers-that-be to determine what to do about the prisoners.

He ordered Manchester to find a spot with sufficient ice depth to land the Osprey. As soon as the aircraft settled down, he loaded the bomb, the prisoners, and his men on board. They lifted, heading back for the *Kitty Hawk*.

As soon as they took off, the Russian submarine slowly sank under the surface and disappeared. There was nothing left except Vaughn's blood and the rapidly retreating freighter.

CHAPTER 17

Area 51, Nevada

RESUME

Without their leader, the eleven remaining members of Majestic-12 were jockeying as much for position as for solving the problem of his disappearance. They sat around the long table at which they—and their forebears—had decided the course of the United States for over half a century, politically and economically.

They were so engrossed in their in-fighting none of them noticed the odorless gas that wafted in through the ventilation system. The first indication of trouble came when the oldest man in the room—the current director of the CIA, grabbed his chest in distress.

When the second man did the same, the others scrambled for the door, only to find it locked. Within two minutes every man in the room was dead.

8th Army Headquarters, South Korea

"Sir, we have a reversal of several key indicators. Elements of the KPA I Corps are reported to be standing down. Three merchant ships that we have been tracking that were suspected to have KPA Special Forces troops on board have turned back."

Patterson nodded. He knew that the message he had just received from the Pentagon had quite a bit to do with that. Apparently the Confederation of Independent States had talked to their former friends in North Korea and informed them that it would not be in their best interest to conduct offensive operations against the South. There had also been a veiled reference from General Morris that the *Kitty Hawk* Battle Group had been involved in a joint U.S.-CIS operation that affected events here. Reading between the lines, the message between had been clear to Patterson: don't complain about the deployment of 7th Fleet elements anymore.

For the time being, things on the peninsula would stay the same—a wary watching across barbwire and antitank trenches. "Inform all units to reduce to a level four alert status."

South Pacific Sea

"You failed," Araki said.

The sun was shining, and Fatima stood on the wing of the bridge, feeling the rays warm her skin. It was the first nice day they'd had since leaving Antarctica. She looked forward to getting back to the Philippines.

"We did not fail."

"The Koreans—" Araki began.

"The Koreans failed," Fatima said, "which actually was what I was hoping would happen. Otherwise I would have had to use my men aboard this ship to kill them all."

Araki stared at her. "You never planned on letting the Koreans do whatever they planned with the bomb."

"That's right," Fatima said. "It would be the worst thing that could happen if a nuclear weapon went off, killing innocent people. In this my uncle was wrong: terrorism at a high level only succeeds in stiffening the resolve of those you fight against. The battle must be much more subtle and psychological."

"So what did you achieve?" Araki asked.

"I showed you something," Fatima said with a slight smile. "Things are not as clear as they were for you."

"You did not do this just to show me that there is some Organization out there pulling strings."

"No. I did this to hurt that Organization. The base is gone. With the Russian submarine here and the American forces, I think this spilled out of what is easily contained and compartmentalized by the Organization. We caused it problems. We won't really know the results of what we did for a while."

"And in the meanwhile?" Araki asked.

Fatima closed her eyes and lifted her face to the sunlight. "We continue the fight."

USS Kitty Hawk, *Off the Coast of Antarctica*

"I told them about Logan, but they insisted they had to take us directly back here." Tai fumed. "They said they would send some planes out to recover his body."

Vaughn shrugged. He wasn't as worried about the dead as the living. He was propped up on the bed, his chest swathed in bandages and an IV hooked into each arm. He'd been unconscious ever since they'd brought him in from surgery, waking only minutes ago. The doctor had said his prognosis for recovery was good.

There was a Marine guard outside the wardroom door, and Tai had been pacing back and forth for the past fifteen minutes, ever since Vaughn had woken up. He was too weary to say anything right now. According to her, no one had said anything to them since they'd been picked up. Vaughn had a feeling they were waiting for someone to arrive who would have the "word," whatever it was.

"Burke?" he asked.

"He's sleeping in a room they assigned him," Tai said. "More like a prison. They have a Marine on his door just like they have one on yours."

"We'll find out—" Vaughn began, but stopped as the door opened. A man wearing a simple black suit and white shirt stepped in. He was nondescript: a bland face, thinning blond hair, pale blue eyes. He carried a metal briefcase, which he placed on the table on the opposite side of the bed from Tai.

"Good morning," he said. "Major Vaughn. Captain Tai." The man stood there looking at the two of them for a little while, then spoke again. "We've recovered Mr. Logan's body. Tentative cause of death is ruled as extreme hypothermia."

The man pulled one of the plastic chairs over to himself and sat down. "It is interesting to see both of you so healthy, or relatively healthy, considering you were both reported as killed in action."

"Royce—" Vaughn began, but the man interrupted.

"Royce apparently did what he needed to. There are other issues of more importance. We have a problem here that also happens to be your problem. To put it bluntly, the word 'Citadel' must never be mentioned publicly."

"Why not?" Vaughn asked.

The man didn't even blink. "Let me explain the facts to you. First, the Citadel doesn't exist any longer. We've landed men there to sterilize what little is left, to include the reactor.

"Second, you have no record of the base existing. The pictures from the Records Center have been taken care of. As a matter of fact, you might say the circumstances surrounding the deaths of your party are very unclear. We have only your word on that issue. There are some who might say the two of you had a hand in their deaths, especially Mr. Logan's. At the very least you might be found negligent in his death."

Vaughn just continued to stare. Now was not the time or place to fight. The fact that the man was laying this out meant they would be able to walk away from it. "What's the deal?"

The man seemed to relax for the first time. "As I said—no word of the Citadel." He opened the briefcase and removed a piece of paper. "A Xerox of tomorrow's headline in the Washington Post."

He handed it to Vaughn. Tai leaned over his shoulder to read:

DIRECTOR CIA, SECDEF, 9 OTHERS KILLED IN PLANE CRASH

Vaughn looked at the man. "And?"

"Let's say you did a service to your country. Exposed something dangerous. And it was dealt with."

"A service to my country?" Vaughn repeated.

The man stood. "So to speak." He walked to the door and stopped. "I will assume I have your agreement." He stepped out.

Vaughn looked over at Tai, giving her a weak smile. "Are we having fun yet?"

Tai rubbed a hand through the tangle of her dark hair. "You think they'll just let us go?"

"Yes." Vaughn closed his eyes briefly. "Because they think we're working for Royce. And Royce is still working for them. In some form or another."

"So what exactly did we accomplish?" Tai asked.

Vaughn felt the pain in his chest. He was very tired. Exhausted down to his core "I don't know exactly. Remember on the ice? The cracks and then the killer whale coming through?"

"Yes."

"I think we've started some cracks in the ice that protects the Organization."